Meant to Be Christmas

JAMEY MOODY

Meant to Be Christmas

Edited: Kat Jackson

Visit my website or sign up for my mailing list here: www. jameymoodyauthor.com.

I'd love to hear from you! Email me at jameymoodyauthor@gmail.com.

As an independent author, reviews are greatly appreciated.

✿ Created with Vellum

Also by Jamey Moody

Stand Alones

Live This Love

One Little Yes

Who I Believe

* What Now

See You Next Month

Until We Weren't: A Story of Destiny and Faith

The Your Way Series:

* Finding Home

*Finding Family

*Finding Forever

The Lovers Landing Series

*Where Secrets Are Safe

*No More Secrets

*And The Truth Is ...

*Instead Of Happy

The Second Chance Series

*The Woman at the Top of the Stairs

*The Woman Who Climbed A Mountain

*The Woman I Found In Me

Sloan Sisters' Romance Series

*CeCe Sloan is Swooning

*Cory Sloan is Swearing

*Cat Sloan is Swirling

Christmas Books

*It Takes A Miracle

The Great Christmas Tree Mystery

With One Look

Meant to Be Christmas

*Also available as an audiobook

For the believers

This is a story about the magic of Christmas.

There's just something about the twinkling lights, the holiday aromas, and the festive music.
And then there's the parties, so many Christmas parties.

Our story begins with a sprinkle of magic that all started with a Christmas date.

For you non-believers: what's meant for you will find you.

One

"COME HOME, KENDALL. I NEED YOU!"

Kendall chuckled and rolled her eyes as she stared at the screen of her phone. "I wonder what Hector has to say about that."

"She needs you, Kendall!" Hector's face appeared on her screen. "Come home!"

"Not you, too!" Kendall couldn't contain her laughter.

She watched as Hector grabbed the phone and his face filled the screen. "Seriously, Kendall. I'm going to be out of town so much in December, it would be the perfect time for you to come stay with us. Jasmine misses you and so do I."

Jasmine wrestled the phone back from her husband. "You can work from anywhere. Come on! You'll have the house to yourself during the day while I'm at work."

"I'll be home on weekends," Hector said, leaning into the frame. "It'll be like old times."

"We're thirty-five years old!" Kendall exclaimed. "I know for a fact you don't stay up past midnight on the weekends. When was the last time you watched Saturday Night Live on a Saturday night?"

"There are too many commercials!" Hector whined. "You know what I mean. We had so much fun being together on weekends and doing whatever we wanted."

"We know what you two were doing," Kendall deadpanned. "*I* was studying."

"Yeah, right," Jasmine said sarcastically. "What were you studying? How many times you could make Dia Hall come on a Saturday night?

"Jasmine Herrera!" Kendall yelled.

Jasmine shrugged. "You know it's true," she said, rolling her eyes.

"Uh, if we could circle back to the moment at hand," Hector said.

"Someone was circling something," Jasmine mumbled, giving Kendall a pointed look.

"If you don't stop..." Kendall warned then burst out laughing.

As their laughter died down Kendall heard a familiar song in the background begin to play. She saw Hector grab his phone and answer it.

"Was that music I heard for his ringtone?" Kendall asked.

Jasmine rolled her eyes and laughed. "Yes, could you tell what song it was?"

"Hey babe, Marley is going to bring her famous pecan pie to Friendsgiving," Hector said loudly.

"Great," Jasmine replied.

"Famous pecan pie?" Kendall asked.

"Oh, yeah." Hector's face appeared next to Jasmine. "She makes the best pecan pie. You'll be here to find out for yourself."

"Wait a minute," Kendall said. "Did I hear 'Moves Like Jagger' playing when your phone rang?"

Hector smiled broadly. "Hell yeah, my girl Christina Aguilera steals that song!"

Kendall chuckled. "Are you kidding me! You used to parade around the living room singing that song to Jasmine!"

"Yeah, and it's my ringtone," Hector said. "I've got the moves, Ken, and you know it."

Kendall burst out laughing. "Oh my God, Hector! You're killing me."

"Come home and it'll be like this every weekend in December," he replied.

Kendall regained her composure and smiled at her friends. It was true, she could work from anywhere and only went into the office for special clients. The idea of spending the holiday season with her best friends was tempting. She'd been in a funk lately. Her life had become nothing but work and she didn't see that changing anytime soon. Was that all she had to look forward to in the future? Surely there had to be something more.

"Okay," she said.

Jasmine and Hector stared into the phone in surprise then looked at one another and back at Kendall. "Really?"

Kendall nodded. "How can I say no to both of you? Hector obviously needs me if he's using a song from college as his ringtone. And you need me, Jaz, if you're letting him!"

Jasmine leaned over and kissed Hector on the cheek. "Way to go, babe. Your goofiness won her over again!"

"Hey," Hector said. "You'll finally get to meet Marley."

"That's right," Jasmine said. "I can't believe our closest friends have still not met each other."

Kendall shrugged. "From what you've said, I want to meet her pecan pie."

"Does that mean you'll come for Friendsgiving this year?" Jasmine asked. "You know we throw the best party in town."

"I do know that," Kendall replied. "I used to help you throw those fabulous parties."

"Yeah!" Hector stood up and began to dance in a circle. "The gang is getting back together."

Kendall laughed. "I thought you were going to be gone. That's the whole reason I'm coming—to stay with Jaz."

"I'll be back for the weekends," Hector replied.

"Okay, you two," Kendall said with a smile. "I've got plans to make if I'm going to get there in time for Friendsgiving."

"This is going to be so much fun," Jasmine said. "Who knows, it may be time for you to leave The Big Apple and come home."

Kendall sighed. "Why do you think that's my home? Dallas is where we went to college. It's not home."

"I disagree," Jasmine said. "Dallas is where you are happiest. Your home is waiting."

Kendall rolled her eyes. It did no good to argue with her. "Whatever," she replied. "I'll let you know when I can get there."

"Love you, Ken," Jasmine said. "You've given me the best Christmas present."

Kendall couldn't keep from smiling. "Love you, too."

She ended the call and sat back against her couch. A smile was still on her face as her gaze wandered around the room. This tiny one-bedroom apartment cost more than Jasmine and Hector's monthly mortgage. It was just an apartment to her, but their place was a home. Maybe it would be a good thing to spend the holidays with her best friends.

She and Jasmine had been roommates the last two years of undergraduate and decided to get their masters degrees when they found out about scholarship funds available at the university. Jasmine met Hector their senior year and he became a fixture at their house every weekend. Kendall loved him like a brother.

He'd grown up outside of Dallas and often talked about his best friend from home, Marley. She'd gone to college in a different city, but came to visit Hector several times over the years. It just so happened that whenever she was visiting, Kendall went home for the weekend. In the fourteen years since Hector had come into her life, Kendall and Marley had never met.

Now that she thought about it, it was rather odd since Marley lived near them now. Jasmine and Hector talked about her often.

"Hmm," Kendall murmured. "I wonder if they talk about me?"

She got up and went into the small kitchen for a drink before her next appointment. It had been a few years since she'd made one of Jasmine and Hector's Friendsgivings, but they made a point to see each other several times a year. Sometimes they would come to New York to visit her and other times she went to visit them.

Kendall shared a large group of extended friends with Hector and Jasmine. She heard from them regularly, but Jasmine was her best friend. It would be good to see everyone together. The more she thought about it the happier she was to be going home, as Jasmine liked to say.

❄

Marley Jacobs smiled as she opened the oven door. The aroma of decadent sweetness hit her along with the warmth from the oven. She carefully set two pecan pies on top of the stove.

"I hope you taste as good as you smell," she murmured.

A knock at her front door had her shedding the oven mitts and exiting the kitchen.

"Hi, Alicia," she said cheerfully as she opened the door.

"Oh my God!" Alicia exclaimed as she walked into the house. "You're bringing pecan pies to dinner."

"Yep," Marley replied with a grin.

"They smell amazing." Alicia sniffed the air as she passed through the living room into the kitchen.

"I just took them out of the oven."

Alicia went over, gazed at the pies, and inhaled deeply. "Mmm, if I didn't love Hector's turkey so much I'd start dinner with your pecan pie this year."

Marley chuckled. "He does make a good turkey."

"It seems there will be a bunch of us this year."

"Yeah, Hector was afraid we'd cause a traffic jam on their street," Marley said. "Thanks for picking me up."

"No problem. You are right on my way to their house."

Marley waved her hand over the pies. "These need to cool for a little bit."

"I'm bringing rolls," Alicia said. "No, I didn't make them, but that's because Sister Schubert's dinner rolls are so good."

"I totally agree," Marley said. "My mom taught me how to make these pies. I can't make much else."

"You're just saying that because you're nice," Alicia said. "That reminds me, did you finally have that coffee date? Was she from your work?"

"We don't work in the same building, but we're in the same division," Marley explained. "We met for a drink after work last week."

"How was it?"

"It was okay." Marley sighed. "I'm over the whole dating thing."

"What?" Alicia exclaimed. "Why do you say that?"

"She was nice, but there was no spark. I mean *none*," Marley emphasized. "I can't seem to meet anyone who interests me or someone I have a connection with. I'm done."

"Whoa," Alicia said.

"I don't mean forever." Marley shrugged. "I'm declaring this the holiday of me."

Alicia smiled. "Okay." She chuckled. "Would you care to explain what that means?"

"I'm not dating, so don't try to fix me up with anyone," Marley said. "I'm taking a break and enjoying the holiday."

"You know how many holiday parties we'll get invited to," Alicia said.

"I do and I'll attend them."

Alicia raised her eyebrows. "Okay, but what if I come across someone at work that would be perfect for you?"

"They'll still be there after the holiday," Marley said. "Enough about me, what's going on with you and Evan?"

It was Alicia's turn to sigh. "That guy can be so much fun and at the same time shy. I've hinted, but he hasn't asked me out."

"So ask him out," Marley said.

"I could, but you know, I'd like for him to take the lead," Alicia said.

Marley nodded. "Hmm, he should be there today. Maybe I'll give him a little encouragement."

Alicia grinned. "I'm not saying no."

Marley chuckled.

"There are supposed to be a few new people there, I think," Alicia said.

"Yeah, but it's new people our friends are dating," Marley said.

"Come to think of it, the number of singles in our group is shrinking," Alicia said. "Oh wait! Kendall is here. She's staying all month."

"I know," Marley replied. "Hector told me she'd be here today."

"Oh fun," Alicia said. "It's been a while since I've seen her."

"We've actually never met."

Alicia looked at Marley and furrowed her brow. "You've never met Kendall? How can that be?"

Marley raised one shoulder. "It's just the way things have worked out. I've heard about her for years, but we've never been in town at the same time."

Alicia nodded. "That is crazy, but you know, I see a lot more of Jasmine and Hector now that Jaz and I work together."

"Yeah, it's funny how that happens, isn't it," Marley remarked.

"What I love about our friend group is that we may not see one another for a while, but we always pick right back up," Alicia said. "You and Kendall will be friends. I mean, you have to be, Hector is your best friend and Jasmine is Kendall's."

"Yeah, I'm looking forward to meeting her."

"You'll be doing more than meeting her since she'll be here for the entire month of December," Alicia said. "I'm a little surprised Jasmine talked her into staying that long. Imagine how beautiful New York City is at Christmas."

"Maybe she misses her friends," Marley said, gently touching the top of one of the pies. "These are almost ready."

"She must be single or why else would she be spending Christmas with us," Alicia said.

Marley shrugged.

"Aren't you curious?"

"Why would I be?"

"Hey, you and Kendall should have a lot in common."

Marley scoffed. "Oh no you don't. I can see what you're thinking. Kendall is Jasmine's best friend."

"So what?"

"I'm Hector's best friend. That's a disaster waiting to happen."

Alicia tilted her head. "I guess I see what you mean. But still, you'll love Kendall and she'll love you."

Marley smiled. "I'm sure I will. Now, let's load these pies up and go feast with our friends."

Two

KENDALL LOOKED through the window into the oven. She'd come to check on the dressing and to also catch her breath. The living room was full of her friends and also a few new faces she'd just met.

"Oh, my God, it's true!" a man exclaimed, looking around the corner into the kitchen. "You are really here!"

Kendall laughed and turned to smile at one of her favorite people. "I just talked to you last week, Evan."

"But I haven't seen you in months!" he exclaimed.

"Then get over here and give me a hug!" Kendall said, holding out her arms.

"I've missed you." Evan hugged her tightly. "Is it true? Are you really staying for the entire month of December?"

Kendall smiled and nodded. "Yep. I have to go back the week before Christmas, but only for a day."

"I don't know how Jasmine talked you into this, but I'm so happy right now," Evan said.

"It will be fun to see everyone and not have to cram everything into a single weekend," Kendall said.

"Maybe this will make you stop working all day and every evening."

"It will. You know all work will stop once Jasmine gets home." Kendall chuckled.

"Perhaps you'll find someone interesting to spend some of those evenings with," Evan said, wiggling his eyebrows.

Kendall smirked, but it would be nice to spend evenings away from her work. Even if it was just her and Jasmine or a few of their friends, maybe it would drive this lonely feeling away. "Hey, that reminds me, Alicia works with Jasmine now. Have you finally asked her out?"

"Well…" Evan's voice trailed off.

"Come on, man," Kendall said, playfully hitting him on the arm. "What are you waiting for?"

Evan looked at his feet then back up at Kendall. "I'm not all confidence and charisma like you, Ken."

"You don't have to be," Kendall said. "She already knows you and likes to hang out with you. Take the woman on a date!"

"Oh," Evan said as he looked out over the living room. "There she is now."

Kendall smiled and saw Alicia standing across the room with another woman. Something about the woman made Kendalls's heart catch in her chest. "Whoa," she murmured. "Who is that with Alicia?"

"Huh?" Evan said, giving her a confused look. "That's—oh wait, that's right—you've never met Marley. Come on, I'll introduce you."

They made their way around several people as they crossed the room, but Kendall's eyes never left the woman with Alicia. She had long brown hair with warm golden highlights that framed her face. Kendall could tell that she had expressive dark brown eyes because they were staring back at her, sparkling

11

with delight. Instead of looking away, Kendall found herself smiling right back at the woman.

Before Evan or Alicia could say a word Marley said, "You have to be Kendall."

"Do I have to be?" Kendall quipped. "Only if you're Marley."

Marley's smile widened and she offered her hand. "It's so nice to finally meet you."

Kendall took Marley's hand and appreciated her firm grip. "You too."

"Uh, hey Kendall," Alicia said sarcastically. "How's it going?"

Kendall slowly pulled her hand away and glanced over at Alicia. "Sorry," she said, holding out both her arms. "How are you?"

Alicia chuckled and hugged Kendall. "It's great to see you."

"Is this really the first time you two have met?" Evan asked.

"It is," Kendall said, meeting Marley's gaze with another smile.

Marley wrinkled her brow and Kendall immediately registered the cuteness in her expression.

"I don't know how you two managed this since your best friends are married," Alicia remarked.

"I don't either," Marley replied. "But we've met now and I'm looking forward to you being here with us for a month."

"Aw, thanks," Kendall said. "I'm happy to be back."

"Drinks," Evan said, clapping his hands. "I'll get drinks for us." He turned to Alicia. "Will you help me?"

"Sure," Alicia replied with a smile.

"They didn't ask us what we're drinking," Marley said as she and Kendall watched them walk away.

Kendall chuckled. "I don't know why he won't ask her out."

"I know!" Marley exclaimed.

"I was just talking to him about courage. Maybe Alicia will ask him."

"I don't know," Marley said as she leaned in a little closer. "She's waiting for him to take the lead."

Kendall raised her eyebrows in surprise. "Oh yeah?"

Marley nodded. "Her words. We were talking about him earlier."

"Good to know." Kendall smiled and ran her teeth across her bottom lip. "I'll get on that."

Marley chuckled. "Are you a matchmaker?"

Kendall looked over at her. "Kind of." She watched as Marley's brow did that cute little wrinkle-thingy again.

"Jasmine and Hector failed to mention that," Marley said.

Kendall chuckled. "It's my job."

"I thought you were a financial advisor."

"I am," Kendall said. "But I'm with a company that focuses on matching women with a financial advisor that connects with them. We all have different needs and I help match women who want to invest with women advisors who share the same interests to reach their financial goals."

"That sounds empowering," Marley said.

"It can be."

"We need to talk more about this while you're here," Marley said. "You're not on vacation, right?"

Kendall chuckled. "To hear Jasmine tell it, I am. But no, I'll be working during the day. Most of my work is on the computer with video chats and the like." Kendall smiled. "I'd be happy to talk about investing if you're interested."

Marley nodded. "I am."

Kendall stared into Marley's eyes and noticed they were almost the same color as her own. "You don't have to do that, Marley."

Marley scoffed. "Honestly, I'm interested. Jasmine and

Hector said you were a financial planner. They didn't mention your matchmaking abilities." She smiled warmly.

"With your help, maybe we can do a little matchmaking with our friends," Kendall said as Alicia and Evan walked up with drinks.

"We forgot to ask you what you wanted to drink," Evan said with a wince. "So, we brought a glass of wine."

"And a beer," Alicia added, holding up a bottle.

"You choose," Kendall said. "I like both."

"No, no," Marley protested. "You're here visiting, you choose. I'm fine with either as well."

"Okay, thanks," Kendall said. "I think I'll have wine." She took the glass from Evan and turned to Marley, "I hear we're having a famous pecan pie for dessert and I'm not sure beer would go with it."

Marley smiled. "Famous?"

"That's what Hector said," Kendall replied.

"He's right!" Alicia said. "Marley's pecan pie is the best."

"Hey everyone!" Hector yelled from the middle of the living room. "I have the Christmas party calendar." He waved a piece of paper over his head. "I have several already on it, but if you're planning to have a party or know of one, please add it. I'll email this to everyone tomorrow."

Several people surrounded Hector as the noise level rose. Kendall saw excitement on most of her friends' faces, but noticed Marley simply sipped her beer. Maybe she wasn't a party person, Kendall thought while taking a sip of her wine.

❄

The meal was excellent along with the good company. Marley was glad she got to catch up with several friends she hadn't seen in a while, but she was really happy that she finally met Kendall. Jasmine and Hector had talked about her so often.

Marley wasn't sure what she was expecting, but Kendall was much prettier in person than the pictures she'd seen.

Her short brown hair was cut in an asymmetrical bob that was trendy and chic. She had lighter, almost blond highlights on top, but when Kendall would run her hand through her hair, Marley noticed a deep brown color underneath. She was a couple of inches taller than Marley with brown eyes that almost matched the color of Marley's.

She'd enjoyed talking to Kendall when they met and had found herself locking eyes with her and sharing a smile several times during the evening. Kendall would run her hand through her hair and Marley couldn't look away. Maybe she'd made a new friend.

As a few people began leaving the party, Marley walked into the kitchen to help Jasmine and Hector clean up. She found Kendall at the sink doing dishes.

"They put you to work," Marley said, stepping beside her. "Let me help." She grabbed a towel and began to dry the pots and pans.

"They have a dishwasher, but all this won't fit," Kendall said. "Thanks for helping."

"After that delicious turkey Hector prepared for us," Marley said, "the least I can do is a few dishes."

"I don't know," Kendall said. "Your pecan pie may have been the star of the meal. Hector told me it was the best, but I had no idea."

"Aw, thanks."

"Hey," Alicia said, walking up to them. "I'm about to leave. Are you ready?"

"Uh–um," Marley stammered. "I wanted to help clean up."

"Do you need a ride?" Kendall asked.

"Yeah. We rode together to keep the number of cars down out front," Marley explained.

"Go ahead, Alicia," Kendall said. "I'll give Marley a ride home."

Marley hesitated. "Are you sure?"

"Yeah." Kendall nodded. "I'm using Hector's car while I'm here."

"Okay, thanks," Marley replied.

"Love you both," Alicia said, putting her arms around them for a quick hug. "Glad you're home, Kendall. Happy Holiday of Marley."

"Did she just say Holiday of Marley?" Kendall asked with a confused look.

Marley winced. "Yep."

"You have your own holiday?"

Marley gave Kendall a measured look but saw nothing but kindness in Kendall's eyes. *Why not?* She shrugged. "I haven't had the best luck in the dating game lately."

"Ugh," Kendall groaned. "I hear you."

"I've decided to take a break from the apps and dating for the holiday," Marley said.

"Gotcha," Kendall said.

"Could your matchmaking skills for business work for dating too?"

"If they did, I'd have a girlfriend," Kendall said, raising a brow at Marley. "However, if I didn't work all the time, maybe I could meet someone."

"Oh, I keep trying," Marley said. "But there's no spark, you know?"

Kendall looked over at Marley. "Maybe it'll happen when you least expect it."

Marley smiled. Kendall had the warmest brown eyes and they were sparkling—oh no, they were off limits. *This can't be happening.*

"Hey, you two," Jasmine said, putting an arm around each of them. "Thanks for cleaning up."

"Of course," Marley said, turning around and handing Kendall a towel to wipe her hands.

Kendall smiled and took the towel. "You hosted and cooked."

"Marley cooked too," Jasmine pointed out.

"I always help clean up." Marley chuckled. "Hector can cook, but cleaning up is not one of his strengths."

"So true," Jasmine said.

"Hey," Kendall said. "I told Marley I'd give her a ride home."

"Aww," Jasmine said. "Babe," she yelled into the living room. "Look, our besties are becoming besties."

Marley looked at Kendall and raised her brows.

Kendall rolled her eyes and shook her head. "Sometimes she's a bit much."

Marley chuckled.

"Come sit down for a minute," Hector called from the living room.

They all went into the living room to find Hector sprawled on the couch.

"Scoot over." Jasmine playfully smacked his legs.

Hector sat up, making room for Jasmine and Kendall to sit down, while Marley sat in a chair opposite them.

"Another wonderful Friendsgiving is done," Marley said. "Way to go."

"Bring on the Christmas magic," Hector said.

Marley groaned. "Don't start, Hector."

He laughed and Marley noticed the confused look on Kendall's face. "Did I miss something?" Kendall asked.

"Marley doesn't believe in the magic of Christmas," Hector said.

"Oh?" Kendall raised her eyebrows and looked at Marley, who shrugged and gave Hector a menacing look.

"We've already had our first Christmas miracle," Hector

JAMEY MOODY

proclaimed.

"What!" Marley exclaimed.

"Kendall!" Hector replied. "It's a miracle she's here!"

Kendall laughed and Marley felt the rich sounds wrap around her heart. *What the...?*

"He's right, Marley," Jasmine said. "It is a miracle I finally got her to come home. And an added bonus is you two have finally met."

Marley knew she wouldn't win this time. "Okay, okay, it's a miracle Kendall is here." She turned to Kendall and asked, "Do miracles drive?"

Three

KENDALL LAUGHED AND NODDED. "Come on, I'll take you home."

Marley got up and hugged Jasmine and Hector. "Thanks for a lovely day."

"It was, wasn't it?" Jasmine said with a smile.

"See you next weekend," Hector said, hugging his friend.

"Next weekend?"

"I'll be gone all week," he replied.

"Oh, that's right," Marley said. "Be safe."

"I'm sure you'll get up to all kinds of shenanigans without me," he said.

Marley chuckled and grinned at Jasmine. "I'm sure we will."

Kendall looked on and felt a warmth spread through her chest. All she felt was happiness. Maybe Jasmine was right: It was good to be home.

They got in the car and Marley gave her directions to her house. At a stoplight, Kendall glanced over at her. "You never told me about your work. All Jasmine and Hector said was something about the supply chain."

Marley smiled. "I run one of the big distribution centers in north Dallas."

"Really?" Kendall asked. "Do you mean one of those huge buildings that can hold several football fields?"

Marley chuckled. "Yeah, there's a lot of square footage under that roof."

"I can't even imagine," Kendall said. "I've always wondered what they look like inside. It seems like they go on and on forever."

"I'd be glad to show you while you're here."

"Seriously?" Kendall asked excitedly.

"Yes," Marley replied. "Except I'm a little surprised. You live in New York City where there are skyscrapers."

"I know," Kendall replied. "They go up. Your buildings go out. They look large enough to have a small town under their roof."

"It's not that big, but really, I'd be happy to show you."

"Thanks," Kendall said, glancing over at her. She paused for a moment and didn't feel like she needed to fill the silence between them. That was new. Oftentimes with clients she had to pull information out of them and silence could be uncomfortable.

"Hey, what is this thing about Christmas magic Hector obviously loves tormenting you about?" Kendall asked as she turned at the light.

"Ugh," Marley moaned. "I don't know what I dread more, the magic of Christmas," she said, making air quotes with her fingers, "or the endless parties."

"Right!" Kendall made a face showing her displeasure. "And you can't miss the parties," she added. "They're our friends so you have to go."

"Exactly," Marley said. "If you come with a date there's the awkwardness of introducing her to everyone."

"What about the awkwardness of walking into the party

alone?" Kendall countered. "Then they immediately try to introduce you to someone that'll be perfect for you."

"Which ends in disaster," Marley said.

Kendall looked over at Marley. She was so easy to talk to and already felt like a friend. "Since you shared your dating woes with me..."

Marley met Kendall's gaze and raised her eyebrows.

"You can't tell Jasmine, but I've been feeling a bit empty of late," Kendall confessed. "If she knew, she'd be setting me up with every single woman she knows."

"And that's the last thing you want or need right now," Marley said.

"Exactly," Kendall replied. "Don't get me wrong, I love my job. It is so rewarding setting women up with other women who want to see them succeed financially. But I have no one to share that with."

"These dating apps are full of very nice women," Marley said. "But I'm looking for a connection, a spark."

Kendall could feel Marley's eyes on her. She wondered if the spark Marley was talking about was like what she'd felt the moment their eyes met. Or maybe was it how easily they'd both opened up to one another? "You're staring at me."

Marley narrowed her eyes and tilted her head. "I have an idea."

"Is it a way to make party season survivable?" Kendall asked, raising her brows.

"How about we go together?" Marley said. "Then we won't have to worry about dates for all the parties."

"That's a great idea." Kendall smiled. "Are you sure?"

"Yes!" Marley exclaimed. "We'll be at the same parties anyway and this way we can enjoy them."

Kendall gasped. "Enjoy a Christmas party! That would take some of the magic you obviously don't believe in."

Marley raised an eyebrow. "Are you saying you do?"

Kendall shrugged. "It's not the Christmas season yet, is it?"

"It absolutely is," Marley said. "Didn't you see the decorations come out after Halloween?"

Kendall chuckled. "Oh, I did, but Jasmine is strict about the fall holiday schedule. She does not skip Thanksgiving."

"Imagine that." Marley grinned. "I guess that's why she's always hosted Friendsgiving."

"Surely you've heard her proclaim the atrocities of Christmas coming earlier and earlier every year."

Marley giggled. "I may have heard a rant or two, but I'm fine with it. Jasmine and Hector are relationship goals."

"You think?"

"As far as making each other happy and bringing out the best in one another? Yes," Marley said.

Kendall nodded and gazed at Marley as she pulled into her driveway. "Yeah, you're right."

"Thanks for bringing me home," Marley said.

Kendall wasn't ready to say goodnight to Marley just yet. "You're really easy to talk to."

Marley smiled. "So are you."

Kendall raked her teeth over her bottom lip. "Uh, this," she said, pointing between the two of them, searching for words.

"Is the beginning of a beautiful *friendship*," Marley finished, stressing the last word. "Our best friends are married."

"Right." Kendall nodded. "And I'm only here for a month."

"You have an expiration date."

Kendall laughed. "I thought we were Christmas dates."

Marley chuckled then sighed. "We are. Definitely."

"About that spark—" Kendall said.

Marley opened the car door, cutting her off. "Good night, Kendall. Thanks again for the ride. I'll see you soon."

Kendall giggled and smiled at Marley as she closed the door.

"Yep." Kendall sighed. "She felt it, too. Maybe there's something to this Christmas magic, Marley Jacobs."

Kendall enjoyed the drive back to Jasmine and Hector's house while moments from the day filtered through her head. She liked Marley and looked forward to getting to know her new friend.

"Any problems?" Jasmine asked as Kendall walked into the house and set the car keys on the table by the door.

"Nope," Kendall replied, looking from Jasmine to Hector. "Just because I don't have a car in New York doesn't mean I forgot how to drive."

"Yeah, but I didn't want you to get lost," Jasmine said.

Kendall held up her phone. "I won't get lost with this. Besides, I'm familiar with the area where Marley lives. It's not far from where I worked one summer."

"I can't believe all the Christmas parties on this calendar," Hector said, tapping on the keyboard of his laptop.

"We have a lot of friends," Jasmine commented. "Let's see, who can we set Kendall up with first?"

"No need," Kendall said. "I have a date."

"I didn't even say which party we were going to," Jasmine said.

"It doesn't matter," Kendall said. "I already have a date."

"With whom?" Jasmine asked, narrowing her eyes.

"Marley." Kendall smiled. "We're going to the Christmas parties together."

"She's not your type," Jasmine stated. "You're all business and besides, you like blondes."

"I can be fun," Kendall said, defending herself. "And I don't have a type."

Jasmine chuckled. "Sure, okay. But Marley is easy-going and, come to think of it, she likes blondes. Hey babe, doesn't Marley like blondes?"

Hector looked up from the computer. "Hmm, now that you mention it, I guess she does. Her last girlfriend was a blonde and I think maybe the one before that, too."

"Hair color doesn't matter," Kendall protested.

"You say that, but why are most of the women you go out with blonde?" Jasmine countered.

Kendall shrugged. "I don't have a type."

"How would you know!" Jasmine exclaimed. "It's been so long since you've gone out with anyone."

Kendall knew she was right, but she and Marley had made a deal and she was sticking to it. Besides, she enjoyed talking to Marley and felt comfortable around her from the start. "I thought you wanted Marley and me to be friends."

"We do, but not those kind of friends," Jasmine said.

"I'm only going to be here for a month, Jaz," Kendall said. "I'm not falling in love or even looking for someone to date."

"Exactly," Jasmine agreed. "I want you to have a little fun."

"I think I'll have fun with Marley," Kendall said. "We did tonight."

Jasmine sighed with frustration. "Not that kind of fun!"

"Jaz!" Kendall exclaimed. "You know I'm not the hook-up kind of gal."

"You could be."

Kendall narrowed her gaze and gave her best friend a wry smile. "You could, too."

"Wait—what?" Hector said, looking up at Kendall then his wife.

"I have my forever hook-up right here," Jasmine said, taking Hector's chin in her hand and kissing him with a loud smack.

Kendall chuckled. Marley was right. Jasmine and Hector were relationship goals.

"How did you and Marley come up with this Christmas date thing?" Jasmine asked.

"We were talking about how it can be awkward walking into a party by yourself," Kendall said. "You know I hate that."

"But you're so confident," Hector said.

"I can look confident and not feel it inside," Kendall said. "Then there's our well-meaning friends who try to set us up with people so we'll have a date for the party." She gave Jasmine a pointed look.

"We just want you to have a good time," Jasmine said.

"Marley told me she's taking a break from dating over the holidays," Kendall said.

"Yeah, she's not having much luck with the apps," Hector added.

"It seemed like a perfect solution for us both," Kendall explained. "We'll get to know each other better, which should make you both happy, and we'll have dates for the parties. It's a win-win. We'll all have fun."

Jasmine studied Kendall for a moment.

"I'm all for it," Hector stated. "It's not like you're dating. My besties will be having fun."

Kendall chuckled. "I'm sure we will."

Hector's phone pinged and he reached for it on the table.

Kendall looked at Jasmine and smiled. "What are you thinking?"

"I don't know yet," Jasmine said as Hector laughed. "What is it?"

"That's a text from Marley. She said that Kendall is her date for the Christmas parties and not to give her a hard time." Hector chuckled. "She knows us so well."

"What if you meet someone at one of the parties?" Jasmine asked. "You won't know everyone at every party."

"It'll be okay," Kendall said. "It's not like we're dating, remember."

Jasmine nodded. "Okay, but if—"

"No, Jaz," Kendall said firmly. "That's the reason we're doing this. We don't want to be set up. Let us go together and enjoy the parties."

Jasmine huffed and sat back against the couch, crossing her arms.

Kendall smiled. "Stop worrying about me and my love life. It'll happen when it's supposed to."

"Hey, maybe Christmas magic will take care of it for both of you," Hector said.

"I know Marley doesn't believe in it, but I do, Hector," Kendall said.

"That's my girl." He nodded and grinned.

"Let the Christmas season begin," Jasmine said.

Four

KENDALL SAT BACK in her chair and smiled at her laptop. She had just done a follow-up with a client and financial planner she'd matched a month ago. Rebecca, the client, wanted to begin saving money to send her two young kids to college, but was unsure how to do that and still have enough money for living expenses. Camila, the financial planner, not only had several ways to help Rebecca make this happen, but she also was saving for college for her own kids.

It gave Kendall such joy when a partnership like this started successfully and she was quite sure it would continue that way. She loved her job and had been recruited by the company five years ago when they were just starting up. At first, she was tasked with finding financial planners that fit within the company's goals, could think outside the box, and wanted to be part of something new and innovative.

Kendall was now responsible for matching clients with planners, but she also researched other markets. Their work was done mostly via computer, but some face-to-face meetings could be arranged. One thing she looked at when making a match was geography, but it didn't play a big part. While she was in the Dallas area she hoped to meet with a few financial analysts she'd been in contact with about making a move to the company.

She sighed as her gaze was drawn to the front window in the living room. Her work area was set up on the dining table and as she looked out the window, she noticed what a nice sunny day it was. Yesterday, she and Jasmine had spent a lazy day catching up and seeing Hector off on his first trip of the month. They'd talked about the Friendsgiving party and Marley's name was mentioned several times.

Kendall wasn't sure why, but a smile played across her lips when she thought of Marley. They'd agreed to this Christmas date thing, so Kendall knew they'd be seeing each other while she was in town for the month. But every time she thought of Marley and their plan, she also thought of their best friends. Was it such a bad idea for them to go on a real date?

The implication that a relationship between Kendall and Marley was off limits because of their best friend status with Jasmine and Hector had Kendall wondering if that's why Marley seemed to ignore the spark between them Saturday night. Yet Kendall couldn't help but wonder what if. There was definitely a spark. *Right?*

She exhaled a deep breath and the mail truck caught her eye as it stopped in front of the house. After a moment it sped off to the next house. Kendall got up and put a hoodie on and walked to the front door.

A lot of time in her job was spent in front of a screen. She had a stand-up desk in her office at home, but here she got up and walked around now and then. A trip to the mailbox was welcome on this rather warm day for December in Texas.

Kendall looked up at the blue sky and let the sun warm her face. She opened the mailbox and gathered the envelopes and flyers. When she closed the box she noticed a little dog walking down the sidewalk towards her.

"Hey, there, little fella," she said with a smile as she stepped onto the sidewalk.

The dog stopped in front of her, wagged its tail and, if a dog could smile, it smiled up at her.

She leaned down, extending the back of her hand to let the dog smell her fingers. "Am I okay?" she asked.

Kendall gently ran her fingers over the top of the dog's head and scratched behind its ears. Her family had always had a dog or cat when she was growing up. She missed it and gravitated towards her friends' pets when she visited.

The dog was brown and white with a few small spots on its legs and feet. It didn't have a collar, but appreciated Kendall's attention.

"Do you live around here?"

The dog licked Kendall's hand and looked at her with soulful brown eyes.

She stood up, not knowing exactly what to do. "You'd better go home," she said as she started back towards the front door. The dog followed her then stopped when she stopped.

"Okay," she said. "I'll get you a drink then you'd better be on your way."

Kendall went inside and found a plastic bowl. She filled it with water and half expected the dog to be gone when she stepped out onto the front porch. The dog was calmly sitting and looked up at her. She set the bowl down and the dog took a drink. While he was drinking, Kendall pet along his back and scratched behind his ears.

Once the dog was finished it laid down on its back offering Kendall its belly to rub.

"Aren't you something," she chuckled. "I can see you are indeed a fella."

Kendall rubbed the dog's belly then stood up. "I've got to get back to work, pal. But thanks for brightening my day."

The dog sat back up and Kendall gave it one more smile

before going back into the house. She was sure the dog would be on its way and hoped it lived nearby. Surely such a sweet dog belonged to someone.

Kendall opened her computer and got back to work. She watched the markets and monitored funds they liked to invest in for specific types of investors. Research was something she'd always enjoyed and still spent a little time each day searching for the next great opportunity for her clients.

After her last meeting of the day she glanced at her watch and knew it wouldn't be long until Jasmine would be home. They'd cook dinner together or maybe they'd go out. There were still a few leftovers from their big Friendsgiving meal, but they'd had turkey two days in a row.

Kendall got up, put her hoodie on, and walked to the front door. She remembered the little dog and thought surely by now he'd found his way home. When she opened the front door she saw the small bowl of water. She'd meant to bring that back in with her.

She walked out onto the porch then down the steps to the sidewalk. It was colder now that afternoon had turned to evening and the sun was going down. She put her hands in her pockets and started back towards the house when she saw the little dog sitting on the top step waiting for her.

"Where did you come from?"

As she made her way to the porch she noticed Jasmine pulling into the driveway. Kendall stopped and waited for her friend to come around the car.

"Who's your friend?" Jasmine asked.

Kendall looked down and the little dog was sitting next to her. He looked up at her and did that doggie-smile thing again and leaned over, resting against Kendall's leg.

"He wandered up when I got the mail earlier today," Kendall explained. "I thought he was gone, but he reappeared just now when I came out to get the bowl I gave him water in earlier."

"Hmm." Jasmine reached down and gave the dog a pat on the head. "No collar, huh."

"Nope."

"I don't recognize him," Jasmine said. "There are a few dogs in the neighborhood, but he's new."

"Do you think he's lost?"

"Maybe." Jasmine shrugged.

"What should we do? I hate to leave him out here all night. It'll be cold," Kendall said.

"I'll tell you what," Jasmine said. "Let's go in and call Marley. She volunteers at a rescue shelter; she'll know what to do."

❄️

"Hi y'all," Marley said, opening her front door. "Come in."

Kendall was holding the little dog in her arms and let Jasmine walk in first.

"I know how much you love leftovers, so I brought dinner," Jasmine said, holding up a sack.

"Aw, thanks, Jaz," Marley said. "I do love a good turkey sandwich." She turned to Kendall and smiled then offered her fingers to the dog. "Aren't you a cutie?"

"He is." Kendall smiled at the dog.

Marley gave the dog's head a couple of strokes with her hand. "So he just wandered up?"

"Yeah," Kendall said, sitting down on the couch. "He came strolling down the sidewalk. He smiles. Look at him. Do dogs smile? I think he's smiling."

Marley chuckled as she watched Kendall's face light up when she looked at the dog. "I think dogs smile and he is definitely smiling at you." Coupled with the strands of hair that

31

had fallen over one eye, the delight in Kendall's eyes gave her face an ethereal glow. Marley's heart did a little skip when Kendall's eyes met hers. *What a beautiful woman.*

"What do you think, Marley?" Jasmine asked, coming in from the kitchen.

Marley cleared her throat, not trusting her voice after gazing at Kendall. "Uh, if he has a chip we can hopefully find him in the system and identify who his family is."

Kendall furrowed her brow. "How do you do that?"

"I can take him to the shelter and they can read the implanted chip," Marley explained.

"Does he have to stay there?" Kendall asked warily. "I feel bad taking him away from the neighborhood. Maybe he lives around there."

"I've never seen him before," Jasmine said.

"He can stay here with me tonight," Marley said. "I'll take him by the shelter tomorrow."

"What happens if he doesn't have a chip?" Kendall asked. "I mean, we can't just leave him there."

"I know you're not thinking of taking him back to New York with you," Jasmine said, soberly. "Your apartment is tiny."

"You'd be surprised at how many people have pets in apartments in New York," Kendall said.

"On second thought, maybe that's a good idea," Jasmine said. "You'd have to get out of the apartment to walk him and maybe you'd see someone besides the people on your computer screen."

"Ha ha," Kendall deadpanned.

"Work is her mistress," Jasmine said to Marley. "Wait, that's not right. You'd have to have a girlfriend to have a mistress."

"I'd never cheat on my girlfriend," Kendall said defensively.

Jasmine chuckled. "I know that. Work is your girlfriend."

"I do love my job and get satisfaction from it, but no, it's not a girlfriend," Kendall said. "There's no…"

Jasmine raised a brow and smiled. "Benefits?"

Kendall smirked then grinned.

"You won't be working all the time this month," Marley said. "We have parties to attend and look—you've already rescued a dog."

"I don't think I've rescued him yet," Kendall said.

Marley smiled and tilted her head. "Maybe he's rescuing you."

Kendall looked at Marley and raised a brow. "Do I need rescuing?"

"We all need it," Marley replied. "Sometimes we just don't know it."

Jasmine cleared her throat and Marley tore her gaze away from Kendall's. She saw Jasmine cautiously look from her to Kendall. "Do you have anything to drink around here?"

"Oh," Marley said, hopping up from the couch. "Yes, is wine okay?"

"That would be perfect," Jasmine said. "It was a Monday at work."

"I hear you," Marley said from the kitchen. "We had several shipments messed up today."

She came back into the living room and handed Kendall and Jasmine each a glass of wine. "How was your day?" she asked Kendall.

Kendall smiled and looked down at the dog. "Mine was good, thanks to this little fella."

"Maybe I can make it even better," Marley said. "I have a piece of pecan pie left we can all split."

"Yum," Jasmine said.

"I'll trade you my turkey for a bigger piece of the pie," Kendall said.

Marley chuckled. "That would be quite a compliment if I didn't know you two were tired of turkey."

After they'd made and eaten their own custom turkey sandwiches and split the pie, Kendall helped Marley clean up while Jasmine had another glass of wine.

"Y'all turned this rather crappy day into a very nice evening," Jasmine said.

"Yeah, thanks for helping us with the dog, Marley," Kendall said.

"I haven't helped yet," Marley said. She looked over as Kendall bent down and smoothed the dog's fur.

"Marley is really nice and she'll take good care of you," Kendall said softly to the dog. "We'll find your family."

Marley had such a rush of emotion at the tenderness in Kendall's voice. *Why does she have to be Jasmine's best friend?* Marley shook the thought from her head. "Would you like to go with me tomorrow when I take him to the shelter to check his chip?"

"Could I?" Kendall asked.

Marley grinned down at her and nodded. She'd do just about anything to keep that sparkle in those brown eyes.

Five

KENDALL PULLED into Marley's driveway, but she wasn't home yet. Marley had texted Kendall the door code if she happened to get there first.

Kendall could hear the dog barking on the other side of the door as she entered the code. Once she opened the door, the dog jumped up on her legs, wagging his tail.

"Hey, little fella," Kendall said, patting the dog's head. "I hope you remember me and are not so welcoming of strangers. Guard dog may not be one of your strengths."

Kendall looked around the room and was tempted to snoop a little. She liked Marley and couldn't deny wanting to know more, but nosing around her house wasn't the way. Marley stirred something inside Kendall with those cute little smiles and those eyes— they were so rich and brown. It almost felt like a warm hug when she looked at her sometimes.

She sat down and the dog immediately sidled up next to her and leaned into her lap. "So," Kendall said as she stroked the dog, "is she as great as I think?"

The dog looked up at her and smiled.

"I know, I know," Kendall said, carrying on with the one-sided conversation. "She's pretty, but have you seen those eyes? Yeah, they are a beautiful shade of brown, almost like liquid caramel."

The dog settled next to Kendall and put his head on her leg.

"You have beautiful eyes as well," Kendall said. "You see, here's the problem. Our best friends are married and sometimes it's considered a no-no for the best friends of best friends to think about dating." Kendall sighed. "Yeah, I don't get it either. I mean, sure, it could be awkward if things didn't work out, but that's not a very positive attitude going in, is it?"

The dog licked Kendall's finger and continued to watch her.

"And then you add in that I'm only going to be here for a month."

The dog sighed and let out a quiet whimper. "Don't worry, it'll be all right," Kendall assured the dog.

Satisfied, the dog laid his head back down on Kendall's leg.

"But there was a spark," Kendall said. "I know she felt it because I could see it in her eyes."

Just then the front door opened and Marley came rushing into the room. She stopped when she saw Kendall and the dog relaxing on the couch. "Sorry, I got sidetracked when I was leaving."

"Excuse me?" Kendall said, offended. "What could be more important than this little fella?"

Marley stared at Kendall wide-eyed then smiled. "Nothing is more important than our little friend here," she replied, reaching over and scratching underneath the dog's chin. "But a stray automated forklift had other ideas."

"Oh, no!" Kendall exclaimed. "That sounds kind of scary."

"It's fine," Marley said casually. "Were you two having a nice conversation?"

Kendall furrowed her brow. Surely Marley hadn't heard her.

"I thought I heard you talking when I came in," Marley clarified.

Kendall noticed the amused yet sweet smile grow on Marley's face. "Like you didn't talk to the dog after Jaz and I left last night."

Marley chuckled. "Of course I did. What asshole doesn't talk to a dog?"

Kendall laughed. "You're definitely not an asshole."

Marley shrugged. "Are you two ready to go?"

"Let's go find out where your family is," Kendall said, getting up. "I know they're missing you." She leaned toward Marley and said quietly, "They'd better be."

Marley gave her a lopsided smile and nodded. "Hang on," she said. "I have a collar and a leash I keep for emergencies."

"There are dog emergencies?" Kendall asked as Marley went into the kitchen. She could hear her rummaging in a cabinet.

"Yes." Marley came back into the room and expertly slipped the collar on the dog. "One emergency almost cost me my best friend."

"What?"

"Come on," Marley said. "I'll explain in the car."

Kendall followed her out of the house and took the leash when Marley handed it to her. It had turned colder overnight and they quickly got into the car.

Once they were belted in and Marley had backed out of the driveway she said, "We didn't meet at Jasmine and Hector's wedding because I wasn't there."

"Oh, yeah," Kendall said, trying to bring back a memory. "Didn't you miss a flight or something?"

"Yep," Marley said. "I have a friend in Staten Island—"

"Staten Island!" Kendall exclaimed.

Marley laughed. "Yes, the Staten Island near you. My friend runs a rescue there. They are associated with a shelter in Puerto Rico. From time to time they bring dogs over here to be adopted."

Kendall looked over at Marley as she continued the story. She had her hair pulled back in a ponytail, but a few wisps had escaped. Kendall wanted to reach over and curl the hair behind her ear. Ugh, she had to stop thinking of Marley this way.

"My friend always has someone go with her when she's picking up dogs, but on the weekend of Hector and Jasmine's wedding no one was available. So, she called me and begged me to go with her."

"Did you think about saying no?" Kendall asked cautiously.

"Of course I said no!" Marley exclaimed, looking over at Kendall like she'd lost her mind.

"Okay, okay," Kendall said. "So what happened?"

"She assured me that we would be back the day before the wedding, so I agreed to go with her," Marley said.

"Oh no," Kendall said.

"Yep." Marley nodded. "Everything that could go wrong did and I got back here after the wedding. The only thing that saved me was that they were at the airport waiting to leave for their honeymoon when my plane got in. I ran down to their gate and saw them before they got on the plane."

"You knew when they were leaving?"

"Hell yeah," Marley said. "I helped Hector with all the honeymoon arrangements."

"Wow!" Kendall exclaimed.

"They forgave me and we had a drink in an airport bar before they left," Marley said. "It turned out to be really lovely."

"Nice save," Kendall said, impressed.

"Thanks," Marley looked over at her and grinned. "Here we are," she said as she pulled into the parking lot.

As they entered the shelter, Kendall heard a random bark. The entrance had a sweet smell masking a muskier odor.

"Right over here," Marley said.

Kendall followed her into an office, but didn't see any other people.

"They're already closed for the day, so I'm sure whoever is here is checking on the animals before locking up," Marley explained.

Kendall watched as Marley looked into the bottom drawer of a desk and pulled out some kind of hand-held device.

"This is a scanner," she said. "It will tell us if he's chipped."

Kendall nodded and heard a door close, then a woman appeared in the doorway to the office.

"Hey," she said.

"Hi, Jane Ann," Marley said. "This is my friend Kendall."

"Hi," Jane Ann said. "You're the one with the lost dog Marley told me about."

"That's me," Kendall said. "Thanks for helping us find his home."

"I'm happy to help," Jane Ann replied.

"I'll wave this over the little guy's neck and if he's chipped it'll beep and give us a number," Marley explained.

Kendall heard the device beep and her eyes widened.

"There it is," Marley said, holding the device where they could all see the number displayed.

"Now what?" Kendall asked.

"I'll write this down and tomorrow I'll search the databases and see if we can find a match," Jane Ann said.

Kendall released a deep breath she hadn't realized she was holding. "Fingers crossed you'll find a match."

"I'll call you when I find something," Jane Ann said.

"Okay, we'll get out of your way," Marley said.

Once they were back in the car Kendall felt Marley staring at her. "What?" she asked.

"Is that how you do it at work?" Marley asked. "Cross your fingers and hope they match?"

Kendall smirked. "There's a little more to it than that."

Marley grinned. "I was just teasing you, Ken. You were so uptight in there."

Kendall sighed then chuckled. "I had no idea this would be so stressful."

Marley reached over and pet the dog's head. "It doesn't seem to be bothering him."

Kendall smiled down at the dog. "You know, maybe a little Christmas magic will help us find his home."

"Oh no," Marley said. "Technology will help us find his home. It has nothing to do with Christmas miracles."

"Who said anything about miracles?" Kendall said. "It's magic."

Marley cut her eyes over at Kendall and Kendall couldn't keep from chuckling. "I was just teasing," she said, mocking Marley's earlier words.

Marley smirked and shook her head. "Hey, would you like to stay and finish off that bottle of wine we opened last night?" Marley asked.

"Yes!" Kendall replied. "I mean, I should make sure he's settled in and all."

Marley smiled. "Right." She nodded. "It isn't like he spent last night or anything."

Kendall chuckled. "I'd love to stay, Marley."

"Uh, should we text Jasmine?" Marley asked.

Kendall could hear a hint of reluctance... Or was that nervousness in her voice? "Uh, yeah. Let me..." She got out her phone and quickly sent Jasmine a text. Neither of them said anything as they waited for her reply.

This was not the comfortable silence Kendall had experienced when she and Marley first met.

Kendall's phone pinged with Jasmine's reply. "She says for us to have fun, but she's going home."

"Okay," Marley said.

Kendall looked over at her just as Marley gazed her way. She smiled and saw Marley's shoulders relax. Was that relief knowing Jasmine wasn't joining them? Before Kendall could consider her own feelings, Marley pulled into her driveway.

"So what are we going to call this little fella?" Marley asked as they started back to her house. "You should name him; you found him."

"Ha," Kendall scoffed. "It's more like he found me. But..." She thought about it for a moment. "I'd name him Frank, because frankly, I don't need a dog."

Marley laughed as they got out and went inside. She poured each of them a glass of wine and they settled on the couch with the dog between them.

"Is that empty feeling you told me about going away since Frank appeared in your life?" Marley asked as she took a sip of wine.

Kendall smiled. "Maybe, but someone else may have helped with that as well."

"Don't you dare say a word about Christmas magic," Marley said with a faux glare.

Kendall chuckled and sipped her wine. After a moment she said, "What about this first Christmas party? We're supposed to be working on Evan asking Alicia out."

"Right." Marley nodded. "You're turning your match-making skills to love."

"You're supposed to be helping me."

"I already did," Marley said. "I told you Alicia is waiting for Evan to ask."

"Okay, I'll meet up with him tomorrow and get this done," Kendall said.

"Listen to you," Marley said. "I love your confidence."

"It's not just confidence. There's another reason," Kendall said. "Doesn't everyone know they want to be together, but are too afraid to ask each other out?"

"Yeah," Marley confirmed.

"Just imagine how happy everyone will be to see them at the party together," Kendall explained. "That way they won't be looking at us."

"Will they be wondering what's going on with us?" Marley asked.

Kendall shrugged as a smirk grew on her face. "Let them."

Marley chuckled. "As long as Jasmine and Hector are okay with it."

Kendall tilted her head. "Yeah, something about that feels wrong. I mean, why do they have a say?"

"Well, they don't really, I guess," Marley said. "But..."

"But?"

"A long time ago Hector and I made a sort of pact that we wouldn't date each other's close friends. He'd been burned when a good friend dated his sister. It didn't end well," Marley explained. "Of course, it wasn't a hardship for him because most of my close friends were gay and he met Jasmine not too long after that."

"But I'm Jasmine's best friend," Kendall said.

Marley smiled. "Yes, and you're very close to Hector, too. Besides, you're only going to be here a month. Remember?"

Kendall nodded but held Marley's gaze with her own.

"Hey," Marley said, changing the subject. "Next weekend the shelter is having an event. Would you like to come or maybe even help with it?"

Kendall smiled. "Yeah." She looked down at the dog

sleeping between them and rested her hand on his back. "What is it?"

"At Christmas time the shelters in the area do an event to try and get as many animals adopted as possible."

"Oh, you adopt from the shelter instead of a pet store or breeder," Kendall said.

"That's the hope," Marley said, reaching to pet the dog.

Kendall looked down at both their hands stroking the dog's back while he slept peacefully. She stilled her hand and was surprised when Marley's hand gently covered hers. Their little fingers momentarily entwined then Marley pulled her hand away.

"Are you hungry?" Marley asked, standing up and walking into the kitchen.

Six

MARLEY NEEDED to put a little distance between herself and Kendall. She didn't know why she reached for Kendall's hand. Maybe it was the universe testing their loyalty to their best friends. They couldn't pursue anything because, duh, their best friends are married, but she couldn't stop herself. She wanted to touch Kendall, feel their connection.

If it was a test then she didn't know if they'd passed or failed it. Because there was definitely a spark. She felt it every time their eyes met and when they touched, a jolt of electricity flew up Marley's fingers. No, that wasn't quite right. It was more of a warmth that flowed through her.

"Do you like chili?" Marley asked, looking into the refrigerator. She didn't dare look into Kendall's eyes for fear of what she'd see.

"I love chili!" Kendall exclaimed, walking into the kitchen with Frank trailing behind her.

"I make it and freeze it so I'll have it for cold winter days, like today," Marley said, getting the container out of the refrigerator.

"I don't know when I last had it," Kendall said. "Are you sure?"

"I wouldn't have offered if I didn't want you to stay." Marley gave her a smile. "Besides, all I have to do is heat it up."

"How can I help?"

"Uh, you can look in the fridge and get out what you want to top your chili with," Marley suggested.

"Okay," Kendall replied, opening the door to the refrigerator. "Do you like shredded cheese? Sour cream?"

"I don't have sour cream, but there's Greek yogurt," Marley said.

"That's what I eat," Kendall said. "I sweeten it with honey for breakfast in the morning or use it as sour cream for baked potatoes." Then she added, "Or chili."

Marley chuckled. "Me, too." As she stirred the chili on the stove she could feel Kendall's eyes on her. She looked up and Kendall didn't look away. "What?"

"I'm trying to decide if you eat onions on your chili," Kendall said cautiously.

Marley gave her an amused look. "Is this some kind of test?"

"I'm not sure." Kendall chuckled. "What do you think, Frankie?" she said to the dog.

"Well, I do not care for onions on anything," Marley said. "I wouldn't call myself a picky eater, but it's a hard no on onions." She scrunched up her face.

Kendall nodded and took the yogurt out of the fridge.

"Well?" Marley asked.

"Well what?"

"The onions? Did I pass?"

Kendall chuckled. "Who said it was a test?"

"I don't know," Marley said with a hint of frustration in her voice. "It felt like it was."

"I don't like onions either," Kendall admitted. "But it's not like I wouldn't be your friend if you liked them."

"Oh, so you're my friend," Marley said with an easy smile. Why hearing Kendall say that made her heart happy was something she'd think about later.

"I am," Kendall said. "Aren't you mine? I mean, don't we come with the package?"

"What?" Marley furrowed her brow, reaching in the cabinet for bowls.

"Jasmine used to tell Hector we were a package deal," Kendall said. "When I objected, she quickly explained that as her best friend he had to love me if he loved her." She shrugged.

"Oh!" Marley said, now understanding what Kendall meant. "Yeah, I guess I came with Hector, but Jasmine and I got along from the beginning."

"Yeah, that's me and Hector," Kendall said. "I love that guy."

Marley stopped and stared at Kendall. "Does that mean we were friends before we even met?" she asked. "Like, by default?"

"Hmm, I guess, but that's not what I meant," Kendall said.

Marley smiled. "Right. I don't like onions so you'll be my friend." She looked down at the dog. "Some friend."

"I did not say that!" Kendall exclaimed.

Marley laughed and got two glasses out of the cabinet. "Would you like something to drink? I guess I could open another bottle of wine."

"How about iced tea?"

"Okay, here's another test," Marley said with a grin. "Sweet or unsweetened?"

Kendall narrowed her eyes and gave Marley an exaggerated

smirk. "I may be from the south, but it's unsweetened tea for me, darlin'."

Marley giggled. "I love your Texas drawl. Where did that come from?"

"We're talking serious stuff here," Kendall said.

"We're in trouble, friend," Marley said. "I'm unsweetened all the way, too."

"I knew we'd be friends." Kendall paused. "But what about ketchup on your chili?"

"Absolutely." Marley handed Kendall the glasses to pour their tea while she ladled chili into two bowls. They each topped their chili and Marley led them to the table.

"Will you look at that," Kendall said, nodding towards the floor.

Marley looked down and saw the dog lying on the floor under the table. "He seems more like a Frankie than a Frank. "

They dug into their food and were quiet for a few moments. Marley appreciated Kendall's moans of delight as she ate.

"This is delicious," Kendall said.

"Thanks," Marley replied. "I'm glad you like it."

A few minutes went by and as Marley took a sip of her tea she noticed Kendall staring at her with the sweetest smile. Marley raised her brows in question.

"I knew we'd be friends, but I wish we'd met a lot earlier," Kendall said.

"I don't believe in Christmas miracles or magic," Marley said. "But I do believe people come into our lives at the right time."

"Really," Kendall said with surprise. "Are you saying this is the right time for us?"

Marley shrugged.

"I think we're going to need a little Christmas magic," Kendall said, taking another bite of her chili.

"Why?"

Kendall looked up and stared into Marley's eyes. "You know why."

Marley coughed, choking on the bite she was chewing.

"Are you okay?" Kendall asked with alarm in her voice.

Marley reached for her tea and took a drink while staring over her glass at Kendall. She could see the concern in her eyes.

"I'm okay," Marley said hoarsely. She swallowed and took a breath. "I'm curious, do you use magic in your job?"

Kendall smirked. "Maybe it's more like a spark," she said. "I analyze a client's interests and background and hope when I introduce them to an advisor there'll be a spark. Do you think a spark is like magic?"

Marley could feel the heat rising to her cheeks. She had told Kendall about her dating woes and not feeling a spark with anyone. Marley had felt it within a few minutes of meeting Kendall but wasn't sure Kendall had felt it. It was obvious to Marley now that they were both feeling it, but what were they going to do about it?

After taking a deep breath, Marley smiled. "I think a spark can feel like magic."

"Oh, definitely," Kendall agreed.

"I can see you like your job," Marley said. "Your eyes light up when you talk about it."

Kendall smiled and stared back at Marley.

"I guess there's no chance of you moving back here," Marley said tentatively.

"I do like my job, but that doesn't mean I necessarily like New York," Kendall replied.

Marley raised both brows. "Oh really?"

Kendall shrugged. "My office is in New York, but I don't always have to be there. Plus, I'm not actually in the office very much."

Marley nodded and took another bite of her chili.

"What about you?" Kendall asked. "Do you see yourself here forever?"

"Hmm," Marley murmured. "I guess I don't see myself anywhere else, but I haven't really considered it. Forever is a long time. I'll advance in my company so I won't always be at the distribution center, but I like it there for now."

Kendall nodded.

"Where do you see yourself if not in New York?" Marley asked.

Kendall sighed. "Unfortunately my job keeps me busy and I haven't seen into the future."

"That's why Jasmine wanted you to come here," Marley said. "So you wouldn't work all the time."

"Yeah," Kendall replied. "She thinks I work too much, but I don't want it to be that way. Someday, I want what she and Hector have."

"Someday?"

Kendall nodded. "It's hard to see that in your future when you don't go out and meet other people or use dating apps like you do." She smiled. "There's always the hope of a Christmas miracle."

Marley smirked. "Hector never should've told you my feelings about Christmas miracles and magic. You like to tease me."

Kendall chuckled. "I do, but maybe I want to make you a believer."

"And how are you going to do that?"

"I'm going to point out miracles as they happen," Kendall replied. "The first one has already happened and I'm hoping to put the next one in motion tomorrow."

"The first one has already happened?" Marley asked, raising her brows. She thought back to the things that had happened since meeting Kendall at Jasmine and Hector's a few days earlier. "If you're thinking the miracle is you and I finally meeting, you're wrong. It was bound to happen sooner or later. It just took longer than anyone expected."

"I agree with your logic," Kendall said. "The first miracle is that I'm here at all. I haven't been back here for Christmas since we graduated."

"I'm sure the idea of meeting me sealed the deal for you." Marley smirked.

Kendall laughed. "You've got jokes. I love it! Yes, the idea of finally meeting the amazing Marley Jacobs is what got me here. Along with Jasmine and Hector's sad pleas on a video call one lonely night."

Marley furrowed her brow. Imagining Kendall in her apartment at night, lonely and alone, tugged at her heart. "We'll make sure you're not lonely while you're here."

"I appreciate that, but no mention of my loneliness to Jasmine, remember?" Kendall warned.

"Of course I remember. We may have just met, but you can trust me, Ken."

Kendall smiled. "I know," she said softly.

"Okay," Marley said, sitting back in her chair. "I'm guessing the second miracle will be Evan asking Alicia to the Christmas party Saturday night."

"That's right," Kendall said excitedly. "You're catching on pretty quick to this miracle stuff."

Marley chuckled and shook her head. "I'm not a believer," she said skeptically, standing up and taking their empty bowls.

"Yet," Kendall clarified.

Marley put the dishes in the sink and turned to Kendall. "I'm all out of pecan pie."

"I couldn't eat another bite anyway," Kendall said. "Your chili was delicious. Thanks for feeding me." She walked towards the sink. "But I can do the dishes."

"It's okay." Marley held up her hand. "I have a dishwasher."

"Okay," Kendall said. "I guess I'd better go."

"You can sit for a minute and make sure Frankie is settled for the night," Marley suggested as she rinsed the bowls.

Kendall smiled then walked into the living room. The dog followed her and jumped into Kendall's lap once she was seated on the couch.

"I think all three of us know that Frankie is just fine in your capable hands," Kendall said, stroking the little dog's back.

Marley finished loading the dishes and joined Kendall and Frankie. "Maybe we like your company."

"What did I keep you from doing tonight?" Kendall asked.

"Oh, very important things," Marley said. "I'd probably be watching TV or reading a book."

"That sounds like my evenings," Kendall said.

"Un uh. From what I've heard, you'd be working."

"Guilty," Kendall replied. "If I was in New York, I would probably be reading advisor and client profiles. But here, Jasmine and I would be watching something on TV."

"I'm glad I could help bring us closer to getting this little guy back to his family," Marley said, reaching over and scratching behind the dog's ears.

"Do you think Jane Ann will find something tomorrow?"

"Hopefully," Marley replied. She could see the anticipation in Kendall's eyes. "I'll let you know as soon as I hear from her."

"Thanks," Kendall said with relief in her voice. "Okay, I really should get going."

When Kendall got up, Frankie plopped down in the spot where she'd been sitting.

"That dog really likes you," Marley said, walking Kendall to the door.

Kendall chuckled. "Good night, Marley. I'll talk to you tomorrow."

"Good night." Marley waited at the front door as Kendall got in her car and backed out of the driveway. She gave her a wave and closed the front door.

"You're not the only one that really likes her," Marley said to the dog.

She sat down on the couch and Frankie crawled into her lap and looked up at her.

"I just don't know what to do about it," Marley murmured.

Seven

Kendall adjusted the cuff on her button down shirt and looked in the mirror. "Not bad," she murmured. She raised one eyebrow and wondered if Marley would notice. "Stop," she said on a frustrated breath.

Kendall had seen Marley every day this week, using the excuse of checking on the dog. She knew Marley felt the connection that was only getting stronger between them, but where could it go? Playing with each others' hearts was something neither of them would do.

She took one last look in the mirror and went into the living room.

"Wow, Ken," Hector said. "Don't you look nice."

"Thanks," Kendall said with a grin.

"Tell me about this dog that showed up," he said. "I didn't get a chance to get the whole story once I got home last night."

"His name is Frankie," Kendall said. "He wandered up as I was checking the mail one day. Marley has been keeping him at her house until we can find his family. We took him to the shelter where she volunteers and she scanned him for a chip."

"Any luck?"

"He has a chip and she could read the number, but the woman at the shelter is having a hard time locating what service the chip came from."

"Kendall doesn't seem to trust Marley with the dog," Jasmine said, walking into the living room while putting on an earring.

"What?" Kendall exclaimed. "Of course I trust Marley!"

Jasmine raised a brow and smirked. "Then why do you have to go over there every day and check on the dog?"

"I thought you wanted us to be friends," Kendall said defensively.

Jasmine chuckled. "I do, but I think Marley has seen more of you than I have."

"You've gone over there with me," Kendall said.

"She's messing with you, Kendall," Hector said. "I knew you and Marley would hit it off."

"I like Marley," Kendall said. "She helped me put a little Christmas magic on Evan and Alicia."

"Did he finally ask her out?" Hector asked.

Kendall nodded and grinned. "They're going to the party together tonight."

"Aww, that's awesome," Hector said. "But Marley won't believe it's Christmas magic."

Kendall chuckled. "I'm working on her. Before I leave she'll be a believer."

Hector looked at her in surprise. "Oh really? I wish you luck, my friend. I've been trying to convince her for twenty years."

Kendall smiled. There was definitely something going on between her and Marley. Whether it was Christmas magic or something else, she didn't know. They had three weeks to figure it out, but every time Kendall felt like they shared a moment, Marley would mention Kendall's expiration date or that they were Jasmine and Hector's best friends.

Kendall could understand why it might not be a great idea to see where this thing between them could go, but it was just getting stronger. Kendall wondered if that was because there was a hint of forbiddenness to it... Or was it because they shared more than a spark?

"Hey," Jasmine said quietly. "Where'd you go?"

Kendall widened her eyes and looked from Jasmine to Hector. "Sorry," she said. "What'd I miss?"

"Are we going by to pick up Marley?" Hector asked.

"No," Kendall replied. "She's picking me up here."

Hector gave her a puzzled look.

"She's my date," Kendall said. "Remember? We're going to the Christmas parties together."

"Yeah, but you could ride with us," Hector said.

The doorbell rang and Kendall got up to answer it. She opened the door and smiled, but when her gaze traveled up and down Marley's body, her mouth fell open. "Wow," she said with amazement. "Marley, you look incredible."

Marley grinned. "This old thing?" she said with a wink.

"Damn, girl!" Hector said over Kendall's shoulder.

"Uh, come in," Kendall said, finding her voice.

Marley was wearing a tight red dress with long sleeves and the hem hit about mid-thigh. Her heels made her almost the same height as Kendall.

"You know everyone likes to dress up for the Stewarts' holiday party," Marley said.

"I wondered when you were going to wear that dress," Jasmine said with a smile. "Good choice."

"Jasmine and I went shopping one day," Marley explained to Kendall. "She wouldn't let us leave the store until I bought this dress."

"I told you it would be perfect for one of the Christmas parties," Jasmine said.

"May as well start with the first one." Marley grinned.

"I was just telling Kendall y'all could ride with us. We could've picked you up," Hector said.

"And I was about to explain to him that they like to stay longer than we do," Kendall said.

"How do you know?" Jasmine asked. "When's the last time you went to a Christmas party?"

"I go to parties in New York," Kendall said.

"Uh huh," Jasmine said, eyeing her. "When?"

"Uh–um," Kendall stammered.

"It doesn't matter," Marley said. "Kendall and I are on the same page about these parties. That's why we're going together."

"Yeah," Jasmine said. "I'm still not sure about that."

"Will you please just go to the party, have a good time with your husband, who you haven't seen in days, and let Marley and me do the party our way?" Kendall pleaded.

"Okay, okay," Hector said. "Marley, you may be looking good, but I have the hottest date to the party." He put his arm around Jasmine's waist and kissed her sweetly on the lips.

"Thank you, babe," Jasmine replied. "We'll see you two there."

"Bye." Marley waved as they walked out the kitchen door to the garage.

Kendall let out a frustrated breath. "Sorry about that."

"It's not your fault," Marley said. "But in all the dress and party discussion I didn't get to tell you that you look gorgeous, Ken."

"Thank you," Kendall replied. She looked down at her skinny pants and tall black boots. The crisp button-down shirt was tucked in and she'd slicked her hair back in a sleek, edgy style. Suddenly she wondered if her outfit was appropriate.

"Your legs are so long and lean," Marley muttered under her breath. "Sexy..."

Kendall could feel Marley's eyes looking her up and down. Maybe she did look okay.

"I almost wore a dress," Kendall said. "But I only brought one with me."

"I love this look on you," Marley said. "Come here."

Kendall followed Marley into the spare bedroom Jasmine and Hector used as an office. She turned the light on and stood in front of a full length mirror that hung on the wall.

"Over here," Marley said, holding out her hand to Kendall.

Kendall took her hand and stood beside her. They gazed into the mirror and Kendall met Marley's eyes. The sexiest smile was on Marley's face.

"We look fucking hot," Marley said, her smile growing.

Kendall giggled. "Yeah, we do."

"I wasn't sure what you'd wear, but I wasn't expecting this," Marley said, holding Kendall's gaze in the mirror.

"I hope it's okay," Kendall said.

"It's more than okay."

"Thanks."

"I hoped everyone's attention would be on Evan and Alicia tonight, but we may draw a few looks our way," Marley said.

"I love Jasmine and she's my best friend, but Hector was wrong," Kendall said. "I have the most beautiful date for the party."

"Mmm, I may have to disagree." Marley winked.

They gazed at themselves in the mirror for a moment longer then Marley said, "Are you ready?"

Kendall nodded. "Let's do this."

❄

They hadn't been at the party long when Evan and Alicia pulled them over away from the crowd.

"Hey," Evan said. He glanced over at Alicia and then back at Kendall. "Thank you for giving me a much needed kick in the ass."

"I don't know what you're talking about," Kendall said.

"It's okay, Kendall," Alicia said with a smile. "Evan explained to me that he wanted to ask me out for a while now, but his delicate ego was in the way. He needed your gentle encouragement."

"I don't know why we don't encourage one another more," Kendall said. "We should begin all of our get-togethers with a compliment. It's not hard to do and it can make such a difference."

Marley felt her heart melt. "What a great idea," she said.

"You look amazing in that dress," Alicia said to Marley.

"Thank you," Marley replied. "Have you seen my sexy date for the evening?" She put her arm through Kendall's and gave her a wink with a smile.

Kendall chuckled. "Oh, okay. I'm so proud of my friend Evan for finding his courage."

Evan grinned. "So am I!" He put his arm around Alicia and gave her the sweetest smile.

"We didn't realize so many of our friends hoped we'd end up going out," Alicia said.

"Thanks again for the encouragement from both of you," Evan said.

Kendall grinned. "I'm glad it's working out."

"I need another drink," Evan said.

"I'll go with you." Alicia smiled at him. "We'll see y'all later."

Marley watched them walk away and smiled. "We did a good thing, Kendall. Your matchmaking abilities are top notch."

"Yeah, I think we did," Kendall replied. "What should we do for the next party? Another match, perhaps?"

Marley chuckled as Jasmine and Hector joined them.

"Are you having fun?" Hector asked.

"Yeah," Kendall replied. "We were just talking to Evan and Alicia. That seems to be working out well."

"Good for them," Jasmine said.

"Marley, did you see Jacob come in?" Hector asked. "He'll be teasing you before the night's out."

"I saw him," Marley said dully.

"Why does he tease you?" Kendall asked.

"He likes to make fun of my name, especially around Christmas," Marley said. She watched as confusion came over Kendall's face. "He likes to call me Jacob Marley instead of Marley Jacobs."

"Oh!" Kendall said, nodding. "The Dickens' *Christmas Carol* thing, right?"

Marley nodded. "Some people think it's funny. I've been hearing it for all of my thirty-three years."

"Wasn't Marley the ghost of Christmas past?" Kendall asked.

"Yep, he was," Marley replied.

"This is a ghost of a Christmas party past," Jasmine said, walking up behind them.

"What are you talking about, babe?"

"Look around," Jasmine said. "Most of the people here were at our Christmas party our last year in college."

"I wasn't there," Kendall said.

"Yeah, but I was," Marley said.

"Oh, that's right," Jasmine said. "Isn't that when you met Leah?"

Marley nodded. "That was a party I wished I hadn't gone to. Just imagine the heartache I could have spared myself."

Kendall tilted her head. "Heartache?"

59

"Hector brought several bottles of tequila and we started doing shots," Jasmine said with a chuckle.

"Oh, God," Marley groaned. "I was so hungover the next day."

Jasmine laughed. "Those shots are probably what made you go home with Leah that night."

"Oh, I'm sure they did!" Marley exclaimed. "And they blinded me to the red flags I later ignored."

Jasmine patted Marley on the shoulder. "We all have to live and learn."

Marley looked at Kendall and noticed her confusion. "I dated Leah and later moved in with her. Let's just say it didn't end well."

"Oh, sorry." Kendall winced. "Let's make this party better, then."

"Yeah," Jasmine said. "There's no Leah and you're here with Kendall. That's a definite upgrade."

"Gee, thanks," Kendall said.

Jasmine chuckled. "I didn't mean it that way, but you're definitely an upgrade from Leah. How about we liven things up with shots!"

"Oh, no," Marley said. "I'm not doing that again. I learned my lesson."

"It's okay," Kendall said. "I won't let you go home with anyone but me."

Marley smiled and gazed into Kendall's brown eyes. Sometimes it felt like the warmth she saw there taunted and dared her to give in. Did it matter that Kendall would only be here a few weeks? Would Jasmine and Hector be upset if they went on an actual date? Did they have to know? So many questions, all with potentially dreadful answers.

Kendall smiled and Marley felt that spark shoot through her entire body.

"Okay, no shots," Jasmine said. "Let's get a refill. Come on."

Marley swallowed and reluctantly pulled her gaze away from Kendall's. Jasmine didn't seem to notice, but when Marley looked over at Hector, he was staring at her with one eyebrow raised.

Uh oh?

Eight

"THAT WAS FUN," Kendall said, holding the front door open for Marley.

"Yeah, it was," Marley agreed.

"Would you like a drink?" Kendall asked.

"I'd like water," Marley said. "That seems like the wise choice."

Kendall chuckled and got each of them a bottle of water from the kitchen. "At least we got out of there before Jasmine started with shots."

"Thanks," Marley said, taking the water from Kendall and sitting on the couch.

"Hey," Kendall said, sitting on the other end of the couch. "I was wondering..."

"Yes?" Marley said when Kendall looked at her.

"Have I been coming over to your house too much? Jasmine made the comment that you've seen more of me this week than she has. Hector said she was joking around, but it got me thinking—"

"No," Marley said. "As cute as it is to watch you fret over this—"

"Fret?"

Marley laughed. "My grandmother used to say that." She scooted closer to Kendall. "When you worry or fret, you get this cute little wrinkle between your brows." Marley slowly reached up and smoothed the wrinkle away.

An easy smile settled on Kendall's face. She focused on Marley's eyes as she gently touched the space between Kendall's brows. They sparkled with delight and Kendall felt her breath catch in her chest. Her eyes drifted down to Marley's lips and she couldn't help but wonder how they'd feel pressed to hers.

When Marley dropped her hand, Kendall said, "I wanted to check on Frankie, but I like spending time with you."

Marley smiled. "I like it, too."

"You'd tell me if I wear out my welcome," Kendall said.

"That's not going to happen."

Kendall sighed. "I wonder if Jasmine may be rethinking me staying all month. Did you see them cuddling in the corner not long before we left? They may want some alone time."

"How about we make lunch for them tomorrow? Then we'll find something to do so they'll have the afternoon together before Hector leaves tomorrow night."

"Okay," Kendall said. "But do we have to cook?"

Marley shrugged. "What are you thinking?"

"Pizza," Kendall stated. "We loved to order pizza on Sundays and laze around the house."

"Okay," Marley said, nodding. "But pizza from where?"

Kendall scoffed. "Neony's, of course."

Marley laughed.

"Do you really think Jasmine and Hector would let us order from anywhere else?"

"They are kind of pizza snobs, aren't they?" Marley said.

"Yep, but it's so good," Kendall said. "Great idea."

They sat there for a moment both drinking their water.

"Evan and Alicia looked very pleased with themselves." Marley said.

"They did," Kendall replied. "I hope it works out for them." She paused. "Isn't it funny how sometimes we need a little encouragement to do the thing we want to do even though we're a little scared?"

"I was sure you were going to call it a Christmas miracle," Marley said.

Kendall chuckled. "Well," she said, raising her brows. "That might be a stretch."

"Is that what you do? Encourage people?" Marley asked.

"That's what I did with Evan." Kendall smiled. "I guess I kind of do that in my job, too."

Marley nodded. "Who encourages you?"

"Uh, friends," Kendall replied, putting her arm on the back of the couch.

"Hmm, like Jasmine?"

"Yeah, but you're my friend now," Kendall said. "Wouldn't you encourage me to do something if I was scared?"

"Not if it would hurt you!" Marley exclaimed.

Kendall chuckled. "Well, duh. I know you wouldn't want me to get hurt."

"Is there something you might need encouragement about?"

Kendall stared into Marley's eyes. She could feel the pull between them. There was no doubt Marley felt it, too. When they walked into the party, Kendall had offered Marley her arm. After that, Marley had put her arm through Kendall's several times throughout the night. Kendall liked the feel of Marley's hand in the crook of her elbow.

They both slowly began to lean towards each other when the back door suddenly opened.

"Hey!" Hector shouted cheerily.

Kendall took a deep breath and reluctantly turned away from Marley. "Hey," she replied.

"What are we drinking?" Jasmine asked, coming into the living room. She swatted Kendall on the leg to make room for her on the couch. Kendall closed the distance between her and Marley.

"Water," Marley replied.

"Oh, come on," Hector said, plopping into a chair across from the couch. "We started doing shots!"

Kendall raised her brows. "Was Jasmine the bartender?"

"You know it," Hector replied.

Kendall shook her head. "Marley, have you ever wondered how Jaz keeps from getting drunk while doing shots?"

Marley chuckled. "Oh, I know, Ken. Isn't it funny how she's always the bartender?"

Jasmine laughed. "Everyone has a good time. What's the harm?"

"You keep filling everyone's glasses and only take a sip of yours!" Kendall explained. "How is that fair? We're all supposed to be taking the shots together."

Jasmine shrugged. "Someone has to fill the glasses."

Kendall grinned and slapped her on the thigh. "Hey, Marley and I are making lunch tomorrow for all of us. Then I'll scram so you and Hector can have some time together."

"Oh, what are you cooking?" Hector asked.

Kendall exchanged a look with Marley and grinned. "Well, how about pizza?"

"You're making pizza?" Hector asked skeptically.

Marley chuckled. "No, we're ordering pizza."

"It has to be Neony's," Jasmine said.

"Duh," Kendall said.

"You don't have to leave after we eat," Jasmine said.

"Yeah, if it didn't bother us that you were in the next room when we lived together before, why would it bother us now?" Hector said.

"Yeah, but before..." Jasmine said, raising her eyebrows at Kendall.

"Nope," Kendall said, waving a finger back and forth at Jasmine. "We are not going there."

"Oh yes we are," Marley said with a big grin on her face.

Jasmine and Hector both laughed.

"Let's just say we weren't the only ones being loud in the house," Hector said.

"We weren't loud!" Kendall exclaimed.

"Who is *we*?" Marley asked with amusement in her eyes.

Jasmine chuckled. "Well, there was Dia."

"I remember Paige," Hector said. "She was fun."

Kendall dropped her head and closed her eyes. "Do we have to do this?"

Marley bumped her shoulder to Kendall's and grinned.

"That's all," Jasmine said. "This one studied all the time." Jasmine put her arm around Kendall and squeezed. "How many times have we been eating pizza on a Sunday afternoon while watching a movie and I called you, wishing you were here?"

Kendall smiled. "So many times."

"That's right," Hector said. "It's the three of us most Sundays." He nodded at Marley and Jasmine. "You're finally here, so let's do it."

Kendall raised her brows. "When you get sick of me it's going to be your own fault. Just remember that I offered to give you alone time."

"We could never get sick of you, Ken," Hector said.

Kendall grinned and looked over at Marley. "And you?"

"I won't get sick of you either," Marley said.

"I didn't mean that." Kendall chuckled. "Let's hear about *your* girlfriends."

"Well," Hector said, drawing the word out.

"Stop!"

"Oh, no," Kendall said. "I had to suffer through it, so do you."

"We already mentioned Leah," Jasmine said.

"The last one was Arianna," Hector said. "I'm glad we don't have to see her very often."

"Why would you see her if she's Marley's ex?" Kendall asked.

"She's part of our extended friends group," Hector explained. "She'll show up at one of the Christmas parties. You'll see. That's one of the hazards of friends dating friends."

"Ugh," Marley moaned. "Maybe she won't come this year."

"Doubt it," Jasmine said. "I heard she has a new girlfriend and you know she'll want to show her off."

Kendall looked over at Marley and winced. "Sorry."

"Why?" Marley said. "It's okay. I was over her as soon as we broke up. Just add that to the list of my poor decisions when it comes to women." She looked over at Kendall and raised her brows. "However, my date for tonight's Christmas party was a good decision."

Kendall gave Marley a sweet smile.

"I have to agree," Jasmine said. "You two look good together and it was fun to see other people's reactions when you walked into the party."

"It's okay, Marls," Hector said. "You'll find your person."

"So will you," Jasmine said, squeezing just above Kendall's knee.

"Ouch!" Kendall exclaimed, jumping up. "You know I'm ticklish there."

"That never gets old." Jasmine chuckled.

"You are such a bitch," Kendall said with faux venom.

"And you love me," Jasmine added.

Marley laughed at them. "I hate to leave this love fest, but..." She got up and started for the door.

"What a friend," Kendall said. "You're going to leave me with them."

Marley chuckled. "I've got to get out of here before they start on me again."

"Smart," Kendall said. "I'll walk you out."

"See y'all tomorrow," Marley said, waving to Hector and Jasmine.

Kendall walked Marley to her car. "I guess we don't have to find anything to do tomorrow after all."

"You're going to come see Frankie, aren't you?" Marley asked, opening her car door.

"Yeah, I'll come over and we can go pick up the pizza." Kendall smiled softly and reached for Marley's hand. "Thank you for being my date to the party. I had a wonderful time."

"I did, too," Marley said.

Kendall leaned over and kissed Marley on the cheek. "I hope that's okay," she said when she pulled away.

Marley nodded. "I'll see you tomorrow."

Kendall smiled and stepped back. Hector's comment about friends dating friends echoed in the back of her mind. She watched Marley drive away and said quietly. "Are *we* a good decision?"

❄

"This was even better than I imagined," Hector said as the movie ended. "Let's do this every Sunday."

Marley chuckled. "We do this most Sundays."

"No," Hector said. "I mean while Kendall is here. We have to do this every Sunday. We can take turns choosing the movie."

"I'm not surprised," Jasmine said. "I knew y'all would

become friends. We love y'all so why wouldn't you like each other."

"I do like Marley," Kendall said. "We are dating, you know."

Marley laughed. "That's right."

"Ha ha," Jasmine said. "I'm not sure I like this idea of yours."

"Why?" Kendall asked.

"You know why," Jasmine said, giving Kendall a pointed look.

"You said last night that we look good together."

"But you're not really dating," Jasmine said.

"Oh yeah," Kendall replied, leaning back in her chair. She gave Marley a look. "Jaz wants me to hook up with someone while I'm here."

"What's wrong with that?" Jasmine exclaimed.

"Okay," Kendall said. "Let's ask Hector and Marley. I'm supposed to find someone to date for a few weeks while I'm here, have sex, and then go back to New York. Is that right, Jaz?"

Jasmine smirked and nodded. "Again, what's wrong with that?"

Kendall scoffed. "Can you see me doing that?" she asked, looking from Hector to Marley.

"Uh," Hector said, stalling. "I feel like this is a trick question and I'm about to get into trouble."

Kendall rolled her eyes.

Marley wasn't sure what to make of Kendall's comments. She hadn't known her long, yet she did know her; at least it felt like she did. Jasmine and Hector talked about her often. Marley cleared her throat. "Uh, it sounds like Jasmine worries about you working too much, Ken. Maybe she doesn't realize casual sex isn't your thing."

"Just because it's not her thing doesn't mean she can't try it," Jasmine said, staring at Kendall.

"Why are you so worried about me having sex!" Kendall exclaimed.

"It's not the sex, Kendall," Jasmine said. "How are you ever going to meet someone if you don't try? I wanted you to come here because I hoped you wouldn't work such long hours and maybe we could find someone that's interesting to you."

"With all the Christmas parties and the new people we meet at each one," Hector said, "we thought it would be a good chance for you to meet someone."

"What about Marley?" Kendall asked. "Did you want the same thing for her?"

Hector looked over at Marley and smiled. "Yeah, we did. That's why we weren't too excited about your plan to go to the parties together."

Marley knew her friends were only trying to help, but why couldn't they see that there could be something between her and Kendall? She took a deep breath and wondered what they would think if she and Kendall went on a date.

Nine

∞∞∞

KENDALL HOPED the talk about Christmas parties and dates would end. Hector and Jasmine might not like the idea, but she did and she planned on keeping her dates with Marley.

"Yikes!" Hector exclaimed. "I've got to get ready to go to the airport." He jumped up and left the room.

Jasmine looked at Kendall and then at Marley. She sighed. "We hoped you both might meet someone this Christmas. I promise we only want you both to be happy. We love you so much."

Marley looked over at Kendall and shrugged.

"How about no more talk about dates and meeting people," Kendall said.

"Yeah, let's just enjoy the holiday together as one big happy family," Marley added.

"Oh, I love that idea," Jasmine said. "One big happy family! That's what we were this afternoon."

Kendall and Marley nodded.

Jasmine jumped up. "I'll tell Hector. No more date talk. One big happy family," she said as she ran out of the room.

Marley blew out a frustrated breath. "I wonder if they've ever considered setting us up together."

"I don't think so," Kendall said. "They told me that I wasn't your type."

"What? I don't have a type."

"They think we both like blondes," Kendall explained.

"Hair color doesn't matter," Marley replied.

"I know." Kendall sighed. "Do you remember when I gave you a ride home after Friendsgiving?"

Marley nodded.

"Jasmine told me then that she wanted me to have some fun." Kendall made air quotes with her fingers. "I told her I'd had fun with you." She chuckled, remembering Jasmine's response.

Marley peered at Kendall. "What's funny?"

"Jasmine said she didn't mean for me to have *that* kind of fun with you."

"Oh!"

"Yeah." Kendall exhaled a big breath. "Thanks for defending me on the casual sex thing."

Marley shrugged. "I can tell that's not you, but…"

Kendall raised her eyebrows.

"I think it's clear that they don't want us to go on a date, however… Do they have to know?" Marley said.

Kendall chuckled. "That right there makes it a bad idea."

"Why?"

"We'd be hiding something," Kendall said. "How long do you think that would last?"

"You could tell Jasmine you were just doing what she wanted," Marley said.

Kendall scoffed. "Excuse me! Are you asking me on a date or to have some fun?"

"Well, we should start with a date, but you never know where it could lead."

Kendall stared at Marley. *Is she kidding or does she mean it?*

"Did you have as much fun as Hector did today?" Marley asked.

"I did," Kendall replied warily, wondering where Marley was going with this. "It brings back memories, but it was also different. It felt good to hang out with friends."

"Was it enough to make you think about moving back?" Marley asked tentatively.

"Whoa, where did that come from?"

Marley shrugged. "I don't know. Just imagine, we could be doing this all the time."

Kendall smiled, enjoying the idea. Just like that, Marley had painted a picture of lazy Sunday afternoons spent together with friends.

"I think it would not only do away with your expiration date, but it could ease that loneliness you feel."

Kendall chuckled. "Expiration date," she murmured. The way Marley was looking at her made Kendall feel like Marley was inside her head or maybe her heart. "Most of my friends in New York," she began, unsure why she was telling Marley this, "are people I work with."

Marley nodded and waited.

Those brown eyes were curious, but also full of kindness. Kendall didn't talk much about her life in New York when she was here. "People are always so busy there," she continued. "I work a lot because that's what I had to do when I joined the company. One day I realized that the few acquaintances I'd made were no longer around and the only people I had any kind of friendship with were co-workers. That sounds so sad."

"No it doesn't," Marley said. "If those are the people you're spending most of your time with, it seems they'd become your friends."

"But that's not how it is for you," Kendall said.

"When I got out of college and moved here for work, I

already had friends here," Marley said. "Like Hector. He's been my best friend since we were kids. I know that's kind of weird, but we get each other."

"It's not weird," Kendall replied. "Jasmine and I hit it off immediately and have been close ever since. It's rare for a day to go by without a text or call from her."

Marley nodded. "I have great friends, a great job that I like, but I get lonely, too, Ken."

"Yeah?"

Marley nodded. "That's one thing that led me to volunteer at the shelter. Those animals will fill your heart with love."

Kendall smiled. "I'm trying not to fall in love with Frankie because he has a family somewhere."

"That's hard not to do, isn't it?" Marley said. "He's got an expiration date, like you."

"Yeah, I guess he does," Kendall said. She stared at Marley and couldn't keep from wondering if Marley meant something else with that comment. Was she trying not to fall for Kendall? All this talk of expiration dates made her wonder. What if she wasn't going back to New York or, more realistically, if she did, could they do long distance?

With their best friends against the idea, why would they even risk going on a date? Was it meant for disaster before it even started? But what if it was magical? A soft smile played over Kendall's lips. So many questions were flying through her head.

Marley narrowed her gaze. "Why are you looking at me like that?"

"I'm waiting for a little Christmas magic," Kendall said. She tried to shake the thoughts from her head hoping she wouldn't have to explain further.

Before Marley could say anything, Jasmine came back into the room. "What are y'all talking about?"

74

"Expiration dates," Marley said with a twinkle in her eyes.

"What?" Jasmine asked. "Like for food?"

"No, for me and Frankie," Kendall said.

Jasmine gave her a confused look.

"Marley has pointed out that I have an expiration date because I'll only be here for the month of December," Kendall explained.

"And Frankie will leave us when we find his family," Marley added.

"Well, that's depressing," Jasmine said.

"Kind of," Marley agreed. "But, Kendall, how was your first week here?"

"It was wonderful," Kendall replied. "I expect each week to be even better."

"Maybe it will convince you to come visit more often," Jasmine said.

"Or get rid of that expiration date," Marley said, winking at Kendall.

Kendall smirked.

"Hey, Hector!" Marley yelled. "Got any of that Christmas magic we could use on Kendall?"

Hector rolled his bag into the living room and reached for his laptop. "*You* are asking me for Christmas magic?" he said in disbelief.

"Here's your chance to make me a believer," Marley said. "Can you bring back a Christmas miracle on this trip?"

Hector narrowed his eyes at Marley. "What is this about?"

"Expiration dates," Jasmine said with a grin. "Come on, I'll explain in the car." She stopped in front of Kendall. "I haven't mentioned you moving back in ages. Please remember that Marley is the one who brought it up. Be forewarned."

Once Hector and Jasmine had gone into the garage, Kendall glared at Marley. "Do you realize what you've done?"

Marley chuckled. "I know exactly what I've done. Don't act like you're mad at me. I can tell you've thought about coming back."

"Not until you put that image in my head of sweet Sunday afternoons and the four of us together," Kendall said.

Marley shrugged. "You know Jasmine is going to try and talk you into moving back. She gave you a break the first week because she didn't want to scare you away."

Kendall chuckled. "If I moved back, would that take my expiration date out of the equation for us?"

"Oh, I didn't realize we had an equation," Marley said.

"Maybe that's not the right word," Kendall said. "Our friends don't want us together and I'm here for a limited time. That's two things against us. Yet, you asked me on a date."

Marley smiled. "Maybe I like a challenge?"

"Oh, yeah?"

Marley nodded. "I solve them all the time in my job. You're a sort of matchmaker in yours. Surely we can figure this out."

It was Kendall's turn to smile. "We have several Christmas dates to look forward to."

"Jasmine and Hector know about those, too," Marley said.

Kendall nodded. "I am suddenly looking forward to our next party."

"Oh, hey," Marley said. "I almost forgot. There's a Christmas community event in a nearby suburb Tuesday evening. The shelter is going to have a booth with dogs available for adoption. I'm going to work it and wondered if you'd like to come."

"I'd love to," Kendall said.

"You won't have to work the whole time," Marley said. "You'll be able to enjoy the other things, too. Let's get Jasmine to join us. It'll be fun."

"She loves stuff like that," Kendall said. "Hey, we'd better go check on Frankie. You've been gone all afternoon and he'll wonder why I haven't been over to let him outside."

"You haven't gotten tired of going over to my house every day while I'm at work, have you?" Marley asked.

"Not at all," Kendall said. "I have lunch then I go over to your house, let Frankie out to pee, and then we play for a little while," Kendall explained. "Do you mind having someone in your house without you there?"

"You're not just someone," Marley said, getting up from the couch. "Right now, you are Frankie's person."

"Uh, I think *we* are Frankie's people," Kendall corrected her. "He does live with you right now."

"I've really liked having him there," Marley said.

"Why don't you have a dog?"

"My work schedule would mean the dog would have to stay outside all day or inside all day," Marley explained. "I rarely come home for lunch. This has worked out great with Frankie because you go see him every day."

Kendall nodded. "It's made me miss having a pet."

"Well, when you move back," Marley said with a grin, "you can get a dog."

Kendall smirked and shook her head. "It would take Christmas magic and a miracle for that to happen. And we both know you don't believe in either one."

"Hmm," Marley murmured. "I thought you were going to make me a believer."

"Do you know what Christmas magic is?" Kendall asked.

"A fantasy? A myth? A coincidence?"

"It's all the things that transport you to a world where anything is possible," Kendall said. "With all the festivities, decorations, and gift-giving at Christmas, it's easy to believe anything is possible. Isn't it?"

Marley stared at Kendall for a moment. "Hector has never explained it like that," she said thoughtfully.

"Keep your eyes and your heart open, Marley," Kendall said. "Anything is possible."

Marley smiled and nodded. "We'd better go."

Later that night Kendall was lying in bed, staring at the ceiling. She was thinking about Marley and how she was such an unexpected surprise. Kendall smiled. It was almost like getting an early Christmas gift. Yes, they'd met a week ago, but it felt like they'd known each other much longer. At first Kendall thought it was because they'd heard Jasmine and Hector talk about them for years. Now, she wasn't so sure about that.

Marley could make her heart skip a beat or speed up with a simple look. As much as Kendall loved Jasmine and enjoyed spending time with her, it was Marley she looked forward to seeing each day. Kendall was sure Marley must be feeling the same way. After all, she'd practically asked her on a date that afternoon. Maybe the obstacles didn't matter.

She chuckled at the thought. "Since when do people have expiration dates," she muttered, then sighed. "What are we going to do about this?"

The last thing she or Marley wanted to do was cause problems for Jasmine and Hector. Kendall tried to think back over the women she'd dated and Jasmine's reactions to them. She could remember a couple of times when Jasmine didn't think a woman Kendall had gone out with was good enough for her. That was just Jasmine being Jasmine, but Kendall knew that she loved Marley, which made her wonder...

Kendall had been having these thoughts off and on since meeting Marley a week ago. There was something about her. Kendall would catch herself wondering what Marley was doing in the middle of the day. Or she'd look at the clock checking to see how long it would be until she saw Marley again. She hadn't felt this way about another woman in a very long time.

She sighed, rolled over, and fell asleep with Marley Jacobs on her mind.

Ten

MARLEY HAD BEEN LOOKING FORWARD to this evening ever since she'd told Kendall about it. The idea of working side by side with her as they tried to find forever homes for adorable animals made Marley's heart melt.

Speaking of adorable, why did Kendall have to be so cute when she furrowed her brow? Marley couldn't stop her finger from smoothing the cute little wrinkle that appeared from Kendall's unwarranted worries the other night. The idea that Marley could ever get tired of seeing Kendall. Come on!

Marley sighed as she turned onto Jasmine's street. How many first dates had she'd been on in the past year trying to find a connection with another woman? She'd only actually met Kendall a little over a week ago, but she'd felt the spark immediately. At first she thought it was excitement from finally meeting Jasmine's best friend. Marley now knew that wasn't true.

From the moment their eyes had met at Friendsgiving, she and Kendall had had something pulling them towards each other.

"Oh my God!" Marley exclaimed. "This can't be the friggin' Christmas magic Kendall was talking about. Holy fuck! No, no, no!"

Wide-eyed, Marley pulled into Jasmine's driveway. She saw Kendall come bounding down the front porch.

"Hey!" Kendall exclaimed as she opened the car door. "I've been excited about this all day."

Marley tried to soften her expression, but she wasn't quick enough.

"Are you all right?" Kendall asked. "What's wrong?"

Oh, God. There's that cute little wrinkle!

"Nothing," Marley replied, trying to smile. "I'm excited too. Where's Jasmine?"

"Jasmine is going to meet us there," Kendall said. "She couldn't get away from work early. Alicia is coming, too."

"Oh, that'll be fun."

Kendall narrowed her gaze and tilted her head. "Are you sure everything is all right?"

Marley nodded. She took a deep breath and exhaled. This time her smile was genuine. "I'm glad to see you."

Kendall grinned. "Me too."

Marley backed out of the driveway and smiled as Kendall began to ask her questions about her day and the event.

Once they'd found a parking space, Marley led them down the sidewalk towards the town's square. "We should be right over here."

"Nope," Kendall said. "This way."

Marley felt Kendall reach for her hand and their fingers interlaced like they'd done this many times before. Sure enough, Kendall had spotted the shelter's banner and stopped them in front of a row of pet carriers.

"Hey," Jane Ann said. "You found us. They thought this would be a better location."

"It is," Marley said. "What do we need to do?"

"We were about to set up the play area," Jane Ann replied.

"They gave us this grassy spot so we can set up our little fence and people can pet the dogs."

"We can do it," Kendall said, raising her eyebrows and grinning at Marley.

"Okay." Marley chuckled at Kendall's exuberance. They had the temporary fence pieced together in no time.

"We can take the dogs out of their carriers and set them inside the pen," Marley said.

Kendall followed Marley's instructions, setting each dog down, letting them get used to the pen, and making sure they couldn't jump over the barrier.

"We can put them on a leash if someone wants to pet them individually," Marley said.

"If you two can watch the dogs, I'll put our information pamphlets out on the table and store the kennels underneath it so they're out of the way," Jane Ann said. "Our other volunteers should be here soon."

"Okay," Marley said, smiling at Kendall.

"Look at all this," Kendall said. "It's so festive."

"Yeah," Marley said. "They really go all out for Christmas. Maybe we'll get a chance to walk around later."

"Hey," Kendall said. "Thanks for letting me be part of this. I'm beginning to understand why you volunteer."

"I hope to push all of that loneliness out of you," Marley replied.

"You already have," Kendall admitted.

Marley smiled and felt her heart speed up a little as Kendall's brown eyes sparkled.

People began to stop by and pet the dogs as the event officially began. Several other volunteers joined them. Kendall was quick to refer people with questions to Marley.

"You're doing a great job," Marley told Kendall as she put one of the dogs back into the pen.

"How hard is it?" Kendall grinned. "I get to play with these cuties."

Marley chuckled. "How many are you going to take home?"

"All of them!" Kendall exclaimed. "I don't know how you keep from bringing one home every time you volunteer."

"It's challenging at times," Marley said.

"Oh, but you love a challenge, right?"

Marley met Kendall's gaze and knew she was talking about her comment from the other night. She smirked. "I do."

"Hey!"

Marley and Kendall turned around to see Jasmine, Alicia, and another woman walking towards them.

"They are so cute," Alicia said, bending down to pet a dog Marley had on a leash.

"Sadie," Jasmine said to the woman standing next to her. "This is Marley and my best friend, Kendall."

"Hi," Sadie said with a big smile. "I've heard so much about you, Kendall."

"Oh," Kendall said, widening her eyes. "I don't know if that's a good thing."

"Believe me," Sadie said, "it was all good."

"Sadie works with me and Alicia," Jasmine explained.

Marley saw Kendall nod. She had an uneasy feeling in her stomach as she watched Alicia stand up.

"I saw the cutest dog sweater at the store across from here," Sadie said excitedly. "Let me show you, Kendall."

Before Marley knew what was happening, Sadie grabbed Kendall's arm and was leading her across the street.

"Wait," Kendall said, turning to look at Marley.

"You go ahead," Marley said with a small smile.

"She can catch up with us later. Come on, Alicia," Jasmine said, pulling her away and falling into step behind Kendall and Sadie.

Marley watched them disappear into the crowd. If she wasn't sure about her feelings for Kendall before, she was now. A lump of stinging jealousy settled in her stomach. She could feel her cheeks heating up. Marley wasn't a jealous person, so she was unsure where these feelings were coming from.

"Are you going to let that woman take Kendall away?" Jane Ann asked quietly.

Marley hadn't seen or felt Jane Ann walk up beside her. She was too focused on Kendall.

"She looked back at you for help," Jane Ann said.

Marley scoffed. "What? No she didn't."

"How long have we been working at the shelter together?" Jane Ann asked. "Five, maybe six years now?"

Marley nodded.

"Over the years, you've brought several of your friends to help out," Jane Ann said. "Your face lights up when you're around Kendall. You've never done that with any of the others."

Marley sighed. She knew what Jane Ann said was true. "Jasmine is Kendall's best friend and her husband, Hector, happens to be my best friend," she explained. "It's made things challenging for us."

"I didn't believe you when you told me you two had only met last week," Jane Ann said. "There's a familiarity between the two of you, like you've been friends much longer."

"Our friends have talked about us to one another for a long time, but we were surprised at how easy things were between us from the beginning," Marley said.

"I don't think Kendall really wanted to go, but didn't know what to do," Jane Ann said.

"I think Jasmine is trying to set them up," Marley said.

"She's been talking about it all day at work," Alicia said from behind Marley.

"Where'd you come from?" Marley said, turning around.

Alicia smiled. "I came to see if you can get away."

"I'd better stay here," Marley said.

Jane Ann raised a brow and walked back over to the table.

"You don't want to watch Sadie throw herself at Kendall?" Alicia asked with amusement.

Marley smirked.

"You know what I've noticed since you met Kendall at Friendsgiving?" Alicia asked.

"No, but I'm pretty sure you're going to tell me."

Alicia chuckled. "You look at Kendall the way I look at Evan."

Marley stared at Alicia and shook her head.

"What's even more interesting is that Kendall looks at you the way Evan looks at me," Alicia added.

"How can you say that when you only have eyes for Evan?" Marley said.

Alicia smiled. "I almost messed up by waiting for Evan to finally ask me out. I don't want you to miss your chance."

"What chance?" Marley said. "Kendall isn't going to be here that long and Jasmine obviously has other ideas for her."

"I understand why you're hesitant," Alicia said. "Evan and I are really good friends and one thing we talked about before we went on our first date was not messing up our friendship. Why should Jasmine and Hector have a say in who you and Kendall date?"

"They don't really," Marley said. "But they are our best friends."

"Who should want you to be happy," Alicia said. "How wonderful would it be if you found happiness with each other?"

"I know," Marley said. "But what if we didn't? What then?"

"Do you want to spend your life wondering what if?"

Alicia asked. "Or do you want to find out and be grown-ups about it, however it turns out."

Marley sighed. Did Kendall look like she wanted Marley to come with them or save her? "Just a sec," Marley said to Alicia. She walked over to Jane Ann and smiled. "I'm going to find Kendall and have hot chocolate," she said. "We'll be back to help load all the animals."

Jane Ann smiled. "Have extra marshmallows in your hot chocolate."

Marley chuckled. "Yes ma'am."

Alicia led them back to where she'd left Kendall and Jasmine.

"You know, we're all very happy for you and Evan," Marley said.

Alicia put her arm through Marley's and giggled. "I'm going by there after I leave here."

Marley grinned. "Good for you."

"You know, your friends would be very happy for you and Kendall, too."

"Nothing has happened yet." Marley chuckled.

"That doesn't mean it won't," Alicia said in a playful voice. "Just look at that face."

Marley looked over at Alicia and followed her gaze. Kendall was staring at Marley with the brightest smile on her face.

"Hey," Marley said. "Who wants hot chocolate?"

"I do," Kendall replied.

Marley watched as Kendall pulled her teeth over her bottom lip. If she had any idea what that simple gesture did to Marley's body. Heat warmed her from the inside. It didn't matter how cold it was this evening.

"I have a connection at the hot chocolate stand," Marley said with a wink.

"Let's go." Kendall stepped next to Marley and bumped

their shoulders together as they made their way down the sidewalk.

Marley smiled at Kendall and felt the knot in her stomach fall away.

After they all had steaming cups of hot chocolate with extra marshmallows, Marley asked about what all they'd seen.

Jasmine, Alicia, and Sadie shared what they'd purchased and the cute decorations they'd seen as they made their way back towards the shelter's booth.

"Do you have time to go in a few of the shops?" Kendall asked.

"No, I told Jane Ann I'd help her get the dogs loaded in the van and take the table down," Marley said.

"I've got to go," Alicia said. "A certain someone is waiting for me."

"I bet we know who that is," Kendall said.

"Thanks, y'all," Alicia said. "This was fun."

"I'd better get going, too," Sadie said. "I'll walk out with you."

"It was nice to meet you," Kendall said.

"It was nice to meet you both," Sadie said to Kendall and Marley.

"Are you ready to go?" Jasmine asked Kendall as they stopped at the dog pen.

Kendall glanced over at Marley. "I rode with Marley."

"I know, but I'm going home," Jasmine said. "There's no need for Marley to bring you to the house."

"I'm going to help get everything packed up," Kendall said.

"You don't have to," Marley said.

Kendall smiled. "I want to."

Jasmine looked from Kendall to Marley and narrowed her gaze. "Okay," she said. "I'll see you at home."

"Bye, Jaz," Marley said. "Thanks for coming out."

Jasmine nodded and walked away.

Eleven

As soon as Jasmine walked away, Kendall turned to Marley with a pained look. "I'm so sorry about that."

"About what?"

"Leaving you here," Kendall said. "I would've waited until you could've gone with us, but Sadie and Jasmine were—"

"It's okay," Marley said with a smile.

Kendall let out an exasperated breath. "I love Jasmine, but she knows I don't want her to set me up with anyone."

"You could've ridden home with Jasmine," Marley said.

"I wanted to stay with you," Kendall said. "If that's all right and you don't mind taking me home."

"You know I don't mind."

They both looked up to see Jane Ann walking over to them. "I think it's time for these cuties to go back to the shelter," she said, gesturing to the dogs.

"Okay," Marley said.

"Take the larger dogs to the van," Jane Ann said. "Their carriers are inside it."

Kendall and Marley got to work and with the help of the other volunteers it didn't take long until the van was loaded.

They said their goodbyes to Jane Ann and Marley drove them to Jasmine's house.

"Hey, I was wondering something," Marley said.

Kendall looked over at her and smiled. "What's that?"

"You know when you said Christmas magic was all the things that made you think anything was possible?" Marley said.

"Uh huh," Kendall murmured.

"Could some of those things seem bad but turn out to be good?"

Kendall furrowed her brow. "I'm not exactly sure what you mean."

"You said that you didn't really want to go with Sadie and Jasmine," Marley said.

"Right."

"Well…"

Kendall looked over at Marley and could see she was contemplating her next words. "Well?"

Marley sighed. "I didn't really like how Sadie grabbed your arm and pulled you away."

"Oh, you didn't." Kendall smiled.

"No," Marley said. "Jane Ann said you looked back at me for help."

Kendall chuckled. "I did! It shocked me when that happened and I didn't know what to do."

"I didn't really know what to do either," Marley said with a relieved grin.

"When we got to the store, I tried to come back," Kendall said. "I told them I didn't have my purse. I was going to come back and get you," she explained. "But Jasmine said she had money if I wanted to buy anything."

"Of course she did," Marley muttered. "Alicia came back

to the dog pen and said it was kind of obvious what was going on."

"Sadie was nice, but I'm not interested," Kendall said. "I will make that clear to Jasmine when I get home."

"Not interested," Marley murmured.

Kendall looked over at her. "I'm not interested in being set up with anyone," she clarified.

Marley quickly glanced at Kendall and smiled. "I think I know what you're saying."

Kendall turned to her and narrowed her gaze. "Let's go back to your question."

"About Christmas magic?"

"Yes. Are you becoming a believer?"

"Hardly," Marley said.

"You asked if something bad could turn into something good," Kendall said.

"Right."

"You are being rather cryptic, Marley."

Marley grinned. "I don't mean to be. It's just..."

"What are you trying not to tell me?" Kendall asked.

"Oh what the hell," Marley said. "I didn't like Sadie dragging you away like that, but now that I know that you didn't like it either—well, it started out bad, but now it's good."

"Marley," Kendall said. "Were you jealous?"

Marley sighed and then winced. "Maybe?" she said in a squeaky voice. "But I'm not usually like that!"

Kendall reached over and squeezed Marley's forearm. "It's okay," she said. "Why do you think I cared that she took me away from you?" Kendall chuckled.

"I'm not sure what we're doing, Kendall," Marley said as she turned onto Jasmine's street.

Kendall knew what she wanted them to do. "I'm not sure either," she said. "But I do know we have a Christmas date this weekend and I'm looking forward to it."

Marley pulled into Jasmine's driveway. "Me too. I seem to always have fun with you," Marley said.

"Tell Frankie I'll see him tomorrow," Kendall said.

Marley chuckled. "I will."

Kendall looked into Marley's eyes. She wanted to lean over and kiss her softly on the cheek, but decided against it. "You still haven't shown me around your distribution center," she said instead.

"I know," Marley replied. "I was thinking about one day next week."

Kendall reached over and squeezed Marley's hand. "I had fun tonight," she said. "Well, most of the time."

Marley laughed. "Thanks for helping out."

"I should be thanking you," Kendall said. "I'll see you tomorrow."

"Bye."

Kendall got out of the car and knew Marley would wait until she was in the house to drive away. When she stepped on the porch, she turned around and gave Marley a smile and a wave.

Kendall took a deep breath and opened the front door. She found Jasmine in the kitchen pouring wine into a glass.

"Hey," Jasmine said. "Did you get all the dogs back to the shelter?"

"Yeah."

"I'm having a splash of vino to end the evening," Jasmine said. "Do you want some?"

"No thanks," Kendall said tersely.

Jasmine looked up and raised an eyebrow at Kendall. "Is everything all right?"

"What was that tonight, Jasmine?" Kendall asked curtly.

"What was what?"

"Don't act all innocent," Kendall replied. "You know what I mean." She raised her eyebrows. "Sadie?"

"Oh," Jasmine said. "When Alicia and I were talking at work about the Christmas thing on the square, Sadie walked up. I thought you two might hit it off so I invited her to come with us."

Kendall let out an exasperated sigh. "How many times do I have to ask you not to set me up with someone?"

"I know, I know," Jasmine said, holding up her hands. "You're not here to fall in love, but really, Ken. Why are you getting so upset about this? It's not like Sadie wasn't fun."

"Why am I upset?" Kendall said, putting her hands on her hips and leaning forward. "You were rude to Marley!"

"When?"

"When you introduced Sadie," Kendall said. "She grabbed my arm and pulled me away then all you said was Marley can catch up later."

Jasmine shrugged and took a sip of her wine.

"I thought Marley was your friend, too," Kendall said. "You barely said hello to her."

"Marley was busy with the dogs," Jasmine said defensively. "We've been to events with her before and she meets us when she can."

"That's no reason to be rude," Kendall said, walking into the living room and sitting on the couch.

"Did Marley say something?" Jasmine followed Kendall into the living room.

"No," Kendall said. "It was obvious what was going on. I went there with Marley to work the event. Then you and Sadie showed up and dragged me away."

Jasmine narrowed her gaze. "You keep saying we dragged you away," she said. "You didn't have to go with us."

Surprise covered Kendall's face. "Right." She nodded. "I'd hate to imagine what you would've done then."

"You're really upset about this," Jasmine said.

"Yeah, I am."

"I'm sorry, Ken," Jasmine said sincerely. "No more set-ups."

"Thank you," Kendall replied. "I have a date with Marley this Saturday to the next Christmas party and we're all going to have a great time."

"Understood," Jasmine said, nodding. She took the last sip of her wine and studied Kendall over the top of her glass. "Why do I feel like there's more going on here?"

It was Kendall's turn to shrug.

❄

Marley pulled into Jasmine and Hector's driveway. Nervous butterflies had been fluttering in her stomach since she left her house. She was looking forward to her date with Kendall even though this Christmas party was a little different.

She knocked on the door and there stood Kendall in all her sexy glory.

"Hi," Marley said softly. The butterflies were now buzzing through her entire body.

"Hey." Kendall greeted her with a smile. "Jaz," she yelled. "Marley's wearing sexy leggings with boots."

Marley raised her eyebrows as she walked into the living room. "Uh, is something wrong with what I'm wearing?"

"Not at all," Kendall said quietly.

Marley looked into Kendall's eyes and saw a sexy smile across her face. She smirked and looked Kendall up and down. She, too, was wearing leggings along with a red sweater "You don't look so bad yourself."

"I wasn't sure what to wear to a bowling party," Jasmine yelled from down the hall.

"Who has a Christmas party at a bowling alley?" Kendall asked.

Hector chuckled while walking in from the kitchen.

"Frannie and Blake do. They went to a birthday party there for one of their kids and thought it would be fun."

"I'm sure it will be," Kendall said. "But I haven't been bowling in years."

"Neither have we!" Hector laughed. "That's the fun of it."

"If you say so," Kendall said.

He eyed them both. "So what did you two get up to this week?" Hector asked suspiciously.

Marley quickly looked away from Kendall and approached Hector. "Did Jasmine not tell you?" she asked. She patted him on the arm and grinned. "If she didn't tell you then we can't tell either."

"Wait—what?" Hector looked from Marley to Kendall. "Babe?" he said, walking down the hall.

Kendall chuckled. "You shouldn't do that to him."

Marley laughed. "Believe me, he deserves it."

"But Hector's so sweet," Kendall said.

"Most of the time," Marley replied. "Hey, I was thinking, why don't you spend the night with me tonight?" The look on Kendall's face made her chuckle.

"Uh, I know this is our second date, but I'm not that kind of girl," Kendall said.

"Oh yeah?" Marley said. "What kind of girl is that?"

Kendall giggled. Marley hadn't heard Kendall giggle too many times, but it was quickly becoming one of her favorite sounds.

"We have to be at the shelter early in the morning," Marley explained. "This will be your chance to give Jasmine and Hector alone time."

"They may need it after—"

"Okay, you two," Jasmine walked into the room with Hector on her heels. "Tell him what we really did this week."

Marley looked at Kendall and raised her eyebrows. "Well, we met at a different bar for happy hour each day after work."

"No we didn't!" Jasmine exclaimed.

"What's wrong with happy hour?" Kendall asked.

Jasmine tilted her head. "Nothing," she said. "That's actually a good idea. Why didn't we do that?"

"We've got this week," Kendall said.

"Wait a minute," Hector said. "What are y'all talking about?"

Jasmine chuckled and put her arms around Hector's neck. "All we did this week was take turns hosting dinner and watching trashy TV. We'd either go to Marley's or she came here."

"Don't forget we did the Christmas thing Tuesday night," Marley said.

"Shhh," Jasmine said. "I don't think Kendall has forgiven me for that yet."

"What did you do?" Hector asked.

"I tried to set her up with a woman from work," Jasmine admitted.

"And?" Kendall said.

"I was rude to Marley," Jasmine said dolefully.

"No you weren't," Marley said.

"Yes she was!" Kendall said.

"And I apologized," Jasmine said. "Which I will do again." She walked over and gave Marley a hug. "I'm sorry we left you at the booth."

Marley chuckled. "It's okay." At the time Marley didn't like Jasmine and her co-worker whisking Kendall away, but it worked out all right. The three of them had spent every evening together since and had fun.

"Let me pack a bag and I'll be right back," Kendall said.

"Pack a bag?" Jasmine asked.

"Marley will explain," Kendall said, leaving the room.

"Kendall is going to stay with me tonight," Marley began.

"We have to be at the shelter early in the morning for the adoption event."

"Oh, okay," Jasmine said.

"And she also wanted to give y'all a little alone time," Marley added.

"That's nice, but we're all still hanging out again Sunday afternoon." Hector smiled and put his arm around Jasmine. "Hmm. I wonder what we'll get up to tonight."

"We do not need details," Kendall said, walking back into the living room with an overnight bag.

Jasmine chuckled. "Let's go bowling."

"I can feel the Christmas magic all around us," Hector said, winking at Marley.

Marley playfully groaned and shook her head. If Christmas magic could help her figure out how she and Kendall could go on an actual date without expiration dates and their friendship with Jasmine and Hector getting in the way, then she'd be a believer.

Twelve

◦◦◦◦◦

"There's still no word on Frankie's family?" Kendall asked Marley as they drove to the bowling alley.

"Not yet," Marley replied. "But I did tell him that I was inviting you to spend the night and he was happy about that."

Kendall chuckled. "I'm sure he was." She looked over at Marley. "Is it weird that we talk about him like he's a person and not a dog?"

Marley quickly glanced at Kendall. "Do you think it's weird?"

"I do not."

Marley smiled. "I don't either, but it can be our secret."

"Oh, I like secrets," Kendall said. "What other secrets do we have?"

"Well, are you a bowler?"

"I cannot remember the last time I've been bowling," Kendall replied.

"I want us to take on Jasmine and Hector," Marley said.

"Are you going to carry our team?"

"Yep," Marley said. "Because Hector is terrible, but he thinks he's good."

Kendall laughed. "I'm always on your team, Marley, and that's not a secret."

Marley smiled. "That's good to know." She pulled into the bowling alley parking lot and they went inside.

"Over here!" Jasmine yelled to them and waved.

"Is someone excited?" Kendall asked, stepping into the seating area behind two of the bowling lanes.

"Don't you want to bowl with us?" Hector asked, setting a ball on the circular table between the lanes.

"Absolutely," Marley said with a big grin. "Kendall and I will take on you and Jasmine."

"Hi, Marley," a woman said, walking into the area.

"Hi, Frannie," Marley replied. "I'd like you to meet my friend, Kendall Malloy."

"Hold up," Jasmine said. "Kendall is *my* best friend."

"She is," Marley said, "but she's also my friend."

"Hi, Frannie," Kendall said. "We actually met several years ago at Lake Grapevine."

"Oh, yeah," Frannie said. "Blake rented a boat and we had the best time."

"I remember that," Jasmine said.

"It was before kids," Frannie added.

Hector grinned. "*We* were still kids."

"I'm trying to remember why I wasn't there," Marley said.

"You had to go home for something," Hector said. "I think it was someone's graduation."

"Probably my brother." Marley shrugged. "That was another time Kendall was in town, but I wasn't."

"Blake almost bought a boat that summer," Frannie said. "Instead I got pregnant and the boat sailed away."

"It's nice to see you again, Frannie," Kendall said. "What an interesting place for a Christmas party."

"I know it's a little unexpected," Frannie said. "But you're going to have a great time. The waitress will come by and take your drink orders." She waved at a couple who walked into the bowling alley. "I'd better go and welcome the others. Save this lane for Blake and me. I'm not sure who is playing with us."

Marley raised her brows at Kendall and winked. She walked over and picked up Hector's ball. "Isn't this a little heavy for you?"

"No," Hector said defensively. "You just wait." He gave her a menacing look.

Marley chuckled. "Yeah, wait and watch me and Kendall kick your ass."

"Uh oh," Jasmine said, leaning towards Kendall. "Here they go."

"I take it they do this often?" Kendall said.

Jasmine chuckled. "They are like a brother and sister. Always competing."

Kendall laughed. "This should be fun."

"Oh, just wait until Hector has a couple of beers," Jasmine said. "His bowling skills get worse but he takes his trash talking up a notch. It's quite entertaining."

Kendall grinned. She looked over at Marley and Hector who had already started in with the trash talk. Suddenly she felt such a nice feeling wrap around her. They were four friends at a party having fun together. She had the same feeling last Sunday in Jasmine and Hector's living room while they watched a movie and shared lunch.

When she agreed to come spend the month with her friends, her expectations were to simply have a little fun. She had no doubts that she'd be ready to go back to New York at the end of the month. But now, she wasn't so sure.

She'd miss spending evenings with Jasmine and Marley. And now the four of them had started a Sunday afternoon routine. Add to that the way her heart sometimes skipped a beat when Marley looked at her. Or how nice it was to feel

Marley's hand on her back when they walked into the bowling alley.

Yeah, going back to New York might not be so easy.

"Hey," Marley said. "We'd better find balls before everyone else gets here."

"Okay," Kendall replied and followed her over to a rack that held all kinds of bowling balls.

"Are you okay?" Marley asked quietly, putting her hand on Kendall's elbow.

When Kendall met her gaze she could see concern in Marley's eyes. "Yeah."

"You had a rather wistful look on your face," Marley said.

Kendall smiled. "I was just thinking about how nice it is to be here with you and Jasmine and Hector."

"Uh oh," Marley said with a playful grin. "Is Christmas magic lurking around the lanes?"

Kendall laughed. "We'll need some Christmas magic if you want me to keep my ball out of the gutter."

Marley raised her eyebrows and reached for a ball. "You'll be fine."

Kendall tried her fingers in several of the balls and with Marley's suggestions she found one that she hoped would stay out of the gutter. To her surprise Kendall found herself wanting to do well for Marley. She didn't necessarily care if they won— although beating Hector would be fun—but she wanted Marley to be pleased.

"Let's get a beer before the games begin," Kendall said.

Marley nodded and Kendall led them to the bar. Kendall ordered them both a beer and Marley leaned closer. "Are you nervous?" she asked softly.

Kendall swallowed and looked at Marley. "Well, I wasn't, but now I'm not so sure." Marley gave Kendall the sweetest smile.

"There's nothing to be nervous about," Marley said. "It's all in fun."

Kendall smiled and tilted her head. "I don't want to disappoint you."

Marley gasped. "You could never disappoint me because of a game of bowling, Ken." When she saw Kendall shrug, Marley leaned in a little closer. "You have no idea what you're doing to my heart right now."

Kendall widened her eyes and smiled. "Be careful, Marley Jacobs. There's Christmas magic floating around here."

Marley chuckled as the bartender set two beers in front of them. "We'll see."

They walked back to their lane and Kendall was sure that Marley had no idea what *she* was doing to Kendall's heart at that moment. "What are we going to do?" she murmured.

"We're going to win," Marley said over her shoulder.

"I wasn't really talking about bowling," Kendall replied.

"I know," Marley said with a wink.

Kendall smirked and didn't know how she was supposed to resist this woman for another couple of weeks.

"Hey Jacob Marley," Hector said as they walked back to their lane. "The last party was from Christmas past. What's this one?"

"How should I know?" Marley said. "You're the Dickens fan."

"This one is the party of Christmas present," Jasmine said. "Because Kendall and Marley are finally present in our lives at the same time."

Marley and Kendall groaned. "You are quite the clever one, aren't you?" Kendall said with a chuckle.

Jasmine laughed. "I always knew you two would be friends," she said. "But this has been better than I imagined. I should've gotten you here a long time ago."

"It's not like I planned to visit when Marley wasn't here," Kendall said. "It just happened that way."

"You could come visit more often," Hector said.

"Well, I'm here now." Kendall grinned. "And we're about to kick your ass, Hector."

Hector threw his head back and laughed. "Oh my God, babe. Marley's taught Kendall how to trash talk."

Jasmine laughed. "Oh, honey, she's not the sweet one you think she is."

"This is going to be fun," Marley said.

"You're up first, babe," Hector said.

"Hector likes for Jasmine to go first," Marley explained to Kendall. "He'll go after her, then you'll go, then me."

"When it gets down to the end we'll know how many pins we have to knock down to win the game," Kendall said.

"That's right." Marley grinned.

The smile on Marley's face made Kendall's stomach do a flip. What is happening tonight, she wondered. Every time Marley looked at her or said something to her, it made her heart flutter or skip a beat.

"Okay, Ken," Marley said. "It's your turn."

Kendall stepped up to the table and wiggled her fingers into the holes of her ball. She faced the pins and tried to remember what to do. Marley's voice played over in her head, *It's all in fun*. Kendall closed her eyes and pictured what she wanted her body to do.

"Any day now," Hector said from behind her.

"Hey, leave my partner alone," Marley chastised him.

Kendall smiled and stepped down the lane while pulling the ball back, then smoothly let the ball go as her arm swung forward. It rolled down the slick wooden surface and pins cracked as they fell down.

"You got seven," Hector said. "Not bad."

When Kendall turned around Marley was smiling and clapping for her. "That's my girl," she said.

Kendall couldn't help but chuckle. Marley was right, this was fun.

They took turns with Hector and Marley teasing each other on every turn. Jasmine and Kendall looked on, totally entertained by their antics.

Kendall was surprised at how good Marley's cheerleading made her feel. It not only gave her pride a boost, it also helped her knock down more pins. Knowing Marley was behind her with encouragement kept the ball out of the gutter—or at least that's what Kendall attributed it to.

"You're falling behind, Hector," Marley said, coming off the lane after rolling a strike.

"We can still catch you," Hector said. "Come on, babe."

Kendall was standing in front of Marley at the back of their area when she heard someone behind them.

"Hi Marley," a woman said.

Kendall turned around and saw Marley smile, but it didn't quite reach her eyes. "Hi Arianna."

"Hey," Jasmine said while she waited for her ball to return. "How are you, Arianna?" She didn't give her time to respond before adding, "Marley, have you introduced Arianna to your girlfriend?"

Kendall raised her brows and stared at Jasmine. Her back was to Arianna, but Kendall gathered herself and turned to Marley with a smile.

"Arianna, this is Kendall," Marley said. "My girlfriend."

"Hi," Kendall said. She stepped closer to Marley and put her arm around her waist.

"I see you're winning," Arianna said, looking up at the score projected on the screen over the table.

"We are," Marley replied.

Kendall pulled Marley into her side and smiled down at her. "It's because you're carrying our team."

"That's not true," Marley said. "You're holding your own."

"We're way down on the other end," Arianna said. "But we're not doing as well as you are."

"Kendall, it's your turn," Hector said.

Kendall dropped her arm from Marley's waist, but she squeezed her arm with her other hand as she turned to the lane. She gave Marley her best smile and winked. "I've got this, babe."

Marley chuckled. "Yes you do."

"Arianna, it was nice to meet you," Kendall said as she reached for her ball. She walked to the lane and lined up her shot. She said a silent prayer to the gods above and rolled the ball down the lane, hoping several pins would fall. To her surprise, all the pins fell down. She'd rolled a strike!

Kendall turned around just before Marley grabbed her in a hug and spun her around in exuberance.

"That was fun." Kendall giggled when Marley put her down.

"Way to go, babe!" Marley exclaimed.

Kendall saw Arianna walking away and looked at Jasmine. "So I'm Marley's girlfriend now?"

"There was no way I was going to let Arianna flaunt her new girlfriend in front of Marley," Jasmine explained.

Kendall laughed. "Now you're okay with Marley and me going to the parties together?"

"I certainly am," Jasmine said. "Besides, y'all look cute together."

Kendall looked at Marley and raised her brows in surprise.

"Oh stop," Jasmine said. "You're not going to let me set you up with anyone, so you can be Marley's girlfriend while Arianna is around."

"Is that okay with you?" Kendall asked Marley.

Marley smirked but Kendall could see the delight in her eyes. "I don't really care what Arianna thinks, but if it gives Jasmine so much joy. How can I say no?"

Jasmine laughed. "I know I'm a terrible person, but I loved the look on Arianna's face when Kendall called you babe."

"Okay, okay," Hector said. "We have a game to finish. It's your turn Marley."

Thirteen

THEY EACH HAD another turn and although the game was close, Kendall and Marley came out victorious by eight pins. Hector immediately had them start another game for a rematch.

"I'll get us another beer," Kendall said after she finished her turn.

"Okay," Marley replied.

"Bring me one, too," Jasmine said.

Kendall nodded and walked over to the bar. She ordered and felt someone walk up next to her. When she glanced to her right, Arianna was standing there smiling. Kendall returned her smile but didn't say anything.

"You're Jasmine's friend from New York, aren't you?" Arianna asked.

"I am," Kendall replied.

"So you and Marley are doing the long distance thing," Arianna commented while watching the bartender pour Kendall's beers. "That must be hard."

Kendall smiled. "We make it work."

Arianna nodded. "Marley's worth it."

Kendall gazed over at the other woman. "Is that regret I hear in your voice?"

"Not exactly." Arianna shrugged. "I think Marley and I both knew our relationship wasn't a long term thing. She's a great person."

"Yes she is," Kendall stated.

"Hey!" Jasmine yelled from across the room. "Your girl is thirsty."

The bartender set three beers down on the bar and Kendall corralled all three in her hands. "I'd better go."

Arianna looked away and placed her order as Kendall walked back to her friends.

Jasmine met Kendall and took one of the beers from her. "I saw her walk up and thought you might need an out."

Kendall shrugged as they made it back to their lane. "She was just saying how great Marley is."

"She *is* great and Arianna missed out," Jasmine said.

"I couldn't agree more," Kendall replied. "Here you go, babe," she said, handing Marley one of the beers.

"Thanks," Marley said, looking from Kendall to Jasmine and the amused grins on their faces. "Did I miss something?"

Kendall and Jasmine both shook their heads.

"It's your turn, Kendall," Hector said.

"You've got this, babe," Marley said with a big grin.

Kendall chuckled, set down her beer, and reached for her ball. Seconds later, she watched as the ball only knocked down two pins. Her good luck had worn off, and soon, Jasmine and Hector took the lead.

"I need that Christmas magic to come back to our lane," Kendall said as she looked up at the score.

"It's okay," Marley said, putting her arm around her. "We have time to catch up."

"Hey, hey," Alicia said, walking up and sitting next to them. "You'll never guess what I heard."

"Let me tell them," Evan said excitedly, plopping down next to Kendall.

Kendall looked from Evan to Alicia and back. "Well, tell us!"

"I heard that Marley has a girlfriend," Alicia said.

"Oh really?" Kendall said dramatically, playing along.

"You'll never guess who," Evan said. He paused, then exclaimed, "It's you!"

Kendall and Marley both rolled their eyes and laughed.

"Why didn't you tell us?" Alicia asked.

"Yeah, we're happy for you," Evan added. "I always thought y'all were hands-off because of Jasmine and Hector."

"It just happened," Kendall said, looking into Marley's eyes.

"Yeah, it did," Marley replied softly.

"Mixing dating with friendships can be tricky," Alicia said. "It's like how brothers don't want their sisters to date their friends."

"My cousin wanted to go out with Marley in high school." Hector chuckled. "Unfortunately for him, she only had eyes for the captain of the volleyball team."

"Oh yeah?" Kendall asked with a grin.

Marley smiled and nodded. "She was hot."

"Yeah she was," Hector added.

Alicia and Evan changed the subject and began to tell stories about their friends bowling on the other lanes. Hector jumped in and told them how close their games had been.

Marley leaned over and whispered to Kendall, "It looks like we have another secret."

Kendall chuckled. "Jasmine is in on this one. Let's see how long it lasts."

Marley grinned. "Oh, she's motivated as long as Arianna is around."

Kendall softened her face. "Are you okay with all this?"

Marley nodded. "You're a good girlfriend, aren't you?"

Kendall smiled. "With you, the best."

Before Marley could reply it was Kendall's turn to bowl again. Luckily for them, Hector had another beer and his bowling prowess suffered. Marley and Kendall were able to catch up. The game was on the line as they all took their last turns.

"Okay, Marley," Hector said. "This is your last ball and you have to knock down nine pins for the win."

"Aw, that's nothing for my girl," Kendall said, putting her arm around Marley and walking up to the lane with her.

"I don't know," Marley muttered.

"We'll win either way," Kendall said quietly.

"Yeah?" Marley asked.

Kendall nodded. "If they win, Hector will be happy, and if we win, we can tease him about this from now on."

"I guess you're right," Marley replied.

"To use the wise words of my girlfriend," Kendall said. "It's all in fun."

Marley laughed. "I like the way your girlfriend thinks."

Kendall winked. "You've got this."

She walked back into the sitting area and stood next to Jasmine.

"I don't know when we've had this much fun," Jasmine said. She slung her arm over Kendall's shoulder. "You've got to come visit more often."

"You're right," Kendall said. "I do." As she watched Marley line up her shot, she couldn't help but think she had a very good reason not to leave in the first place.

Marley's ball careened down the lane and hit just to the right of the center pin which was the perfect spot. The pins flew, then danced in the air, knocking into the others. One of the pins slid across to the two pins left standing. One stayed upright while the other began to totter.

Marley stomped her foot on the lane like she could make it fall from so far away. It appeared she and Kendall were one pin short. Then, as if in slow motion, the pin did a final pirouette and fell next to the others.

Kendall jumped into the air and when she landed she rushed to put her arms around Marley. "You did it!" she shouted as they both jumped in a circle with their arms tightly around each other.

Marley threw her head back and laughed. "I thought it didn't matter if we won!"

Kendall giggled. "I guess it did! You're amazing!"

"What a game!" Hector said, holding up his hand to high-five them both.

"Aw, you're a good sport, friend," Marley said.

"One of us has to be." Hector smirked.

Marley laughed. "Did you want me to let you win?"

"Of course not!" Hector exclaimed. "Kendall could have, though."

Kendall's mouth fell open in surprise.

"I'm kidding," Hector said.

"No he's not," Jasmine said, joining them. "This was fun. We demand a rematch before you leave."

"You can pick the movie on Sunday, Hector," Kendall said.

"Is that supposed to make me feel better?"

Kendall raised a shoulder and winced. "I hope so."

Hector laughed. "When will I learn not to have that last beer until we're finished with the game!"

They all laughed and sat down to change their shoes.

"Maybe it's a good thing you're not coming home tonight," he added. "I'll have time to get over this bitter defeat."

"I'm just as surprised as you are, Hector," Kendall said,

slipping her foot into one of her boots. "It must have been Christmas magic that kept my ball out of the gutter."

"Oh, well, that makes a difference," he replied. "Did you hear that, Marley?"

Marley stood up and looked down at both of them. "It was not a Christmas miracle that helped Kendall bowl tonight."

"We'll see about that when we play again." Hector chuckled.

"Come on, girlfriend," Marley said. "Let's go home."

Kendall giggled and bumped her shoulder into Jasmine's. "She can be so bossy sometimes, but I like it."

"Oh my God!" Jasmine burst out laughing.

"Let's go, babe." Kendall jumped up, grabbing Marley's hand.

As they walked away, Kendall turned around. "See y'all tomorrow."

Hector waved but Kendall noticed he had a curious look on his face. She wasn't sure what to make of that, but before she could think about it Marley said, "I'm kind of hungry."

"Yeah, I snacked a little at the buffet table, but I'm hungry, too," Kendall said. "What are you thinking? Do you want to stop somewhere?"

Marley looked over at Kendall as they got in her car. "I have ice cream at home."

"Ice cream!" Kendall exclaimed. "It's thirty-eight degrees outside."

"Ice cream is a treat to be enjoyed anytime," Marley stated.

Kendall chuckled. "Okay, what flavor do you have?"

Marley smiled. "I have Blue Bell Homemade Vanilla, which is the best flavor, but I also have Rocky Road."

"If vanilla is the best then why do you have Rocky Road?"

"Homemade Vanilla," Marley corrected her. "I like a little variety."

"I see," Kendall said with an amused grin. "I'll remember that."

Marley nodded. "Did you have as much fun as I did beating Hector tonight?"

Kendall laughed. "I don't think anyone could enjoy that as much as you did. But I'm loving these Christmas parties. The magic is real."

Marley scoffed. "Oh really. How so?"

"I have a date to every party and tonight I got a girlfriend!" Kendall exclaimed. "I even get to go home with her and spend the night."

Marley chuckled. "Uh huh, so that's magic."

Kendall looked over at Marley as she turned onto her street. "Does it make my expiration date go away?"

Marley glanced over at her with an amused grin. "If we're going to make this long distance relationship work then it seems to me that you don't have an expiration date."

Kendall clapped her hands together. "Yes! That's one obstacle out of the way!"

"Are you serious?" Marley asked as she pulled into the garage. "The big obstacle is still there. Our best friends happen to be married to each other."

Kendall looked across the darkened interior of the car at Marley's profile. She reached over and gently put a lock of Marley's dark brown hair behind her ear. "I know," she whispered.

Marley turned her head and met Kendall's eyes. "Ice cream?"

Kendall smiled. "Yes, please."

They walked into the house and were met by an enthusiastic Frankie. He seemed to wiggle his butt even more when he saw Kendall.

Marley bent down to pet him. "I told you she was spending the night."

Kendall laughed and kneeled down next to Marley. Frankie happily grunted at the extra attention and kept going back and forth between them.

"Okay, buddy," Marley said standing up. "We're having ice cream. How about a treat for you."

Kendall reached into the freezer and got the vanilla ice cream out. "What are you having?"

Marley gave Frankie a treat then turned to see which flavor of ice cream Kendall had on the counter.

"You're having vanilla?" she asked.

"Yep," Kendall said. "I may not live in Texas any longer, but I know all about Blue Bell Homemade Vanilla ice cream."

"Whew," Marley said. "I'm so glad you know about Blue Bell."

"Was that another one of those tests?" Kendall asked, getting two bowls out of the cabinet.

Marley chuckled. "Maybe." She reached in a drawer for the ice cream scoop and handed it to Kendall.

"Uh," Kendall said. "Was it okay that I got everything out? I mean, it is your kitchen."

"You know where just about everything is now," Marley said. "Of course, it's fine."

"I do come over here every day," Kendall said.

"Frankie is glad you do."

"Is he the only one?"

Marley smiled. "I think you know the answer to that."

Kendall scooped ice cream into a bowl and handed it to Marley before doing the same for herself. "I know you said you're pausing the dating apps for the holidays, but do you wonder if you'll ever find your..." she trailed off.

"Person? Special someone? Partner?" Marley filled in the blank.

"Yeah," Kendall said. "All those things."

Marley took their bowls over to the table while Kendall brought spoons.

"It goes in cycles for me," Marley said. "Sometimes I feel like I'm really trying. I mean, if you don't get out there, how are you supposed to meet someone? So I swipe and meet someone for a drink or whatever. Then there are other times when I feel it's useless and I take a break, like now."

Kendall nodded and took a bite of her ice cream. She closed her eyes and let the cold treat coat her tongue with sweetness. "Mmm, that is so good."

"What about you? Are you having doubts your true love is out there?" Marley asked.

Kendall shook her head. "No, I can feel her."

"What?" Marley said with a confused look.

Kendall sighed. "I have such a longing in my heart that I know she's there, but I haven't quite figured out how to meet her. Does that sound pathetic?"

Marley shook her head. "No. A longing? Is it like the loneliness you told me about when you got here?"

Kendall smiled. "I think the loneliness stayed in New York," she said. "Since I told you about it, I haven't felt it here."

"That's good," Marley said.

"I think I know why." Kendall narrowed her gaze and pointed her spoon at Marley. "It has something to do with a cute little dog and a new friend."

Marley smiled. "You have taken away the desperation I'd been feeling about trying to meet someone."

"Now do you believe in Christmas magic?" Kendall said with a twinkle in her eye.

Marley took a bite of her ice cream and shook her head. "I think it's the magic of friendship."

"Okay," Kendall said. "I'll go with that."

Fourteen

MARLEY GOT up and took their bowls to the sink. She quickly rinsed them and put them in the dishwasher. "We have to be there early in the morning," she said.

"Okay." Kendall grabbed her bag and followed Marley down the hall.

"I'm sure Frankie will dump me tonight and sleep with you," Marley said as Kendall walked into her guest bedroom. "But that's okay. It's so sweet to see how much he loves you."

As if on cue Frankie walked into the room and jumped onto the bed. Marley reached over and scratched behind his ears. "I won't hold it against you, buddy."

Kendall chuckled. "I'm not the only one he loves. He tells me how great you are when I come over and let him out at lunch every day."

"So we've gone to talking about him as a person to now admitting he talks to us," Marley said.

Kendall raised her brows and shrugged.

Marley laughed. "Goodnight, you two. I'll see you in the morning."

"Good night, Marley," Kendall said. "Thanks for letting me stay with you tonight."

"Anything for my girlfriend." Marley winked and walked down the hall to her bedroom.

She left her bedroom door open in case Frankie decided to sleep with her after all. Once she'd finished her nighttime routine she slid under the sheets and sighed.

Sleep didn't immediately come as she thought about the party. Marley wasn't necessarily surprised about Jasmine claiming Kendall was her girlfriend in front of Arianna. But Kendall seemed more than happy to be her pretend girlfriend. The attraction or connection—whatever you wanted to call it — between them seemed to only get stronger. It didn't help that Kendall had looked so sexy in those boots. Or that they shared celebratory hugs when either of them had a particularly good turn. Those hugs had made warmth flow through Marley's body.

Marley wasn't especially keen on the idea of keeping secrets from Jasmine and Hector, but she really wanted to go on an actual date with Kendall. How could they know if they really had a shot at something if they didn't try?

She smiled at the thought of Kendall being right down the hall and getting to see her first thing in the morning. A hint of an idea began to take shape in the back of Marley's mind. It wasn't long until she fell asleep.

❄

Marley stirred and slowly opened one eye. She looked towards the window and saw it was still dark outside with just the hint of the sunrise. Her hand brushed the hair out of her face before she reached for her phone.

At some point in the night she'd gotten up to go to the bathroom and Frankie was waiting when she got back in bed.

The little dog had snuggled next to her, but was now gone. Marley listened and only heard the silence of the morning.

She sat up against the headboard and checked her email. The distribution center where she worked was in motion around the clock. Even on the weekends she liked to check and make sure everything was running smoothly.

"You're up early," Kendall said from the doorway.

Marley looked up and smiled. "I'm not up yet."

"May I?" Kendall asked, nodding towards the bed.

Marley pulled back the covers, inviting Kendall into the bed. "You are my girlfriend after all."

Kendall smiled and settled in. A few moments later Frankie jumped on the bed and curled up between them.

"Thanks for letting me stay last night. I know Jaz and Hector needed some alone time."

"You're welcome anytime," Marley replied.

Kendall nodded. "It was kind of fun last night seeing everyone's faces when word got around that I was your new girlfriend."

"Thanks for doing that," Marley said. "Arianna has a way of looking at me that makes me feel less than."

"What?" Kendall said, turning to her. "No one should ever make you feel that way, Marley. You are an amazing person."

Marley put her hand on Kendall's shoulder. "Thank you for saying that, but I'm okay, Kendall. I know who I am. She just knows how to push my buttons; however, she didn't last night. With you by my side, she gave me a look of... Let me see." Marley narrowed her gaze, trying to find the right words. "Oh hell, she looked at me like I'd scored the most beautiful woman at the party."

Kendall laughed.

"Why are you laughing? I did!" Marley said.

"Right back at you!" Kendall said. She looked away and stared at her hands.

"What's wrong?" Marley asked.

"Nothing is wrong," Kendall said, looking back up at her. "Come to New York with me next weekend," she blurted.

Marley's eyes widened.

"I have to go back for an event. I'll only be there one night, but I'd really like you to come with me." Kendall gave her a hopeful look and continued. "We can fly out Saturday morning and I can show you the New York I love. Later that evening we can go to the party and you can get an idea of what I do."

"I don't have anything to wear to a fancy New York party," Marley said, her head suddenly spinning at the thought of running around New York City with Kendall.

"Your red dress would be perfect," Kendall said.

"But you've already seen it."

"New York hasn't," Kendall replied with a grin.

"Are you wearing a dress?"

Kendall nodded. "My clothes are there. I have a dress here but I'm saving it for the Garcia's Christmas cocktail party. It's Sunday night but we'll be back in time."

"I'll get to see you in a dress Saturday and Sunday night. That gives me something to look forward to," Marley said.

Kendall chuckled. "Please, Marley. Come to New York with me."

"What about Jasmine?"

"She needs the weekend with Hector. I think having me here is a little harder than they expected."

"No it's not," Marley said. "Hector hasn't said a word and believe me, he would."

Kendall shrugged.

"Okay, Ken." Marley smiled. "I'll go with you."

"Yes!" Kendall said, shooting a fist into the air. "This is going to be so much fun."

They both sat back against the headboard. When Kendall sighed Marley looked over at her and raised her brows. "What now?"

"I was thinking about the adoption event today," Kendall said.

"What about it?"

"Do you think we should take Frankie with us?" Kendall replied. "We still haven't found his family. He's so friggin cute, he'd surely get adopted."

Marley reached over and laid her hand on Kendall's. "Don't worry about Frankie. I will keep him until we find his people."

"But what if you don't?"

Marley tilted her head and gave Kendall her sweetest smile. "You have to believe, Ken. We'll find them."

Kendall smiled. "Are you saying you believe in Christmas magic?"

"No," Marley replied, shaking her head. "I believe in good. It was a good thing when Frankie pranced down that sidewalk and found you."

Kendall's face softened. "He does prance, doesn't he." She laughed.

"He does."

"Thank you, Marley," Kendall said, kissing her on the cheek. "That is such a relief."

Marley was surprised by Kendall's reaction, and she could feel the heat where Kendall's lips touched her cheek. "You were really worried."

"I was." Kendall jumped out of the bed. "I'll make breakfast," she said, hurrying to the door.

"Wait." Marley laughed. "You don't know what food I have."

Kendall grinned. "You always have something." She winked. "I'll surprise you."

Marley watched her disappear into the hallway. "You have no idea how you surprise me, Kendall Malloy." Frankie crawled into her lap and she sighed. "What are we going to do when she leaves?"

"I'm not gone yet," Kendall said, sliding into the doorway. "Besides, you're going with me."

Marley laughed as Kendall disappeared once again.

❄

Later that afternoon at the animal shelter, Kendall couldn't keep from watching Marley. She knew Marley was good with the animals, but she had a way with people, too.

To say Kendall was looking forward to going back to New York on Saturday was an understatement. At first, she'd tried to get out of the work party, but her boss wouldn't hear of it. Kendall had planned to fly in, attend the party, and fly out the next morning, but as she and Marley began to spend more time together, it was obvious they were holding back. In New York there wouldn't be any familiar eyes watching them, and they could be with each other however they wanted.

Kendall hoped this would be a real date. They could find out if this new friendship could possibly be more. Yes, there were obstacles, but Kendall had a feeling it would be worth it.

She watched Marley give another applicant's paperwork to Jane Ann as she took the dog they were hoping to adopt back to its kennel.

"You have a real talent for matching people with pets," Kendall said.

"Do I?" Marley asked with a grin.

Kendall nodded.

"I guess you'd know since you're a matchmaker of sorts," Marley said.

Kendall chuckled. She stared at Marley and couldn't keep the smile from her face.

Marley tilted her head. "Why are you looking at me like that?"

"I'm really happy you're going to New York with me," Kendall replied. She leaned a little closer. "I'm hoping since we'll be away from all the people that know us, we can…" she trailed off.

"Go on a real date?" Marley asked, finishing her sentence.

"Would you go on a date with me?"

Marley grinned. "I've already been on two dates with you."

"You know what I mean," Kendall said, raising her brows.

"Well, I was wondering if you'd like to see where I work this week," Marley said.

Kendall's eyes lit up. "Yes! I thought you'd never ask."

Marley chuckled. "I hoped we could do it Friday at the end of the day. Jasmine will be picking Hector up."

Kendall raised her brows. "Are you saying that because you want it to be just you and me?"

Marley reached up and patted Kendall's cheek. "A smart woman is so hot."

Kendall giggled.

"I may have a way that we can make it a real date," Marley said. "Jasmine and Hector will be busy and no one will bother us at my work."

"What about—"

Marley put her finger over Kendall's lips, stopping her mid-sentence. "For now, it'll be our secret. Okay?"

Kendall nodded as a big smile grew on her face.

Marley looked around and grabbed Kendall's wrist, pulling her out the back door of the shelter. "I've seen Hector watching us," she said. "Shouldn't we find out if this could be something before he decides to start asking questions?"

Kendall had been staring into Marley's eyes and they flashed with excitement of what could be. She looked down at her lips then back into her eyes. To say she'd imagined kissing Marley would be the truth, but she never pictured it quite like this.

It was as if Marley's lips were pulling her in and Kendall could no longer resist. She leaned in and pressed her lips to Marley's before she knew what she was doing. Kendall's eyes fluttered shut and her hand went around Marley's waist.

Their lips fit together perfectly. *Of course they did.*

Kendall pulled back but not before Marley's firm, luscious lips were burned into her memory.

"I think this is already something," Kendall said softly.

One corner of Marley's mouth lifted in a smile.

The door to the shelter opened and Jane Ann stuck her head out. "There you are," she said. "We need some help up front."

"We'll be right there," Marley said with a smile.

When Jane Ann shut the door, Kendall turned to Marley. "Why does it suddenly feel like it's a very long time until Friday?"

"I'm giving you time to change your mind," Marley said, raising her brows.

"I'm not changing my mind," Kendall replied. "I'm counting down the days."

"Shh," Marley said quietly, putting her finger over her lips. "It's a secret, but it'll be worth it."

Kendall leaned in and softly brushed her lips against Marley's. "It's already worth it."

Marley smiled, interlaced her fingers with Kendall's and led them to the door.

Kendall grinned and already knew she could kiss Marley's pillowy lips all day long. It would always be worth it.

Fifteen

"THAT WAS SO PREDICTABLE," Jasmine commented.

"Well, yeah," Kendall said. "It's a Hallmark Christmas movie. That's why we watch them, because we know they'll have a happy ending."

"We know how it will end, but what's not predictable is how they get there. That's the fun part," Marley added.

"I usually like the age gap or friends to lovers storyline," Jasmine said.

"I liked this forbidden romance we just watched," Hector said. "I'm a fan. If two hearts are meant to be together then they'll find a way, just like in the movie."

"What do you consider forbidden?" Marley asked.

"Mmm, I don't know," Hector said. "There are workplace romances like the boss/employee thing or there's the teacher/student thing."

"What about friends who date your sister?" Jasmine said.

"Oh, yeah," Hector said. "My sister and one of my good friends went out for a while and when it ended, my friendship with him was never the same."

"Haven't any of your friends dated Jasmine's friends?" Kendall asked.

Hector smiled at Jasmine. "We've been married so long, all of our friends are *our* friends now."

"You're always wanting to set me up, Jaz," Kendall said. "Aren't those people your friends?"

"Well, I'd say they're work friends or someone I know through another friend. You know a lot of our friends, Ken. We've had them since college." Jasmine narrowed her eyes at Kendall. "Are you reconsidering letting me set you up?"

"No," Kendall replied.

"Sometimes when friends date friends in the same friend group—wow," Hector said, laughing, "that's a lot of friends, but you know what I mean. Anyway, it can mess with the dynamic of the group when the relationships end."

"Like with your sister?" Marley said.

"Yeah, and like with you and Arianna," Hector said. "I liked her and we all got along okay, but when you two broke up it was awkward."

"Did you really consider her a friend, though?" Marley asked, giving Hector a pointed look. "And friends date friends all the time."

"Kendall," Jasmine said. "What's that look?"

Kendall met Jasmine's gaze and shrugged. "The other night when Marley and I became 'girlfriends'"—Kendall made air quotes with her fingers—"no one seemed surprised. They were happy about it. I guess I'm wondering... What if we weren't fake girlfriends after all?"

Jasmine laughed. "Don't you think we would have set you two up a long time ago if we thought you were compatible?"

"Duh," Hector said. "Kendall, you're all about work and the big city. You're the opposite of Marley. She loves helping at the shelter and is all about fun."

"Thanks a lot, Hector," Kendall said disdainfully.

"Yeah, thanks a lot," Marley echoed.

"I didn't mean it in a bad way," Hector said, holding up his hands. "You're our best friends. Imagine how awkward that would be if you had a fight."

"You and Jasmine have had fights before and Kendall and I are still your best friends," Marley countered.

"Besides," Jasmine said, "Marley isn't interested in long distance. I'm always trying to convince Kendall to come home, but we all know she isn't going to do that."

Maybe Marley could be the reason I did come back. Kendall wanted to say it out loud, but instead looked over at Marley and sighed.

"You won't even go on a date," Jasmine continued. "The two Christmas party dates you've been on with Marley are more than you've had all year. They weren't even real dates."

"Yeah, and Marley dates all the time," Hector added.

Kendall furrowed her brow and stared at Marley. "They are making us sound like a whole lot of fun to be with, aren't they? I wonder how we could possibly be their best friends."

Marley smiled. "I know."

"You are our best friends and we love you," Jasmine said.

"Yes, we love you," Hector echoed. "Why are we talking about you two dating in the first place?"

"No reason. But this all business, never-dates, fake girl-friend needs another beer," Kendall said, getting up. This conversation wasn't helping her and Marley. "Anyone else?"

"Kendall," Hector said. "Please don't be mad. You are an amazing woman and I love you. Someone is going to be so damn fortunate when you love them."

Kendall smiled and shook her head. "It's okay, Hector. Beer, anyone?"

"Yep," Marley said, getting up. "I'll take one."

"Jaz? Hector?"

"Nope, I'm good," Hector said.

Kendall and Marley walked into the kitchen. Kendall reached into the refrigerator and handed Marley a beer. "Well, that tells us how they feel."

"Yep." Marley nodded. "I think our date should stay our secret."

"Hey y'all, hurry up," Hector yelled from the living room. "We have time for an episode of *Hacks* before I have to leave for the airport."

Kendall looked into Marley's eyes and smiled.

"Or do you think we should tell them?" Marley asked.

Kendall shook her head. "I'm really looking forward to Friday. Do you want to call it off?" Her heart was nervously thumping in her chest. She didn't want to call this date off, but the apprehension in Marley's eyes made her wonder if she did.

"No," Marley said firmly. "I want Friday night to be you and me."

"Okay." Kendall nodded. "It's our secret."

Marley smiled. Kendall wanted to grab her and kiss the worry from her eyes. Maybe they should rethink this, but the idea that they couldn't go on a real date because of their friends made Kendall a little angry.

"Shh." Kendall put her finger to her lips and Marley chuckled. She squeezed Marley's hand before they walked back into the living room.

❄

A couple of days later Marley had a work emergency in the middle of the night. She'd spent several hours trying to get repairs done, trucks loaded, and shipments ready to go out. Finally, around nine o'clock that morning she'd gone home to get a few hours of sleep. She planned to go back and use the afternoon to catch up on her regular duties.

When she'd first gotten home and climbed into bed, Frankie snuggled against her, helping her fall asleep. She'd woken up several times in the middle of dreams. Sometimes Kendall was in them and she vaguely remembered Hector in another.

She smiled as she thought she heard Kendall's voice. Her hand reached beside her to pet Frankie, but he wasn't there. Was she dreaming again? Her eyes fluttered open and she realized Kendall must be there letting Frankie outside like she did every day.

Marley got up and walked down the hall to the living room. She stopped when she heard Kendall talking to Frankie.

"Hi, buddy." Kendall reached down and pet the dog. "Three more days, three more days," she began to sing as she rubbed Frankie's back. "Three more days until our date," she said, dancing around with the dog.

There was no way Marley could have formed words into a sentence because Kendall was dressed in a business suit that looked like it was made just for her. She was wearing heels and her legs went on forever.

Marley cleared her throat.

"Oh my God!" Kendall exclaimed, grabbing her chest. "You scared me to death!"

Marley smiled and tilted her head with amusement.

"Oh, uh, you heard that, didn't you?" Kendall said, wincing. "Are you going to call it off now?"

"What!" Marley exclaimed, walking over to her. "No. Why would I do that?"

"Because now you know what an idiot I am," Kendall said.

"I don't think you're an idiot," Marley replied, putting her hands on Kendall's hips.

"No?"

"Mmm," Marley murmured. She reached up, softly touched her lips to Kendall's, and felt a blanket of warmth

129

surround them. It was quickly followed by the pounding of her heart as Kendall's arms tightened around her shoulders.

This wasn't like their rather brief first kiss. Marley parted her lips and instead of inviting Kendall inside she slowly ran her tongue over Kendall's bottom lip. The softest moan escaped Kendall's throat and Marley thought her heart might stop.

When she felt the tip of Kendall's tongue waiting, Marley pulled Kendall tighter and a wave of sensations flew through her body, accompanied by quiet murmurs of pleasure. The feel of Kendall's lips, the taste of her tongue, the sounds of their breaths and moans: *this is so good.*

Their lips nibbled, their tongues danced and when they finally pulled away they both inhaled deeply.

The softest smile played at Kendall's lips. "What are you doing here?" she asked quietly.

Marley smiled. "A better question is, do you always dress like this for work?"

A sultry smirk crossed Kendall's face.

"You've got that sexy executive look locked down," Marley said then added, "babe."

Kendall chuckled. "I met with a couple of prospective financial analysts we're hoping to recruit."

"Mmm-mmm," Marley murmured. She took in every little nuance of Kendall's cheeks, eyes, and lips as her gaze roamed over her face. "You are so beautiful."

"Thank you," Kendall replied softly. She rubbed her lips together then raised one brow. "You look like you just woke up."

Marley chuckled. "I'll explain in a—" She kissed Kendall, unable to resist feeling her lips on hers. They were so soft and the tingles they made race through her body were thrilling. Warmth spread through Marley's veins like a shot of whiskey and culminated with a flutter then a throbbing in her center.

Marley was suddenly wide awake with none of the dull buzz that followed an interrupted night's sleep. She could feel Kendall's fingers at the nape of her neck, then they were in her hair and the kiss grew even hotter.

Since their chat with Jasmine and Hector about forbidden relationships they hadn't had a chance to be alone. Maybe it was the surprise of finding Kendall in her living room when she woke up. Or the illicit idea of their forthcoming date that caused this impromptu make-out session. Whatever it was, Marley didn't care as long as Kendall's lips were on hers.

The saddest little high-pitched whimper pierced the chorus of their heavy breaths and moans.

They pulled away and looked down to find Frankie standing at their feet.

"Do you need to go out?" Kendall asked.

"It's her fault," Marley said, reluctantly letting Kendall go. "Just look at her in this suit."

Kendall chuckled. "I would've worn this a long time ago if I'd known you'd kiss me like that!"

"Come on," Marley said, walking to the back door. She let Frankie out and looked into the backyard. "Wow, it's a beautiful day."

"Are you all right?" Kendall asked.

"Yeah, let me grab my coat," Marley said, taking a hoodie off the back of one of the chairs in the kitchen. She held the back door open for Kendall. "Shall we?"

Kendall grinned and walked out to the patio.

"The sunshine has made it much warmer today," Marley said.

"You know Texas weather." Kendall shrugged. "One day it's freezing, the next day it's gorgeous."

Marley smiled at Kendall and grabbed the lapels of her suit. "I'm so happy to see you."

"Marley, what's going on?" Kendall asked, raising her brows. "Why are you home in the middle of the day?"

"I had to go to work around two o'clock this morning," Marley explained, letting Kendall go and watching Frankie meander around the yard. "There was a big breakdown on one of the automated lines. It backed things up and almost shut everything down. I was able to reroute some things and—long story short—everything is now back running."

"Oh wow," Kendall exclaimed. She gasped. "Wait, I didn't wake you up, did I?"

Marley gave her a sexy smile. "I like waking up with you around."

Kendall chuckled. "After you nearly gave me a heart attack, I thought it was going to beat right out of my chest when you kissed me."

"Yeah," Marley muttered. She reached over and ran her thumb from Kendall's lower lip down her chin. "You're hard to resist."

"Even when you've worked all night and you're tired?" Kendall grinned.

Marley's face softened. "I'm finding you're hard to resist, period."

"Welcome to my world," Kendall said seductively.

They simply stared at one another for several moments before Kendall asked, "Do you have the rest of the day off?"

"Sadly, no," Marley said. "Wait—what do you have in mind?"

Kendall raised her brows and smiled.

"Mmhmm, so tempting," Marley said. "But I do have to go back and catch up on all the things I needed to do this morning."

Kendall sighed and frowned at Marley.

"Come on, let's sit a minute," Marley said, taking

Kendall's hand and leading them to the chairs around her table on the porch.

Sixteen

"You have a nice backyard," Kendall said. "Do flowers bloom in the spring?"

Marley pointed to her left. "In that flower bed there are tulips and daffodils. And over there are a couple of rose bushes." Marley paused for a moment. "In the spring I have flower pots that I put all around the patio with seasonal flowers planted in them."

"I love marigolds and impatiens," Kendall said.

"That's what I put in the pots!" Marley exclaimed.

"Really!" Kendall said in surprise.

"Yes, they're my favorites and they do well in the summer sun."

"Have you ever thought about having a garden?" Kendall asked. "Like to grow vegetables?"

"Are you going to come help me put it in and tend it?" Marley asked.

Kendall looked over at her and grinned. "I'd love that."

"Do you miss having a yard in New York?" Marley asked.

"Yeah, I tried to grow a tomato plant one summer in my

apartment, but I think I managed to get three small tomatoes from it."

"Maybe you'd have better luck if you had an actual garden," Marley said.

Kendall held Marley's gaze for a moment as images danced through her head: the two of them in shorts and sandals, working in the flower bed or planting marigolds in a pot. She smiled, imagining Marley's sun-kissed skin in a sleeveless top and short shorts.

"That might be a perk of moving back here."

Kendall widened her eyes. "Are you planning a presentation to get me to move back?"

Marley shrugged. "Maybe I will. Jasmine would certainly help me."

Kendall chuckled. "I don't need any other reason to move back here other than the one I'm looking at." She couldn't believe she admitted that so easily, but in her heart Kendall realized it was true.

Marley smiled. "Like it would be that simple."

"You never know," Kendall said. "My company is looking to open offices in other parts of the country. Maybe I could sell them on Dallas."

"Are you serious?" Marley asked.

Kendall nodded.

"So your expiration date was tentative from the beginning?"

"Not exactly," Kendall said. "My boss has talked about expanding into other cities for a while now. When I told her about the women I was having lunch with today she commented that she'd been doing research into this area as a possible site for a new office."

"That would be great!" Marley tilted her head. "Wouldn't it? Do you want to leave New York?"

"I hadn't thought much about leaving New York."

Kendall shrugged. "But in the short time I've been back here I have to say the idea has crossed my mind."

"Jasmine and Hector would be over the moon with happiness," Marley said.

"Would they be the only ones?" Kendall asked.

A slow smile crossed Marley's face. "I'm sure Evan and Alicia would love to see you more often. I mean, you were instrumental in getting them together."

Kendall laughed. "You know that's not true." She ran her teeth over her bottom lip. "You're funny when you're tired. It's kind of like when you're tipsy."

Marley sat up in her chair. "When have you seen me tipsy?"

"I haven't but I've heard from our best friends," Kendall replied. "I'm sure you know things about me."

"I know you like sapphic romance, because Jasmine shares your book recs with me," Marley said. "Let's see, you don't like sushi, but you love pecan brittle." She pointed her finger at Kendall. "Not peanut brittle, pecan brittle," she stated. "You don't like peanuts."

"Wow," Kendall said. "I'm afraid to find out how you know those things."

Marley chuckled. "I don't really like sushi either. Jasmine thinks something is wrong with us and has told me so several times." She smiled. "Whenever we're out and come across one of those shops that sells treats like pecan brittle, she always buys a bag."

"She sends them to me," Kendall said with a grin. "We buy orange slices for you."

"What?" Marley wrinkled her brow.

"You're not the only one who shops with Jasmine." Kendall chuckled. "When she sees orange slices she buys them for you."

"What else?"

"Hmm. You love to spend time at the lake in the summer," Kendall said.

"So do you." Marley grinned. "That's why you visit every summer."

"We seem to know a lot about each other," Kendall said, gazing over at Marley.

"But I want to know more," Marley replied softly.

"Will Friday ever get here?" Kendall asked earnestly.

"That reminds me," Marley said. "I need details of this trip you're whisking me away on. I have to know what to pack."

Kendall's eyes lit up with delight. "Is that how you're thinking of it? I'm whisking you away."

"Aren't you?"

"Oh, yeah," Kendall nodded. "We're going behind our best friends' backs and they don't even know it. That's kind of fun, but also a little scary." She gave Marley a wicked grin.

"But you're showing me what you love about your city," Marley said. "That's special."

"Maybe I need to do a presentation on why you should relocate to NYC," Kendall said.

"Oh, God!" Marley exclaimed. "Jasmine and Hector might kill us both if I did that."

"If things go like I think they will with our weekend away, then they may kill us both anyway."

Marley laughed. "I never expected you would be so dangerous."

"I'm not!" Kendall exclaimed. "It must be you!"

"I wish I was home at this time every day," Marley said with a smile.

Kendall shook her head. "Then I wouldn't have to come by and let Frankie out."

"I can't help it if I like being with you."

"I hope that never changes," Kendall said, "because I like being with you, too."

Marley stared at Kendall for a moment. "Come on, Frankie," she said, getting up. "I have to go back to work."

"I'll make dinner tonight and we'll come to you," Kendall said as they walked back into the house.

"Make sure you're wearing something ugly and loose fitting," Marley said. "Our secret will be out if I kiss you in front of Jasmine."

Kendall reached for Marley and pulled her into her arms. "Then you'd better kiss me now, so I won't be tempted when I come back."

Marley giggled. "How did this happen?"

"Uh, you grabbed me when you walked into the room," Kendall said.

"I did," Marley said, rubbing her lips together.

"If you hadn't given me a heart attack first..." Kendall said, raising a brow.

"Let's make sure your heart is still beating—"

Before Marley could finish her sentence, Kendall captured her lips in a fierce kiss. She felt her heart skip a beat as Marley's hands squeezed her shoulders. Their tongues met and began another dance of exploration. Neither tried to take the lead as they sank into the kiss, letting the pleasure flow through their bodies.

A little moan filtered into Kendall's ears as Marley's arms tightened around her neck. Their chests were pressed together and Kendall slightly moved her thigh to rest between Marley's legs as her hands held Marley's hips to her.

Kendall thought their earlier kisses were possibly the best she had ever had, but this was different. She could feel Marley's heart beating with hers as they shared this moment. Kendall was sure the warmth and electricity she felt rushing through her body had to be flowing into Marley as well.

When their lips finally parted, Kendall stared into Marley's dark brown eyes. They were both taking deep breaths and

Kendall wondered if Marley could see what was happening inside her.

"You'd better go," Marley said softly.

Kendall widened her eyes. "Did I do something wrong?"

Marley smiled and tilted her head. "God, no. I'll be thinking about this kiss until Friday."

Kendall closed her eyes and held Marley to her. She could feel Marley's warm breath on her neck. It wasn't lost on her how well they fit together. They stayed like that for a few moments then Kendall stepped back.

"I'll see you later," Kendall said, walking to the front door.

"You'd better." Marley smiled and raised her brows.

Kendall chuckled. "There's my bossy girlfriend."

Marley laughed. "You seem to like it."

"I do from you." Kendall winked and walked out the door.

She turned around as she got in her car and saw Marley watching her with a captivating look on her face. *Yep, Marley's feeling it, too.* What was supposed to be a date to see if there might be something between them had just become much more.

As Kendall drove back to Jasmine's house, she couldn't keep from thinking of their upcoming date. It had been a while since Kendall had had sex with anyone, but this connection with Marley was so much more than that. Yes, if Marley hadn't had to go back to work and Kendall didn't have a meeting in half an hour they very well could be naked in Marley's bedroom doing much more than kissing.

Had it been so long since Kendall had the attention of another woman that she'd lost her ability to think? Yes, it felt good to be desired by Marley. But what about Jasmine and Hector?

They could stop now and pull this back into the friend

139

zone before they all got hurt. Couldn't they? Did she want to? Did Marley?

Kendall sighed. Why did this suddenly seem to be so complicated? She wanted to be back in the middle of that kiss where nothing mattered but the staccato beating of their hearts and the warmth flowing through their bodies.

A Christmas song came on the radio and Kendall immediately thought about Christmas magic. *Is that what's going on*, she wondered.

Sure, she and Marley knew a lot about each other because of their friends, but she never imagined the connection she felt when they first looked into each other's eyes. Marley definitely felt it too, so it wasn't one-sided.

Knowing Jasmine and Hector were against the idea of them even going on a date should have shut things down, but instead now they were in the middle of a huge secret that could end up hurting them all. Why risk it?

When Kendall thought about it she shrugged. "There's no use fighting it because Marley Jacobs is pulling me towards her." She smiled. "And that's exactly where I want to be."

Kendall drove into Jasmine and Hector's driveway and it hit her. "It must be Christmas magic," she said. With her hands still on the steering wheel Kendall stared ahead, not seeing the garage. What she saw was the look on Marley's face when she drove away.

"I'm falling for her," she mumbled. *No way!*

Kendall closed her eyes and tried to shake the image out of her head. She had never fallen for someone so quickly, but that's what her heart was telling her. Once again, she thought, why fight it? Christmas magic always seemed to get its way.

"Hmm," she muttered. Kendall wondered why Marley didn't believe in it because now she was sure it was definitely working on them.

Seventeen

"Wow," Jasmine said as Kendall walked into the living room. "You look nice."

"Thanks." Kendall was wearing dark jeans with a sleeveless sweater over a button down shirt. Ankle boots completed the outfit. Her hair was swept over to one side with a stray strand or two resting against her forehead.

"You are every queer woman's dream," Jasmine said.

Kendall scoffed. "And how would you know what queer women want?"

"Two of my best friends happen to be lesbians," Jasmine replied. "I've seen who they date, so I have a pretty good idea."

Kendall shrugged. "Maybe."

"Why are you so dressed up?" Jasmine asked. "I thought you were going to Marley's work for a tour."

"I am, but after she shows me around I'm not sure what we're doing." Kendall shrugged. "Are you and Hector doing anything after you pick him up from the airport?"

"Maybe," Jasmine said, her gaze resting on Kendall. "He's always hungry, so we may stop to eat. I'll text y'all."

Kendall reached for her purse, trying to escape Jasmine's

stare. Maybe she shouldn't have tried to look quite so nice for Marley. "Thanks for giving me a ride to Marley's work."

"No problem," Jasmine replied casually. "I go right by there on the way to the airport."

Kendall nodded as they got in the car and began the drive to this very important date. Jasmine didn't have a clue how important this night was to Kendall and she tried to tamp down her excitement. All Kendall needed was for Jasmine to find out this was a real date.

"You know, it's surprised me a little, but I've really enjoyed the three of us hanging out," Jasmine said.

"I like it, too," Kendall replied. "But why is that surprising?"

"I don't know," Jasmine said. "I guess I didn't expect it to feel this easy. Even when Hector is with us, we all get along and it's comfortable."

"Yeah, it is. Maybe it's because we're friends," Kendall said playfully.

"You know what I'm going to say next," Jasmine said, glancing over at Kendall.

"You're going to say that y'all need to come visit me in New York," Kendall replied.

"Not." Jasmine chuckled. "It's time for you to come home!" she exclaimed.

Kendall sighed. "I don't know why you keep saying this is my home. It's not. We met here in college and then lived together until we graduated."

"Well, your parents have moved from Houston to be closer to your sister's family and the grandkids," Jasmine said. "That's certainly not home. I know you work a lot because New York does not feel like home. Kendall, look at me."

Kendall looked over at Jasmine and could see the earnestness in her face.

"I am your home," Jasmine said. "No matter where we are,

we will always have a place for you. You've always been able to count on me and you always will. I am your home."

Kendall swallowed the lump in her throat and didn't know what to say.

"Sometimes when we talk, I can hear the loneliness in your voice," Jasmine said. "You hide it well, but I can hear it. I know you're not always going to stay there. Remember that you always have a place right here."

Kendall smiled. "Would it make you feel better if I told you that the thought of moving back has crossed my mind since I've been here?"

"Not really," Jasmine replied. "I know any time you come to visit you think about it. That's one reason I wanted you to meet someone. I thought that would give you a reason to come back."

"What?" Kendall said. "You're not reason enough?"

Jasmine chuckled. "Of course I am. But think about how nice it's been. You have a friend in Marley now and we're like our own little family. Hasn't it been nice to do things with friends at the end of the day instead of continuing to work?"

Kendall smiled. "Yes, I've loved hanging out. We are like a little family, aren't we?"

"Yeah, and you'd have your pick of jobs. There are plenty of companies right here that could benefit from your talents," Jasmine said.

"But I love my job," Kendall replied.

"You love making people rich?"

"Uh, that's one way to look at it, I guess," Kendall replied. "It makes me feel good to know that I'm helping people prepare for the future they want. It's not just about making money, Jaz."

"I shouldn't have said that," Jasmine replied. "There are plenty of jobs here that would be just as fulfilling."

"I'm sure there are," Kendall said.

Jasmine nodded as she pulled into the parking lot. "I know you'll have fun showing Marley New York this weekend, but don't be surprised if you miss us."

Kendall chuckled. "You won't miss us. I know you have plans for Hector."

Jasmine wiggled her eyebrows and grinned.

"Hey, thanks again for keeping Frankie while we're gone," Kendall said.

"Hector is excited about it," Jasmine said. "I'm sure he'll be wanting a dog by the time you get back."

Kendall smiled and opened her door. "I'll see you later."

If Jasmine could hear the loneliness in Kendall's voice then was it just a matter of time before she'd figure out what was going on with her and Marley? She was Kendall's best friend and had been for years. But the way Jasmine was talking about the four of them being a family made Kendall wonder if she and Marley could have a future together *and* keep their best friends.

She decided to tell Marley about their conversation later. Right now, she couldn't wait to start this date.

"Hi," Kendall said, walking up to the receptionist's desk in the lobby of the building. "I'm here to see Marley Jacobs."

Before the receptionist could say anything a woman walked up from a hallway to Kendall's right.

"You must be Kendall," the woman said. "I'm Kyra, Marley's assistant."

"Hi," Kendall said.

Kyra smiled at the woman behind the desk then turned to Kendall. "Right this way. We've been waiting for you."

"Oh." Kendall grinned as she followed her into an area with several offices. Her heart started to beat a little faster and she felt a flutter in her stomach. That seemed to be happening more and more lately when she knew Marley was near.

❄

Marley hurried out from behind her desk. She'd wanted to meet Kendall at the receptionist's desk but had to stop and answer a quick call.

When she walked out of her office she saw Kyra escorting Kendall her way. Marley couldn't stop the smile that grew on her face. For a moment she lost her breath as she took Kendall in. Each confident stride brought this beautiful woman closer and closer. Wisps of hair fell over Kendall's forehead and Marley wanted to gently tuck them behind her ear as she closed the distance between their lips. *Slow down, you're still at work*, Marley chided herself.

She ran her teeth over her bottom lip and simply said, "Hi."

"Hey," Kendall said with a smile.

Marley was sure she could see the same kind of want and delight in Kendall's eyes.

"Thanks, Kyra," Marley said.

There was a pleased smile on Kyra's face as she said, "Kendall just got here."

"I'm sorry I couldn't meet you at the front," Marley said.

"It's okay." Kendall grinned.

"I'll make sure everything is locked up in the offices," Kyra said. "Enjoy your evening."

As Kyra walked away Marley smiled at Kendall. "She may have helped me with a few things for our date." She took Kendall's hand and led her into her office. Once inside Marley turned to her. "I know this is rather unconventional for a first date, but I'm really glad you're here and we're doing this."

Before Kendall could reply Marley softly touched her lips to Kendall's in a brief kiss.

"As first dates go," Kendall said, "how will we ever forget this?"

Marley chuckled as her nervousness began to subside. She'd imagined this moment off and on all day. Yes, they had already had a couple of dates to Christmas parties, but this was a real first date.

"You look so good," Marley said, stepping away and looking Kendall up and down.

"Thank you," Kendall replied. "To quote our friend, Jasmine, I'm every queer woman's dream."

Marley chuckled. "You are certainly this woman's dream."

"I don't know," Kendall said, walking closer. "You look quite commanding in that suit... boss."

Marley giggled. "I thought you wanted a tour of my work."

"I do. I do." Kendall stepped back and held up her hands. "It's just that we haven't been alone—"

"I know," Marley interrupted her, "since *you* were in a suit. Believe me, I remember."

"Jasmine did wonder why I was dressed like this for a tour," Kendall said.

"What'd you tell her?"

"I said we might go out after," Kendall replied. "She also said something that gave me hope about this date, but I'll tell you about it later. Right now, I want to see this." She held out her arms and looked around Marley's office.

"You really are interested, aren't you?" Marley said.

"Yes," Kendall replied. "I can't get over how huge this place is from the outside and can't imagine everything that goes on inside."

"Okay," Marley said. "Let's start here."

Marley's desk was a large semi-circular shape. It held three monitors across one side of it, a computer with keyboard on the other and in the middle was a space for documents. The wall behind her chair was a giant window that looked out into the distribution center.

"It goes on and on, row after row," Kendall said in amazement.

"We'll get down to the floor, but let me show you this first," Marley said. "These monitors give me real-time data on what's happening over the entire facility. Do you see the graphs and lines that are green, yellow, and red?"

"Mmhmm." Kendall nodded.

"Imagine your maps app on your phone," Marley said. "It works kind of like that. We have goods coming in, being processed, then moving from area to area. At the same time we have goods going out. They have to be located, loaded, and then off they go." Marley touched the screen. "These green lines show everything running smoothly, the yellow ones indicate things slowing, and the red means nothing is happening."

"Oh, just like traffic on the map," Kendall said. "If it's yellow then traffic is slow and red means you're at a standstill."

"Right," Marley replied with a smile. "This is where trucks are being unloaded." She indicated a set of graphs on the far left screen. "These are green and you'll notice we have a few yellows here."

"What about this red one?" Kendall asked.

"It could mean that a truck is backing up to the unloading area and its door hasn't been opened yet," Marley explained. "Once it's opened and the unloading process begins, it will change to yellow then green if all goes well."

"Look!" Kendall said. "It's yellow now."

"Yeah, and..."

"There it goes," Kendall said excitedly. "It's green."

"While this is coming in," Marley said, "other things are going out." She indicated another set of graphs on the far right screen.

"This is fascinating," Kendall said.

"When problems arise we have to reroute or find solutions so everything keeps moving," Marley said. "We have meetings every morning and the various departments report their needs so we can adjust supply and demand. For example, there are times in the year where demand will be higher on the outgoing side of things."

"Like now, at Christmas," Kendall said.

"Exactly," Marley replied with a grin. She could tell Kendall was actually interested in how the facility operated. It gave Marley a thrill to know Kendall cared.

"So you have to make adjustments all through the day," Kendall said. "I can't imagine all the information going through your brain every day and the constant battle to keep things balanced."

"I like to look at it as a big puzzle," Marley said, holding out her hands.

"You must be highly organized and love schedules," Kendall said, grinning. "When you look at these monitors then turn and look out over the floor you must get such a satisfied feeling."

Marley chuckled. "I do, much like you get by helping your clients."

"It's funny you say that because Jasmine commented on my job on the way over here," Kendall said. "She thinks I help people get rich."

"That's not what you do!" Marley protested. "What about the single moms you help make a better life? They're not getting rich."

Kendall chuckled. "Wow, you're defending me."

Marley shrugged. "I guess I am. I've seen how passionate you are about your job."

"I see the delight in your eyes as you explain all of this to me," Kendall said. "It's hot."

Marley's eyes widened. "It is?"

"I didn't mean that in a disrespectful way," Kendall said

quickly. "I don't know how you do this and it's really incredible to me."

Marley smiled. "I'm sure I'll feel the same way tomorrow at your company party."

Kendall grinned. "Let's agree that we're both impressed with one another."

"Are you ready to go down on the floor?" Marley chuckled as Kendall's eyes lit up.

Eighteen

"THIS IS the part of the date I wasn't too sure about," Marley said as they walked through the office complex out into the facility.

"Why?"

"Well, looking at a bunch of boxes, packages, and machinery isn't something you do on a date," Marley said.

"Sure it is," Kendall said, glancing over at her. "You wouldn't expect us to go bowling on a date and we did at the party."

"Yeah, I don't know," Marley said. "Showing me around New York tomorrow will be more like a date."

"I wish we could've walked around the shops that night I helped you at the shelter's booth."

Marley groaned. "Oh, you mean the night I found out I have a streak of jealousy for you that runs through me in the most unattractive way."

Kendall chuckled. "I was just as bad trying to get back to the booth to apologize to you." She turned to Marley. "When we look back on that night, will it be the moment we knew there was more than friendship happening between us?"

Marley shook her head. "I knew it the first time our eyes met."

"I remember," Kendall said, gazing into Marley's eyes. "I saw you walk into Jasmine's living room with Alicia and I asked Evan who you were."

"Our eyes met and I felt my heart sigh," Marley said.

"What?"

Marley smiled. "I knew you had to be Kendall and my heart—it's hard to explain." She paused and put her hand flat on Kendall's chest over her heart. "When our eyes met, my heart softened in my chest like a contented sigh."

"Mine skipped a beat then started pounding so hard I thought you'd be able to see it through my shirt," Kendall said. She put her hand over Marley's, keeping it on her chest. "And then we both started pushing those feelings down."

"Because our best friends happen to be married to each other," Marley added.

"And I have an expiration date."

"Not anymore," Marley said.

Kendall smiled.

"Shall we continue the tour? We have places to go and things to see," Marley said. They had stopped next to a golf cart and Marley got in and patted the seat next to her.

"This just keeps getting better." Kendall grinned and slid onto the seat.

Marley drove them down several aisles, explaining each process as they made their way to the back of the facility. Kendall couldn't get over the expanse of the building and the contents. Marley explained how technology and artificial intelligence were used in every aspect of the entire operation.

"This is so impressive," Kendall said.

Marley chuckled. "You keep saying that."

"*You* are so impressive," Kendall stated, putting her arm over the seat behind Marley.

"Would you still say that if I wasn't driving you through a massive building filled with more stuff than you've probably ever seen in one place?" Marley asked with an amused lilt to her voice.

"Oh yeah," Kendall said softly, staring at Marley's profile.

Marley glanced over at her and smiled. "When you look at me like that..."

"Does your heart sigh?" Kendall asked.

Marley giggled. "Are you making fun of me?"

"No!" Kendall said. "That may be the nicest thing anyone has ever said to me. You do that to me but I didn't know how to say it."

"Sure you do," Marley said. "Tell me."

Kendall smiled as Marley stopped the golf cart and met her gaze. "You make butterflies zoom around my heart in excitement of what's next," she said.

"Yes," Marley said, drawing the word out. "That's how it feels." She grinned. "Well, we're here."

Kendall had been watching Marley and not where she was driving them, but now she looked around. In front of the golf cart there was a blanket spread on the ground along with two pillows. Next to the blanket was a picnic basket.

"Marley!" Kendall gasped.

"I thought we could have a picnic." Marley grinned. She got out of the golf cart and walked around it to Kendall and offered her hand.

"Talk about an incredible first date," Kendall said, taking her hand.

"You're taking me to New York tomorrow." Marley chuckled. "I had to be creative."

Kendall squeezed Marley's hand. "You have no idea how much I'm loving this."

"Yeah?" Marley grinned. "Well, have a seat. I have a few more surprises."

They each sat down on one of the pillows. Marley reached for a plastic candle and turned on the switch. She repeated this with another candle and smiled at Kendall. "It wouldn't be safe to have an open flame in here, but I thought a picnic by fake candlelight could still be fun."

"Oh, Marley," Kendall said, shaking her head. "Christmas magic is all around us."

"What!" Marley exclaimed. "Why do you say that?"

"Because!" Kendall replied. "How many people have you set up a picnic for at your work? Think about how long we've known about each other but it took us years to meet. And when we finally do, we immediately decide to be each other's dates for all the Christmas parties."

Marley smirked. "Are you sure you want to know how many dates I've brought here?"

Kendall felt her heart drop into her stomach as her mouth fell open.

"I'm kidding," Marley said, reaching for both her hands. "I've never had a date at my work, Ken."

"Oh." Kendall sighed audibly. "What is it about you and Christmas magic?"

Marley sighed. "If this is Christmas magic then it's not going to end well for us."

"Why do you say that?"

"Because the magic of Christmas hasn't been kind to me," Marley said. She reached into the picnic basket and took out several containers of food.

"Will you tell me about it?" Kendall asked as she took the lids off the containers.

"Yes," Marley replied. "But first, I made a quinoa salad that I think you'll like."

Kendall smiled. "I love quinoa, but I think you already knew that somehow."

Marley smirked then giggled. "I didn't make this bread,

but it's beyond delicious. Oh, I almost forgot." She reached for her phone, hit a few buttons, and music began to play.

Kendall listened and wrinkled her brow. In a moment she gasped and said, "Is that George Michael?"

Marley nodded. "It's a Christmas playlist with some of the songs from *Last Christmas*."

"I love that movie!"

Marley laughed. "I know you do."

"How?"

"That first Sunday when we watched movies with Jasmine and Hector you said it was your favorite," Marley said. "I knew that little tidbit of information would come in handy someday."

Kendall watched Marley set out the food that she obviously took great care to prepare and if Kendall wasn't sure before she was now. She was falling in love with Marley Jacobs.

"Okay," Marley said, handing Kendall a glass of wine then a plate. "The reason I don't believe in Christmas magic is because I've been broken up with three separate times at Christmas."

"No way!" Kendall exclaimed.

"Yes." Marley nodded. "It all started with the captain of the volleyball team."

"The one Hector mentioned the other day?" Kendall asked. She took a bite of the quinoa and moaned. "This is so good!"

Marley smiled. "Thanks."

"Tell me about this volleyball bitch."

Marley choked on the sip of wine she'd just drank and chuckled. "So now you're defending me?"

"Of course!"

"Okay," Marley said. "Hector was right. I was hot for her and she was into me for a minute. But some guy gave her a heart necklace for Christmas and she dumped me."

"Seriously?"

Marley nodded. "Then in college I had a girlfriend for almost two years who dumped me right after she graduated in December."

"Wow! Graduation and Christmas rolled into one," Kendall said.

Marley nodded. "I didn't graduate until the following May and I really couldn't see a future with us, but it still hurt."

"I'm sure it did," Kendall said.

"Then there was Leah," Marley continued.

"That's the one with the red flags you ignored," Kendall said.

Marley nodded. "She hooked up with someone else at a Christmas party and went home with them instead of me."

"Holy shit!" Kendall exclaimed.

"Throw in that two of my grandparents passed away in December a few years apart and you can see why I don't believe in Christmas magic."

"I can understand why you'd feel that way, but you've made this Christmas magical for me," Kendall said. "Just look at all you've done here." She swept her hand through the air and continued. "You've kept Frankie and are searching for his family. You're going to the Christmas parties as my date. You've done all of this for me, Marley."

"Because I like you, Kendall," Marley replied. "If we'd met in July I'd be doing the same thing. That wouldn't be Christmas magic."

Kendall chuckled. She took a few bites of her food and thought about what Marley said. "You know, we could've met so many times, but we didn't. We met at Christmas time."

"Are you going to make this Christmas magical for me so I'll become a believer?" Marley asked with an amused grin.

"I don't think we have to try," Kendall said. "It's happening to us. I know it's Christmas magic because I've

155

never fallen—" Her eyes widened. She did not mean to say anything about falling in love to Marley; she'd barely admitted it to herself.

"What was that?" Marley asked, her eyes sparkling with delight.

"Uh, forget I almost said that."

Marley grinned. "I reserve the right to ask you about it again at a later date."

"Okay," Kendall said. "What I meant to say is everything has happened so fast and I feel like I've known you forever, but there's still so much to learn and I can't wait." She took a deep breath. "Now I'm babbling, but it has to be Christmas magic."

Marley gave Kendall a measured look. "What about Jasmine and Hector? Is your Christmas magic going to help us keep our best friends if this…"

"If this becomes what we think it is," Kendall added.

"You said Jasmine gave you hope about us," Marley said.

"Yeah, she told me how much she's enjoyed us hanging out and on the weekends when Hector is here we feel like a little family," Kendall explained. "But you know what?"

"I'm listening," Marley said, taking a bite of her salad.

"Why should Jasmine and Hector have a say?"

"They're our best friends," Marley said.

"I know that, but…"

"Do you usually tell Jasmine when you have a date?"

"Yeah, usually," Kendall replied.

Marley frowned. "I tell Hector when I have a date, too."

Kendall nodded. "Will you do something for me?"

Marley raised her brows.

"Will you put them out of your mind for the rest of the weekend? Let's finish this date and do New York as two people extremely attracted to each other, exploring where this connection might take us."

Marley smiled. "I think you said something like Christmas magic takes you to a place where things are possible."

"I did say that," Kendall replied.

"I'll believe in your Christmas magic for the rest of the weekend if it will show us how things might be," Marley said with a smile.

Kendall could feel her face light up as she smiled.

"Oh, and I'll do it if you'll seal it with a kiss," Marley added, setting her plate aside.

Kendall leaned over until her lips almost touched Marley's. "This is the part of the date I've been waiting for," she whispered.

Their lips met in what started as a soft kiss, but once their arms were around each other, all restraint was gone. Kendall's lips hungrily sought Marley's to kiss, nibble, lick, and claim.

Marley responded with all the fervor that Kendall remembered from their make-out session at her house a few days earlier.

Their moans and breaths grew louder and more heated. Kendall pulled away panting. "Is this okay?"

"Well, I made dessert," Marley said with a sexy smile. "But you'll do."

Marley's lips were on Kendall's again in a flash. She could feel Marley's hands cradle her face and all Kendall wanted to do was get closer to this glorious woman.

After several long, slow, sensual kisses, they finally pulled apart and stared into each other's eyes.

Kendall could see it then as Mariah Carey's "All I Want for Christmas" played in the background. Marley's dark brown eyes were gleaming with what had to be love. Or was Kendall seeing a reflection of the love in her own eyes? But that wasn't all. Marley's eyes were dark with desire and her lips were slightly parted. Kendall could feel her shallow breaths on her lips.

Kendall leaned in for another kiss when the music stopped and a notification tone sounded from Marley's phone. At the same time Kendall's phone beeped from where she'd left it in the golf cart.

Nineteen

MARLEY SIGHED. "It's probably our best friends," she said, exasperated.

Kendall reached for Marley's phone and handed it to her.

"Yep," Marley said. "Hector has a new game he wants to show us when I take you home."

"Mmm," Kendall murmured. "I'd rather play with you instead."

Marley chuckled. She'd thought about them going back to her house after they'd finished the picnic, but she knew they'd end up in her bed. It wasn't that she didn't want to get naked with Kendall; it was that she didn't want her to leave. Marley wanted Kendall to stay all night and that wouldn't be possible with Jasmine and Hector expecting her at their house.

"The date doesn't have to be over yet," Marley said. "I really did make something for dessert." She reached into the picnic basket and took out two small containers. "This is a recipe my grandmother makes for Thanksgiving. It's called pink stuff."

Marley opened one of the containers and dipped a spoon

into the pink treat. She held it in front of Kendall's mouth. "Try it?"

Kendall opened her mouth and Marley slid the spoon inside. She saw Kendall's tongue wrap around the bottom of the spoon and felt her heart stop as a rush of heat flowed straight to her core. *Good God!*

Marley swallowed and handed Kendall the container with the spoon. Kendall gave her a sly smile and Marley knew she was reading her mind.

"This is delicious," Kendall said while Marley regained her composure. "What's in it?"

"Cherries, pineapples, whipped cream, and condensed milk," Marley said, opening her container. "I added a few pecans, too."

"Thank your grandmother for me," Kendall said. "This is really good."

Marley smiled and they both dug into their dessert. She watched Kendall with amusement. She didn't dare tell her that she'd already wondered if Christmas magic was at work on them. It was too much fun listening to Kendall and her efforts to make Marley a believer.

"Does the date have to end when we finish our picnic?" Kendall asked.

Marley giggled. What was it about Kendall that made her giggle? That was not something she did often. "The date doesn't end until I take you back to Jasmine and Hector's."

"I should've told them I was staying with you tonight."

"Yeah, we didn't plan that very well," Marley said. "It's okay, we're going to New York in the morning," she added excitedly.

"I'm glad they're keeping Frankie for us," Kendall said.

Marley grinned. "So Frankie is ours now," she said as she started to put the containers back in the picnic basket.

"No," Kendall replied, handing Marley her containers.

"You said I have to believe that we'll find Frankie's family and I do. The same way that you're going to believe in Christmas magic by the time we get back from New York."

Marley chuckled. "Whew," she said. "That's a lot of believing."

They got up and folded the blanket, picked up the pillows, and put everything in the golf cart.

Kendall put her arms around Marley and pulled her close before they got in the golf cart. "I believe in you and me," she said.

Marley smiled and put her arms around Kendall's neck. "Now that's something I can believe in." She leaned up and softly kissed Kendall's lips. "Let's go back to my office."

They got in the golf cart and Marley drove them back to the front of the building. She grabbed the picnic basket and blanket while Kendall carried the pillows back to her office.

"You can put those on that chair," Marley said, tossing the blanket on a couch and setting the picnic basket on her desk.

Kendall turned to her and smiled. "I've had a wonderful time."

Marley closed her office door then walked over and stopped in front of Kendall. She drew her lips together in a sexy smirk and put her hand in the middle of Kendall's chest. "This date isn't over yet."

When Kendall raised one eyebrow, Marley pushed her down to sit on the couch. She straddled Kendall, first with one knee then the other, getting comfortable on her lap.

Marley gently ran her fingers through Kendall's hair, sweeping the strands to one side like Kendall often did. "It is so sexy when you brush your hair off your forehead," she said in a husky voice.

Kendall stared intensely into Marley's eyes while she rested her hands on Marley's ass, pulling her closer.

"The fire in your eyes is burning through my body," Marley said breathlessly.

"Kiss me," Kendall demanded.

Marley raised her brows and grinned. "Who's bossy now?"

Kendall reached up and took Marley's face in her hands.

Wherever Kendall's eyes landed, Marley felt heat. First she stared into her eyes, then her lips, then back into her eyes. Marley couldn't have resisted even if she tried. She bent down and gently bit Kendall's bottom lip. Their locked gaze never wavered.

Marley tilted her head slightly as her eyes fluttered shut and she pressed her lips to Kendall's in a scorching kiss. Kendall's hands dropped to Marley's ass once again, holding her close.

Their tongues met in a sensual slow dance of pleasure. Marley pushed Kendall further into the couch as she tried to get even closer. Her arms were wrapped around Kendall's shoulders in a vise grip of desire.

She pulled away briefly to take a deep breath before claiming Kendall's lips again. Marley saw the haze of pleasure in Kendall's eyes before she began to slowly rock in her lap. Kendall's hands were on her ass, encouraging her rhythm. Marley could feel Kendall's center moving to grind against hers.

"I can't wait until tomorrow night," Marley whispered in Kendall's ear.

"Mmmm," Kendall moaned.

Marley put her hands on Kendall's shoulders and pulled back as she stilled her hips. She stared at Kendall and released a big breath. "I'm going to get up now, but it doesn't mean I want to."

Kendall nodded. "Wait, one more kiss." She pulled Marley's face to hers and gently kissed her lips then smiled up at her. "Best first date ever."

Marley grinned. "Yeah, it is."

She slowly got to her feet and stared down at Kendall, sighing.

A few minutes later they were in the car with the picnic supplies in the back seat and Marley drove them to Jasmine and Hector's.

"Do you want to come in and see Hector?" Kendall asked as Marley pulled into the driveway. "You don't have to."

"I am walking you to the door, Kendall Malloy," Marley said. "It's the proper thing to do."

Kendall giggled. "God, I love everything about this date."

Marley reached for Kendall's hand as they quietly walked up the steps to the front porch.

"Do I get a good night kiss?" Kendall asked softly.

Marley nodded and slowly leaned in, touching her lips to Kendall's. The warmth that flowed through her body made her heart sigh once again. She rested her forehead against Kendall's and smiled.

"My heart is so happy," Kendall whispered.

Just then the porch light came on and they jumped apart, wide-eyed, like they were bugs being zapped. The door opened and Hector took a step back in surprise.

"Oh!" he exclaimed. "I was just turning the light on for you."

"You scared us to death!" Marley exclaimed.

"Sorry." He smiled then tilted his head with a questioning look. "How was the tour?"

"It was beyond impressive," Kendall said, grinning at Marley.

"Good. Now come on," Hector said. "I have a new game to show y'all." He turned to walk into the house. "You're going to love it."

Marley smiled at Kendall as her heart began to calm down. "I already do."

❄

Kendall looked over at Marley as she gazed out the window of the plane. They'd made it to the airport with enough time to have a quick cup of coffee and split a blueberry muffin before boarding. Their plane departed on time and it wouldn't be long until they'd touch down in the city.

"Did you see how Frankie looked at us when we left this morning?" Kendall said. "He looked kind of sad."

Marley smiled and reached for Kendall's hand. "He was in Hector's lap. I'm sure he'll be fine."

Kendall looked down at their hands as Marley's thumb gently caressed up and down her finger. They'd been holding hands off and on since they'd arrived at the airport. Even though they were keeping a secret from their best friends, they could be open with their feelings now that they were away from Jasmine and Hector.

"I don't want him to think we abandoned him," Kendall said. "He's already away from his family."

"I leave him every morning and he knows I'll come back," Marley said. "You go over every day at lunch and he knows you'll be there. Jasmine and Hector will take good care of him. He knows we'll come back." She leaned over and kissed Kendall's cheek.

Kendall smiled. "I know you're right. I'm not going to worry about him. The rest of the weekend, it's you and me."

"I can't believe I'm on a plane, jetting to New York City with a hot woman. When I think about it like that I may have to believe in your Christmas magic." Marley grinned.

"I'm so glad you came with me. I've been in a battle, but not anymore."

"Why?"

"When I'm not with you, I wonder what you're doing,"

Kendall explained. "Then when we are together I'm trying to stop all these feelings that I have for you."

"I know. We don't have to stop them for now."

Kendall tilted her head. "That's why I want this trip to be about us." She gazed into Marley's eyes. "The last thing I want to do is break either of our hearts, but Marley, what if we can make this work? We won't know if we don't try. Are you all in with me?"

"I'm here, Ken," Marley replied. "This is where I want to be and you are who I want to be with. I don't like keeping it from Jasmine and Hector, but once we figure it out then we can tell them."

Kendall nodded. "I don't like it either, but I know we have something that's worth it."

"I do, too!" Marley exclaimed. "What is all this, Ken? Are you having second thoughts?"

"No," Kendall said. "That's just it. I've never been so sure of anything in my life. But I'm asking you to keep something from your best friend. That's big, Marley."

"I'm the one who suggested the secret to begin with," Marley said. "I want this as much as you do."

Kendall nodded and smiled. "We're going to have such a good time."

"I already am."

Kendall grinned. "My boss and co-workers will be surprised when I show up to the party with a beautiful woman."

"I'm looking forward to meeting them," Marley said. "But what are we going to do before the party?"

"Is there anything you want to see?" Kendall asked.

Marley smiled. "I want to see your New York. You've lived here for several years now and must have favorite places."

"I do and I'd love to show them to you." She hesitated.

"And there are a couple of people who would love to meet you."

"Me? How does anyone know about me?"

"Just as my work friends will be surprised I'm bringing someone, I also have a couple of friends who like to encourage me to date," Kendall explained.

"Are you telling me you have matchmakers around you all the time, too?" Marley asked.

Kendall chuckled. "Not really. They make suggestions from time to time. I thought since you were doing the dating apps, your friends weren't trying to set you up."

"It still happens occasionally."

Kendall squeezed Marley's hand and hoped neither one of them would need the dating apps again. "We're about to land."

"Here we go on our second date."

Twenty

MARLEY LOOKED around Kendall's apartment and smiled. "This looks like you."

"It does?" She narrowed her gaze. "You've known me for a couple of weeks."

"I've known you for a long time," Marley corrected her. "We may have only met recently, but I've heard all about Kendall Malloy for years."

"Just as I have heard all about Marley Jacobs."

Marley walked around the room then stopped at the couch, resting her hand on the back of it. She could imagine Kendall sitting here most evenings with her computer in her lap, scrolling through prospective client profiles. "Your apartment is tidy with everything in its place."

"Are you saying I'm a neat freak?"

"You're organized. There's nothing wrong with that." Marley raised one eyebrow. "It's actually very appealing to someone like me."

"Are you saying we're compatible?"

Marley plopped down on the couch, pulling Kendall next

to her. She put her arm around her and gave her a lopsided grin. "I think we already know the answer to that, don't you?"

She gently ran her fingers over Kendall's cheek and stared into her eyes. Marley knew she was falling in love with Kendall almost from the first time their eyes met, but to be away from the daily obstacle, also known as their best friends, had freed her heart. She could look at Kendall and let her feelings show, hold her hand whenever she wanted, and kiss those lips she fervently craved.

Marley touched her lips to Kendall's in a long slow kiss. The familiar scent of Kendall's skin wafted through her nose as she heard and felt the softest hum vibrate from Kendall's lips. When the kiss ended, Marley held Kendall's cheek to hers, letting the unhurried moment wrap them in peace.

She realized whenever they were together like this, Jasmine and Hector were always swirling in and out of their thoughts. They were either supposed to meet them somewhere or be at their house, thus most of their kisses had a sense of underlying urgency. Not today.

This was their day to explore, share, and simply be together. However, the thought of sharing a bed with Kendall later that night was not far from Marley's mind.

"This is nice," Marley whispered.

"Mmhmm." Kendall pulled away and smiled when she met Marley's eyes. "We could just stay here," she said, raising her brows.

"That's tempting, but I want to experience your life," Marley said. "When you're back here and I'm in Texas I'll know where to imagine you'll be."

Kendall smirked. "Instead of me moving home, as Jaz likes to say, maybe you'll be the one to relocate."

Marley widened her eyes. "Dear God, Ken. I'm telling you, Jasmine and Hector would kill us both."

The richest laugh bubbled from Kendall's throat and Marley couldn't help but join her.

"Let's go to my favorite neighborhood deli first," Kendall said. "I want you to meet someone I consider part of my New York family."

Marley smiled and nodded. She quickly kissed Kendall again and then stood up. "I'd love to."

"Let me get my other coat," Kendall said. "I brought my lighter one to Texas, but it's colder here." She took a black double breasted coat out of the closet along with a tan and white scarf.

"That scarf makes your hair look golden," Marley said, putting a red scarf around her neck.

"Yours is festive. Those look like the maids a-milking from 'The Twelve Days of Christmas.'"

Marley looked down at her scarf and the little figures that circled the ends. "They kind of look like gingerbread girls."

"Don't forget your hat," Kendall said, putting the white woolen beanie on Marley's head. She grabbed the ends of the scarf and pulled Marley close. "I'm so glad you're here with me."

"Me too."

Kendall quickly kissed Marley on the lips then led them out the door.

"You don't talk about your family much," Marley said, taking Kendall's hand as they rode the elevator down to the ground floor. "I'm glad you have family here."

"Jasmine hasn't told you about my family?" Kendall raised her brows. "I'm surprised. She doesn't think much of my parents."

"She may have mentioned that they are very involved in your sister's life."

"You could say that. I'm not sure they ever got over me being gay."

"Oh," Marley replied. "Jasmine never mentioned anything like that."

"Don't get me wrong," Kendall said. "They love me and we get along, but I may have ruined their plans to have two successful daughters with perfect husbands and beautiful grandchildren."

"I don't know about your sister, but I know this daughter is successful."

"Thanks." Kendall grinned. "I have a good relationship with my sister and her family, but let's just say I won't be missed at Christmas."

"I thought you were going home for Christmas?"

"Probably not. I'll most likely stay at Jasmine and Hector's if we haven't found Frankie's family yet."

Marley furrowed her brow. "We'll see about that," she murmured.

"My parents moved to be close to my sister and her family. They are very involved in their grandkids' lives," Kendall explained. "That's why Jasmine declared herself and Hector as my home. My sister loves having me around, but it's always strained when my parents are there. It's like they are guarded in everything they do and say when I'm there. I wish it wasn't so awkward, but..." Kendall shrugged.

Marley had the strongest urge to wrap Kendall in her arms and protect her.

"Hector once told me that your family was very supportive when you came out," Kendall said.

"They were and are," Marley replied. "My mom likes to joke that she knew I was gay before I did."

Kendall chuckled. "It must have been the best feeling to be yourself and know you were accepted."

"Your parents didn't accept you when you told them?" Marley could feel anger begin to bubble in her stomach.

"I didn't tell them until I was in college," Kendall

explained. "I snuck around in high school because I wasn't sure what they would do." She bumped her shoulder into Marley's and chuckled. "The captain of the volleyball team was not into girls unfortunately, but the first-chair flute player in the band..." Kendall raised her brows and nodded.

Marley laughed as they walked out of the elevator.

"It's not far," Kendall said, reaching for Marley's hand as they left her apartment building.

At the end of the block Marley saw a flashing sign that read "Sal's Deli."

"Here we are," Kendall said, holding the door open for Marley. "I stop by here for coffee and a bagel whenever I go into the office. Otherwise, I walk down and get a few things to last me when I'm working at home."

"Kendall!" a woman behind the counter shouted. "You've come back to us!"

Kendall smiled and chuckled. "Mrs. Kordian, I'd like you to meet my friend, Marley."

The woman wiped off her hands and came around the counter to stand in front of Marley. "It is a pleasure to meet you," she said, slightly bowing her head.

Marley could hear a thick accent but wasn't sure of the origin. "I'm happy to meet you," she replied with a smile.

"Oh, you are from Texas," Mrs. Kordian said, nodding. "You can't keep my Kendall, but we would love for you to join her here."

Marley's eyes widened with shock then she saw the mischief in the older woman's eyes.

"Mrs. Kordian!" Kendall exclaimed. "How do you know she's that kind of friend?"

She laughed. "I see how she looks at you."

Marley could feel her cheeks warm and she was sure they were now a nice shade of pink.

"It's okay, my dear," Mrs. Kordian said, putting an arm

around Marley. "Kendall does not need to be alone. You are—what do they say—a Christmas miracle!"

The surprise turned to delight on Marley's face as she met Kendall's gaze.

"She doesn't believe in the magic of Christmas, Mrs. K," Kendall said.

Marley felt Mrs. Kordian look her up and down, then an amused smirk rested on her face. "Ah, this one believes," she said, nodding. "I can see it deep in her heart."

Marley couldn't help but suddenly feel vulnerable. Could this woman really see into her heart? If so, did she see the love growing for Kendall as each minute passed?

"Are you taking Marley to your park?" Mrs. Kordian asked Kendall.

"No, it's too cold," Kendall replied.

"Nonsense," Mrs. Kordian said. With her arm still around Marley's shoulders she said, "Come with me, my dear. I'll fix you up a nice little picnic that will also keep you warm."

Marley turned to look over her shoulder at Kendall as Mrs. Kordian led her to another counter in the back of the store.

"We have fresh Kaiser rolls that just came out of the oven," Mrs. Kordian said, taking two rolls and putting them in a bag. "I'll add in a couple of slices of cheese and two containers of soup. You'll be nice and warm."

Marley watched the woman work then glanced over to where Kendall was talking to a man.

"That's my husband," Mrs. Kordian said, following Marley's gaze.

"Is he Sal?"

Mrs. Kordian threw her head back and laughed. "Goodness no! My husband is Lew. His grandfather started the deli," she explained as she poured steaming soup into a container. "He thought more people would come to an Italian deli instead of a Polish one, so he named the place Sal's."

"Kendall told me this is her favorite deli," Marley said.

"She is a special one, your Kendall. When my daughter, Liliana, graduated from university, Kendall helped her get a job. She is in the financial business like Kendall."

Marley smiled. She quite liked the way Mrs. Kordian said 'your Kendall.' "I'm not surprised. Kendall has a generous heart."

"I can also see love in her heart," Mrs. Kordian said, putting the soup containers in a bag. "For you."

Marley met the woman's gaze and smiled.

"I see it in your heart, too." Mrs. Kordian gave her a soft smile. "Don't be afraid to tell her."

Marley didn't know what to say. This woman truly could see into her heart.

"Kendall never brings women in to meet me," she continued. "You're special to her or you wouldn't be here."

"She's special to me, too."

"Then why do I feel like you are both holding back?" Mrs. Kordian asked. Before Marley could explain about Jasmine and Hector, the older woman held up her hand. "It doesn't matter. Tell her. Find a way past whatever you think is in the way."

Before Marley could reply, Kendall walked up and put her arm around her. "Hey, are you telling my secrets, Mrs. K?"

The older woman laughed at Kendall. "Never!"

Kendall grinned. "That smells so good."

"Come up to the front and I'll send two cups of hot cocoa with you," Mrs. Kordian said, putting the smaller sacks in a bag with a handle. "You'll be nice and warm with good food in your bellies while enjoying the park."

They followed her up to the front of the store and when Kendall tried to pay, Mrs. Kordian wouldn't let her.

"No!" she protested. "You always tip too much. This is my

treat. I put a little extra Christmas magic in the soup." She winked at Marley and wiggled her eyebrows.

Marley laughed and shook her head. "It was so nice to meet you."

"I hope to see you again," Mrs. Kordian said.

"Oh, you will," Kendall said, grabbing the bag off the counter.

Marley held the door open so they could exit the deli.

"It's right this way," Kendall said, turning right and walking behind the deli. "I'd hold your hand but my hands are full."

Marley put her arm through Kendall's and held a cup of hot chocolate in her other hand. "I've got you."

"I thought we'd walk by the park, but didn't plan for us to stay."

"I hope you're hungry," Marley said. "Those rolls look delicious."

"Oh, they are." Kendall looked over at Marley and smiled.

"What is it?" Marley asked.

"I walk this street often," she said. "But somehow, everything seems so alive and brighter because you're here with me."

Marley grinned and squeezed Kendall's arm. *Oh yeah, they were definitely falling.*

Twenty-One

"I DIDN'T REALIZE there were green spaces throughout the city," Marley said as Kendall handed her a container of soup. "Is this your favorite bench?"

"I don't really have a favorite," Kendall replied. "But I do like this one because it's away from the sidewalk and surprisingly quiet at times."

"Do you come here often?"

"It's a great place to unwind," Kendall said. "Especially when my small apartment seems even smaller."

"You know, Mrs. Kordian told me you'd never brought another woman in the deli to meet her," Marley said, taking the lid off her soup.

"That's true, but I haven't always lived in this neighborhood."

"What does that mean?"

Kendall put her soup down and turned to Marley. She stared into her eyes and sighed. "Since we got on that plane this morning, I realized there are so many things I want to tell you. Things I want you to know."

"Things I need to know before I get into this?" Marley pointed with her spoon between the two of them.

Kendall chuckled. "Maybe, but my heart feels so open and it feels safe to tell you things. I don't know if that's because we've decided to try this or if it's because we don't have to worry about Jasmine and Hector right now."

"I've felt it too," Marley said. "We have to be guarded whenever they're around and careful of what we say or how we look at each other."

"Yes, because of the secret. Or because we knew they'd lose their shit!"

Marley nodded. "That's why those long slow kisses on your couch earlier felt so damn good."

Kendall widened her eyes. "Why do you think I suggested we stay there?"

Marley giggled. She picked up Kendall's soup and handed it back to her. "So tell me about before you met Mrs. K."

"Oh my God." Kendall grinned. "When I first got here I went a little wild, at least for me."

"Wild?"

"I was a lesbian slut."

Marley's brows flew up her forehead in surprise.

"I dated a lot of women," Kendall explained. She furrowed her brow. "Dated might not be the right word."

"Tell me more," Marley said, amused.

"When I first moved here, I had a roommate and it seemed like we both brought home different women every weekend," Kendall said.

"So, you didn't do the U-Haul thing?"

"No." Kendall chuckled. "That only happened with one woman. We lived together for less than a year. When we broke up, that's when I found my current apartment. By then I was making enough to afford my own place. But my ex and I had a friend group that was made up of your stereotypical lesbians.

Several of the women had dated one another or others in the group."

"I have a few friends like that."

"When we broke up some of the friends went with my ex," Kendall said. "There were a few that I still kept in touch with, but they soon moved to the suburbs and started families. I hear from them occasionally, but don't see them very often."

"Did you stop dating after that?"

Kendall nodded. "I started with my company then and worked longer hours because it was still rather new. When I got home at night, the thought of going out lost its luster. I think when I first got here I was trying to find a friend group like we had in college. It felt easier here and there were so many gay women."

"You didn't feel accepted in college?" Marley asked.

"Not like here. You know how conservative Texas is," Kendall said.

"Well, I accept you for the former lesbian slut you were," Marley said, grinning. "You're a good person, Kendall. I knew this before we met and I'm sure of it now."

Kendall smiled and felt her heart melt a little more. "I can't believe I'm sitting in my neighborhood park with you, eating food from my favorite deli. It feels like we've been doing this forever. Before I came to Texas, I would come here and try to get rid of that lonely feeling I told you about. It still amazes me that I immediately felt comfortable to share that with you when we first met. You have pushed the loneliness from my heart and filled it with possibilities, Marley."

"You are safe with me, Ken. I haven't been through the things you have, but it doesn't mean I don't understand. I may have pushed your loneliness away, but you've given me the connection I longed for. It feels like our hearts were either looking for each other or waiting and finally found each other.

I probably just scared you away and this is too much too fast, but I want you to know what's in my heart."

Kendall smiled. "I think we can be honest because it's just you and me here. If anything, all of this could be Jasmine and Hector's doing. We are their best friends. Why wouldn't we get along?"

"It's more than that and you know it."

Kendall nodded. "Here's what I know. I haven't felt this drawn to another person...ever. I don't mean just physically, either. Believe me, I can't wait until we're back at my apartment tonight after the party. But Marley, it's more than that. I want to know everything, from simple things like your favorite color to complex issues like your thoughts on the gender pay gap."

"Blue," Marley replied.

"What?"

"My favorite color is blue." Marley grinned. "Also, I'm part of a group of women in upper management who meet regularly regarding all the ways the system discriminates against women. We present our findings to our bosses with the expectations that they will address them. Some things have changed, but others need work." Marley paused to take a breath. "I want to have these discussions with you, too. But right now, I'd like to enjoy this amazing Kaiser roll and see more of the things you love here."

Kendall felt her heart fill to overflowing with love for Marley Jacobs.

"You've seen my world and I want to see yours," Marley said, taking another bite of her roll.

"I want us to be in the same world," Kendall said softly.

"That's what we're working on, isn't it? Or is that what Christmas magic is supposed to do."

Kendall's eyes widened. "That reminds me." She grabbed the bag and reached inside. "Mrs. K told me she put a little magic in the bag along with something sweet." Kendall began to laugh as she pulled out a sprig of mistletoe.

Marley joined her laughter. "She's right."

Kendall held the mistletoe over Marley's head, leaned in, and kissed her softly.

"So sweet," Marley murmured.

Kendall began to gather their trash and smiled at Marley. "I think I'll save this," she said, putting the mistletoe in her pocket.

"If that's part of your Christmas magic, we don't need it." Marley leaned over, pulled Kendall in, and kissed her soundly.

"Mmm," Kendall moaned when Marley pulled away and stood up. "That kiss was magic."

Marley chuckled. "Where's your magic gonna lead us next?"

"We have just enough time to go to a nearby Christmas market," Kendall said. "I didn't get to do that with you in Texas, but we can here." She threw their trash away and reached for Marley's hand. "This place is magical, you'll see."

"I'll admit that this day has felt magical," Marley said. "But I don't think it has anything to do with Christmas."

Kendall chuckled and led them out of the park. They only had to walk a couple of blocks before they approached shops on both sides of the street that were decorated with festive lights and greenery.

"Oh wow," Marley said. "I hear Christmas music."

"Isn't it magical?"

Marley chuckled then smirked. "I think maybe you're the magical one, Kendall Malloy."

"Come on, let's look around."

They went into several stores and looked at the decorations, ornaments, wreaths, and other Christmas merchandise.

"Look at this, Ken," Marley said, holding up a St. Nick ornament with a round belly. "It has the year on it."

"Isn't he cute." Kendall's eyes brightened at the rotund likeness of Santa Claus.

"We could start a thing where we get an ornament with the year on it every Christmas." Marley gave Kendall a hopeful look.

Kendall thought about what Marley had said earlier about too soon and too fast, but if anything, all of this felt right. She smiled at Marley and noticed a Christmas village on the table next to her. "Hey, what about this?" Kendall walked over and picked up a small figurine of a woman from in front of a little house. Then she picked up another one standing next to a tree.

"If you put these two women side by side can you tell what they're doing?" Kendall placed the two women in the faux snow next to one another.

Marley chuckled. "Yes, they're holding hands."

"Just like us." Kendall grinned. "I'm not sure that's what the toy maker had in mind, but it reminds me of us."

"Well, who gets to keep them?" Marley asked, furrowing her brow.

"You keep one and I'll keep one," Kendall said. "Then when things work out like we think they will…"

"Oh!" Marley exclaimed. "I get it. These will have a permanent place holding hands in our home."

Kendall grinned. "How's that for too soon and too fast?"

"I think it's perfect."

Kendall leaned over and kissed Marley on the lips. "It is."

They paid for the figurines and the ornament then went back to Kendall's to get ready for the party.

"I'm having such a good time today," Marley said, walking into Kendall's apartment. "And now I get to see you all dressed up. I wonder how long I'll be able to keep my hands off of you."

Kendall set her purse and the bag with their ornaments on

the table. She walked over and put her hands on Marley's hips. "The best part is that you don't have to. Jasmine and Hector are thousands of miles away. We get to hold hands, dance, and kiss whenever we want."

"Dance?"

Kendall nodded. "It's a party. There will be music, drinking, food, probably a photo area, and who knows what else."

"I'll also be meeting your boss and co-workers," Marley said, resting her arms on Kendall's shoulders.

Kendall smiled. "They'll be surprised when I walk in with you on my arm."

"I'm excited to meet them, but also a little nervous."

"Let me take those nerves away." Kendall leaned in and softly brought their lips together. She felt Marley's arms tighten around her neck as a velvety moan wafted around the room. "Come here," Kendall whispered. "We have a little time."

Kendall led them over to the couch and pulled Marley down onto her lap. Their lips met again in a hungry kiss. When their tongues touched, the air in the room was electrified with passion. Moans and heavy breaths provided the music for this particular dance.

Kendall pulled Marley closer and as their lips parted for deep breaths, she whispered in her ear, "I'm so glad you are here."

"Mmm," Marley murmured. "There's no place I'd rather be."

Kendall tilted her head back so she could see into Marley's eyes. "You know what I liked about today?"

"Tell me."

"We didn't do anything special, but today was one of the best days I've had since moving here," Kendall said. "It's because I'm doing this with you."

"That's what we did in Texas," Marley said. "You make the

simplest things feel anything but ordinary. I know it will be different tonight and I can't wait."

Kendall felt Marley's fingers run through her hair as she stared into her eyes. "I want to do everything with you," Marley said with a sexy smile. "This doesn't end tomorrow when we get back on the plane. Okay?"

Kendall nodded. "We're figuring it out."

Marley smiled and sighed. "We are."

"However, I want us to go by my favorite bar on the way to the party," Kendall said, raising her brows.

"Then I need to get up and get ready."

"Wait!" Kendall held onto Marley and smiled. She closed her eyes and tenderly kissed Marley one more time.

Twenty-Two

"WOULD you like to help me choose my outfit for tonight?" Kendall asked as they walked into the bedroom.

"You don't know what you're going to wear? I thought you had a dress in mind."

"I did, but then I remembered I have this suit," Kendall said, opening the closet door.

"Nice closet."

"It's a great closet and bathroom for a one-bedroom in the city." Kendall pushed some hangers aside. "Here it is."

Marley watched Kendall pull out a black suit coat and widened her eyes. "That's a tuxedo!" She ran her hand along the lapel. "Smooth satin," she said softly.

"I got it for a very formal wedding and haven't worn it since," Kendall explained. "It's a one button blazer that I don't have to wear anything under."

Marley raised her eyebrows and gave Kendall a sultry look. "Will you wear a dress for me when we get back to Texas?"

Kendall grinned. "I'll wear a dress only for you, if...you'll take it off of me."

"Why, Ms. Malloy, it would be my pleasure," Marley said with an exaggerated syrupy drawl.

"Oh, no, Ms. Jacobs," Kendall replied. "The pleasure will definitely be mine."

Marley couldn't keep from giggling. "Are we being silly? I know I'm making a big deal of all this, but I don't know when we'll get to dress up again and tonight…" she paused. "Okay, I'm going to say it." She met Kendall's warm brown eyes. "Tonight feels magical."

Kendall gasped and the delight on her face made Marley's heart skip a beat.

"It's a Christmas miracle!" she exclaimed.

"Hold on, Mrs. Claus," Marley deadpanned. "I wouldn't go that far."

Kendall chuckled as they walked out of the closet.

"Are we both getting ready in here?" Marley asked.

"I need to reapply my makeup, but I can get dressed in the living room," Kendall said. "I don't want to crush this magical vibe."

"I can do my makeup with you," Marley said. "I'll do my hair and change while you're in the living room."

"I remember when I saw you in that red dress the first time," Kendall said, walking into the bathroom. "I think my heart stopped and then I realized I couldn't let Jasmine and Hector see my reaction."

"Oh, I saw it in your eyes," Marley said, opening her makeup bag. "I felt the same way when I saw you in that suit at my house."

"Hmm." Kendall opened a drawer and reached for her brush. "That was another time my heart stopped when I saw you. I'm not sure what that says about you."

Marley met Kendall's gaze in the mirror. "Don't worry, I'll always get it pumping again."

Kendall laughed. "Right out of my chest."

They stood side-by-side, brushing eye shadow across their lids, blush on their cheeks, and carefully drawing on eyeliner before finishing with mascara on their lashes. Marley couldn't help but wonder if this was a peek into their future. *God, I hope so.*

"This is fun," Kendall said, grinning at Marley in the mirror.

"I'm pretty sure we'd have fun doing almost anything." Marley winked.

"Does this look okay?" Kendall batted her lashes at Marley.

"You look beautiful." Marley combed her fingers through Kendall's hair, brushing it to one side.

"You like doing that," Kendall said.

"I do."

Kendall smiled. "I'll be in the living room waiting for you."

"I won't be long."

Marley watched Kendall take her clothes and leave the bedroom. She turned back to the mirror and pulled her hair up into a knot. She wrapped and twisted to give it a loose look then pulled several wisps down to frame her face. With a turn to the left and then to the right she decided it would do. Marley wanted to look elegant, but also carefree.

She walked into the bedroom and took her dress from the closet where she'd hung it as soon as they'd arrived at Kendall's apartment hours earlier. This wasn't the same red dress Kendall had already seen her in. This one was a deeper shade of red and form-fitting. It wasn't quite a minidress and hit her at mid-thigh. The long sleeves were tight as she worked them up and over her shoulders. The neckline formed a deep vee which showed off her cleavage.

Marley stepped into her strappy heels and walked into the living room. "Could you zip me up?" she asked Kendall with a sexy smile. The look on Kendall's face was all Marley needed to know she'd not only surprised her date, but pleased her as well.

Kendall's hand went to her chest. "You take my breath away," she mouthed with barely a sound.

Marley smiled then let her eyes roam up and down Kendall's body. "You look even better than I imagined. Get over here."

Kendall chuckled.

Marley watched her slowly step towards her. Each stride oozed a sexy assuredness. "Mmhmm," Marley murmured and turned around.

She felt Kendall's breath on her shoulder before the softest lips touched the base of her neck. Marley took a deep steadying breath as shivers tingled down her spine. How she'd like to turn around, lose these beautiful clothes, and tumble into Kendall's bed.

"There you go," Kendall said, zipping up the dress.

Marley leaned back into Kendall and felt her arms circle her waist. She put her hands on Kendall's and they sank into the moment. "This is nice," she whispered.

"Mmhmm."

Marley took another deep breath and turned to smile at Kendall. Just then both of their phones beeped with an incoming text message.

"Hmm, I wonder who that could be," Kendall said.

Marley reached for her phone and on the screen was a picture of Frankie sitting on Hector's lap. The dog was smiling at them. "Aww, isn't he cute."

"At least we know they're taking good care of him," Kendall said. "Let's send them a selfie."

Marley stood next to Kendall and put her arm around her waist. "Don't give our secret away with your smile."

"God, I know." Kendall held her arm out and took the picture. "What do you think?"

"We look fabulous and also like two people going to a party," Marley said. "Except... What's that sparkle I see in your eyes?"

"I'm going to a party with a beautiful woman who happens to be my date," Kendall replied. "Your eyes are sparkling, too."

Marley hesitated for a moment. She knew this trip was their chance to be themselves and explore their feelings, so she was honest. "My eyes are sparkling because I've had the most incredible day with a woman I'm falling for and it's not over yet."

Kendall looked up into Marley's eyes with surprise.

"Yes, I used that same word you did on our date at my work," Marley said. "I've felt it too, Ken. We're here to find out what this is, but I think we both already know."

Kendall smiled. "Are you afraid?"

Marley shook her head. "I'm not afraid of these feelings or of us, but I am apprehensive about our best friends' opinions."

"But not tonight," Kendall said. "Tonight is for us."

"Why don't you send that picture and let's go dazzle your co-workers," Marley said with a big smile. She watched Kendall fiddle with her phone and couldn't quite believe she'd just proclaimed her love. Sort of. Was this the Christmas magic Kendall loved to tease her about or was she getting caught up in *this*, whatever *this* was?

Maybe it was time for Marley to be honest with herself. Since locking eyes with Kendall, there had been a definite pull. Yes, there were obstacles that went along with it, but when had she ever done anything risky in her life? Not that this was particularly hazardous. Well, it would be if she lost her best friend, but come on. Wouldn't Hector want her to be happy?

She'd seen several peeks into the future today, if she was to believe this Christmas magic thing. Those glimpses were nice, but what she remembered was how she felt. Her heart was happy. Much like it was right now, even moreso.

Kendall's phone pinged, bringing Marley out of her euphoric jaunt into the future.

"They said we look great," Kendall said.

"Great? That's all they could come up with?" Marley scoffed. "Our secret is safe then."

Kendall chuckled, put her phone away, and reached for Marley's coat. She held it open for her and smiled. "Let's have a drink before the party."

"I'm all yours," Marley said, slipping her arms into the coat.

"Oh, be careful," Kendall said. "I may be tempted for us to stay here."

Marley whirled around. "Don't tease. I may have already had that thought today."

Kendall grabbed both their purses. "We seem to be on the same page." She winked and opened the front door.

Kendall held the door open so Marley could walk into the bar. She'd explained it was a small space on a busy corner between her apartment and her office. On one side was a long bar where several patrons were seated with drinks in front of them. On the other side there were high tables against the wall and then a few lower tables sprinkled in divided by an open space which served as a walkway to the back.

"Whoa!" the bartender exclaimed, coming out from behind the bar. "You're either on a hot date or on your way to a party."

Kendall grinned. "Both."

Marley felt Kendall's hand on her waist. She wasn't sure if it indicated protection or possession, but either way Marley liked it.

"Stuart," Kendall said, gazing at Marley, "please meet Marley Jacobs."

"It's a pleasure," he said with a friendly smile. "Is this one charming you this evening?"

"Oh, she's been charming me for a while now." Marley grinned and leaned into Kendall. "It's nice to meet you."

"Let me show you to a table," Stuart said, leading them towards the back and stopping at a table in the corner. "What can I bring you?"

Marley looked at Kendall and raised her brows. "Wine?"

"I have a luscious red that would be perfect for a starter," Stuart said.

"That sounds good," Marley said.

"I'll be right back." Stuart gave them another smile and disappeared behind the bar.

Marley gazed around the bar, taking it all in. She tried to imagine Kendall at the bar or perhaps at a table having a drink on her way home from the office. "Do you come here often?"

"I come here for Stuart," Kendall replied.

Marley looked over at her and furrowed her brow.

"I've lived in the city for ten years now and have followed Stuart from bar to bar," Kendall explained.

"Uh, is there something you haven't told me?"

Kendall chuckled and grabbed Marley's hand. "I dated Stuart's husband's sister for a minute when I first got here. Wow, that's a mouthful. Anyway, their wedding was the reason I bought this tux."

"Oh!"

"When we first met he was managing a bar near my old apartment." Kendall paused as Stuart set a glass of wine in front of each of them and slid into the chair next to Marley.

"I was just telling Marley that I have followed you from bar to bar," Kendall said.

"That's what friends do, right?" He grinned.

189

"He owns this bar," Kendall said.

"Co-owns," he corrected her, "along with the bank. Lord knows if I'll ever get it paid off."

"You will," Kendall said confidently.

Stuart smiled at her. "That's what my financial advisor keeps telling me. What do you think?" He nodded at their wine glasses.

Marley put the glass to her lips and took a taste. She widened her eyes. "You're right. It's luscious."

Stuart nodded then studied Kendall for a moment. "Is that your wedding suit? Stand up."

He walked around the table, took Kendall's hand as she stood, and looked her up and down. "Mmhmm."

"Isn't she gorgeous?" Marley said, smiling at them both.

"So are you, honey," he said, sitting back down. "I saw you rocking that dress when you walked in." He snapped his fingers and duck-billed his mouth.

Marley could feel the heat rush to her cheeks.

"Now, tell me where you've been hiding," Stuart said, leaning towards Marley. "My bestie doesn't bring women to meet me."

"Who said I brought her to meet you?" Kendall scoffed.

Stuart smirked at her and turned back to Marley.

"She definitely brought me to meet you and I've been hiding in Texas," Marley said.

"I thought I heard an accent," he said with a grin. He took a moment to look into Marley's eyes then shifted his gaze to Kendall. "I'm feeling some serious vibes here." He turned back to Marley and asked, "Are you going to convince my girl to move back home?"

Twenty-Three

MARLEY LIFTED her glass and took a sip of wine.

"Maybe you should think about moving here instead. New York could use a hot successful couple like the two of you," Stuart said, raising his eyebrows.

"How do you know I'm successful?"

"Puhleeze," he deadpanned. "I'm a bartender. I can read people like a book."

Kendall looked on with delight. She knew Stuart would be taken with Marley. How could he not be? She was, too. This bar was Kendall's last stop on the way to the airport when she'd left to spend the month in Texas. Stuart had encouraged her to ease up on her work schedule and have a little fun. Kendall had mentioned she was finally meeting her best friends' best friend. He'd laughed and told her not to get any ideas of staying in Texas unless there was a woman involved. She smiled at the memory.

"There's something about your vibe that tells me this is an important date to you both," he said, pointing from one to the other. "You're going to Kendall's work party and meeting her co-workers. Don't worry, Marley, you'll captivate them just as you have me. But there's more going on here."

Kendall caught Marley's gaze and widened her eyes. "He knows I wouldn't have brought you here if you didn't mean something to me."

"Something?" Marley said.

"I can see the way you look at each other," Stuart said. "It reminds me of how my husband looked at me not long after we met." He smirked and stood up. "He wanted to tear my clothes off."

Kendall exchanged a look with Marley, both knowing Stuart's observation was accurate.

"I am so happy to meet you, Marley," Stuart said with a slight nod. "I hope this is the beginning of a long friendship."

Marley giggled.

"I mean you and me," Stuart clarified. "If you have to take her to Texas with you, then you must come back and visit."

"Maybe Kendall doesn't have to be the one to relocate," Marley said, raising a brow.

"Don't tease me," Stuart said, grabbing Marley's wrist. He leaned over and kissed Kendall on the cheek. "Love you."

"Love you, too," she replied.

"Oh my God," Marley exclaimed as Stuart walked away. "I love him. Why have you not mentioned Stuart?"

"Now you know why I've followed him all over the city." Kendall took a sip of her wine. "I wasn't sure we'd have time to come by the bar."

"Or if I meant enough for you to introduce me?"

Kendall smirked. "You've meant enough to me from the first time I met you." She reached for Marley's hand and rubbed her thumb across her knuckles. "I wasn't sure you'd drop everything at Christmas time to come to New York with me."

Marley scoffed. "How could I turn that down? Or you?"

Kendall shrugged. "I know I keep saying this, but I'm so glad you're here. I haven't felt this happy at Christmas in years."

Marley smiled. She reached over and cupped Kendall's cheek with her other hand. She leaned into the touch and they simply stared at each other for a few moments.

Kendall sighed. "Are you ready to party?"

"You are charming me into doing almost anything with you."

"Almost?"

Marley chuckled.

Kendall leaned over, pressed her lips to Marley's, and was sure she felt magic surrounding them. Forget falling, she was already there. Something stirred in her heart. In some ways it felt like she'd known Marley forever. In others this was bright, shiny, and new with all the anticipation of a kid at Christmas, and she couldn't wait for what came next.

"We'd better go," Kendall said softly, pulling away. "I want to dance with you."

Marley raised her brows.

"I'm not a great dancer, but holding you close and moving to the music seems like the perfect thing to do at a party."

"When you say it like that I couldn't agree more," Marley replied.

They got up, waved to Stuart, and headed out into the night. After a short walk, Kendall led them into her office building. She reached for Marley's hand as they got into the elevator.

Once the elevator doors closed, Marley nudged Kendall against the wall and kissed her. "Thank you for inviting me to the party. I'll thank you properly when we get back to your place."

Kendall smiled. "What if you don't have fun at the party?"

"I'll have fun. I'm with you."

The elevator doors opened before Kendall could return the kiss. "Here we go."

Kendall's company took up two floors of the office building. The elevator opened onto the main floor, which was a large open concept working area. The desks and other furniture had been moved back to accommodate a buffet line, a small dance floor, and plenty of room to mingle. The entire floor was decorated for Christmas with lights, wreaths, and trees. Christmas music was playing when they arrived, but the dance floor indicated there would be more upbeat music to come.

Marley gasped. "Wow, is this more of your Christmas magic?"

"It looks very festive, but I think the magic is coming from another place."

"Oh?"

"Kendall!" a woman exclaimed, walking towards them. She was older than Kendall and dressed in a black dress with a full skirt. Her red shoes matched the red Santa hat on her head.

"I know you have connections, Nicole," Kendall said. "But I didn't realize you were one of Santa's elves, too." Kendall put her arm around Marley's waist. "Marley, this is my boss, Nicole Wright."

"Hi," Nicole said, extending her hand. She tilted her head and grinned. "I understand you are the reason it may be hard for Kendall to return to New York."

Marley took her hand and smiled. "I don't know about that. Her best friend is also there."

"Oh, I'm aware of Kendall's connections to Texas. I'm not sure it matters where she is as long as she keeps up her outstanding work. We don't want to lose her."

Kendall smiled. She had talked to Nicole about opening an office in Dallas and mentioned her new friendship with

Marley. The excitement in her voice must have told Nicole it was more than that.

"The bar is open, the food is incredible, and the DJ will be turning up the volume on this party soon," Nicole said. "Enjoy yourselves. This is a party. We can talk about business later."

"It was nice to meet you, Nicole," Marley said.

Nicole squeezed Kendall's arm. "It's nice to meet you, Marley. I'm glad you could join us."

They walked over to the bar and Kendall ordered them both a glass of wine.

"You've been talking to your boss about us?"

"Not really," Kendall said, handing Marley a glass of wine. "Maybe she can see it in my eyes and hear it in my voice. We've talked several times about opening an office in Dallas and I'm sure my enthusiasm is obvious."

"I thought we were forgetting about all the obstacles this weekend."

"We are." Kendall nodded. "Here come my coworkers." She smiled as two women approached them. One looked about Kendall's age and the other was older.

"I'm so glad to see you," the older woman said as she hugged Kendall.

"You see me nearly every day."

"That's on a computer screen."

Kendall chuckled. "Marley, this is Amy Sanderson. We work on the same team. And this is Cassie McDoral, our assistant."

"I'm happy to meet you," Marley said with a friendly smile.

"Tell us how you got this workaholic to slow down," Amy said with a twinkle in her eyes.

"It must be some type of Christmas magic." Marley shrugged and winked at Kendall.

"Oh, I could use some of that," Cassie said. "Could you share it with my girlfriend?"

"You'll have to ask Kendall," Marley said. "She's the true believer."

Amy raised her brows. "You don't believe in it?"

"I didn't, but I may be coming around."

"Whatever you're doing, keep doing it," Amy said. "I like this happy Kendall."

"What?" Kendall protested. "I'm always happy."

"Sure you are, especially when you match an analyst with a client, but this is different," Cassie said.

Marley smiled and put her arm through Kendall's. "I know what you mean," she said. "Kendall has certainly brightened up my holiday."

"Now that we're all happy and gay, let's see what's on this incredible buffet Nicole was talking about," Kendall said.

They all laughed and walked over to the tables of food. Kendall introduced Marley to several other members of her team while they enjoyed the food and drinks. A little later the DJ cranked up the music and several people began to dance.

"Cake by the Ocean" by DNCE came on and Marley grabbed Kendall's hand. "Come on."

"This isn't a hold-you-close kind of song," Kendall said.

"It'll be okay," Marley said.

Kendall followed her onto the dance floor.

"Put your hands on my hips," Marley said over the music. She raised her arms, turned around and began to back up.

Kendall immediately grabbed Marley's hips and they moved to the music. She slid an arm around Marley's middle and pulled her close for a moment. "You are so sexy!"

Marley grinned and turned around in Kendall's arms. "If you only knew what you're doing to me."

"We're in trouble."

"Yeah, we are."

The next song was Madison Beer's "Make You Mine." It was a little slower and the lights dimmed over the dance floor.

Kendall pulled Marley close and they began to sway in time to the music. She inhaled the scent of Marley's perfume and nibbled at her ear. This wasn't exactly what she meant to do when surrounded by her co-workers, but this night was magical. Whether Marley believed it or not, Kendall felt it. This was the night Marley's heart grabbed hers and they fell in love. Kendall would never forget it.

They danced to a couple more songs then Kendall led them off the dance floor. "I want to show you something."

She grabbed Marley's hand, walking them to the elevator.

"Are we going to your office?" Marley asked as they ascended.

"Maybe later." Kendall leaned over and kissed Marley softly. "Are you having fun?"

Marley nodded and put her arms around Kendall's neck. "I had no idea I'd love dancing with you so much."

"I think there are lots of things we haven't discovered yet, but we're going to love doing together."

"Mmm." Marley brought their lips together again just as the elevator dinged and the door opened.

Kendall took Marley's hand and grinned as they stepped out of the elevator and through a door to the stairwell. "I come up here when I need to take a deep breath." They walked up a short flight of stairs and through a door that opened to the roof.

"Oh, wow!" Marley exclaimed.

"I know it's cold, but we don't have to stay long," Kendall explained. "I wanted you to see where I go when I come to the office."

"It's beautiful up here. All the lights!"

"Yeah, it's a great view in the daytime, too."

"When you tell me you're at the office I can picture you

here as well as downstairs," Marley said as she looked out over the twinkling lights of New York City.

"If you look up, you can make out a few stars," Kendall said.

"I want to remember this sky so when we get back to Texas I can find the same stars," Marley said. "We'll be looking at them together."

"That's a sweet thought, but I'd rather be looking at them with you." Kendall sat down on a concrete step and patted the space beside her. She looked into Marley's eyes and took a deep breath. "I know all of this seems fast, but I've been thinking about that and..."

Marley raised her brows in encouragement.

"It's taken us so long to meet that I want to be honest with you. I should hold back because I don't want to scare you away like you said earlier, but since we both acknowledged our feelings, I've fallen hard and fast." She grabbed Marley's hand and held it over her heart. "Can you feel how fast my heart is beating? I don't want to mess this up, but Marley, I'm telling you this because I believe we can make it."

Twenty-Four

MARLEY'S HEART rate matched Kendall's. She could feel the staccato beat under her palm where it rested on Kendall's chest. "I don't know how, but I believe it, too. I think once we both felt that spark there wasn't time to go slow. It's taken us so long to finally meet; we do know each other. But there's still so much to learn together."

"I tried to not let my parents' disapproval of me affect my life," Kendall said. "But honestly, it always has. There's been a part of me that has never felt good enough. I think that's why I work so hard to make these matches count for my clients and their financial analysts. With them, I am enough."

"Oh, Ken," Marley said, putting her hand on Kendall's cheek.

"I've been in love a couple of times," Kendall said, "or at least I thought so. But that feeling of inadequacy was always floating in the back of my mind." She took a deep breath and slowly let it out, then smiled. "I've longed for a partner who accepts me and understands me. Someone who can celebrate holidays with me without the awkwardness."

"Oh, honey," Marley said. "Awkwardness is part of holidays."

Kendall chuckled. "I don't feel it when I'm with you. When we're together, I feel like I belong."

Marley felt like her heart had broken into a million pieces for Kendall. She couldn't imagine growing up and feeling like she didn't belong. To know that she took those feelings away when Kendall was with her put her heart right back together again. She knew right then that no matter where Kendall lived she wanted to be with her.

This was the connection Marley had been trying to find by going on all those dates. Kendall made her heart beat with excitement for what would come next, but also with the familiarity of feeling safe to be herself.

"You're not going to scare me away." Marley smiled. "Since we seem to be going big here, let me tell you that this has been more than like, almost from the beginning," she began. "Yes, I was excited to finally meet Kendall Malloy in person, but I immediately liked you. Then when you showed up at my house with the cutest little dog, something stirred in my heart. That's when I knew I'd get to see you every day and it was such a relief because I didn't have to try to find ways to be around you." She squeezed Kendall's hand. "From then on I have felt closer and closer to you, but I've also found out this connection was already there in some form. Ugh, this is hard to explain." Marley looked up at the stars then back into Kendall's eyes.

"I think our hearts have been waiting for each other. Once our eyes met, it was on! Our hearts went to work and here we are, on a rooftop in New York City on a magical night and I can't imagine anything being more perfect or anyone I'd ever want to be with."

Kendall's eyes widened.

"I know that was a lot and it probably sounded like I was

rambling, but Kendall, I'm thirty-three years old with a couple of serious girlfriends in my history. Most of my friends are either married or in committed relationships. I've longed for that connection you read about in books or see in the movies. I almost thought I was fooling myself, but then I went to Friendsgiving and you were staring at me from the kitchen."

"That was another time when you made my heart stop." Kendall smiled. "Do you remember when we got here and I said the magic may be coming from somewhere else?"

"Yeah, you didn't finish because Nicole walked up."

"I think you're right." Kendall put her hand on Marley's chest and placed Marley's hand back on her chest. "The magic is in our hearts."

"I accept you and like you for exactly who you are, Kendall Malloy," Marley said. "My heart has been waiting for your heart."

Marley reached up and put her hand on Kendall's neck. She pulled her in and meant to kiss her soft and slow, but the emotion of the moment took over. Their lips crashed together in a heated, hungry kiss. She felt Kendall's arms around her shoulders pulling her closer.

Their tongues swirled, teased, and tempted, eliciting moans and groans released on frosty breaths.

Once they pulled apart Kendall rested her forehead on Marley's. "I'd love to dance with you again."

"Oh, yeah?"

"And then..."

A sexy smile grew on Marley's face. "And then go back to your place?"

Kendall grinned. "You do understand me."

Marley giggled as they got up and went back to the party.

When they got off the elevator Marley gazed around the room. "Are all these people matchmakers like you?"

Kendall chuckled. "Not all of them. Some are market analysts, managers, and assistants."

"Did I hear the word matchmaker?" Nicole asked, walking up behind them.

"You did." Marley smiled. "Kendall is quite the match-maker, and not only in her job. She encouraged a couple of friends of ours to go out on a date, and they are now quite happy together."

"They would've figured it out," Kendall said humbly.

"Is something happening down in Texas?" Nicole asked. "Because you two look very happy as well."

Marley's eyes widened as a thought popped into her head. "I guess we can blame our best friends for this."

"Oh?"

"Yeah, our best friends happen to be married to one another," Kendall explained.

"Well, how about that," Nicole mused. "That must be fun."

"Uh, they don't exactly know about us," Kendall said, wincing.

"Oh!" Nicole exclaimed. She furrowed her brow. "Why would they care? You're happy."

"That's true," Marley replied.

"Oh wait, I get it," Nicole said. "If something happens and it doesn't work out, that would be challenging."

"Exactly," Kendall said.

Nicole smiled. "Well, however it turns out I'm just happy you've gotten this one to have a little fun." She squeezed Kendall's arm. "But..." She looked from Kendall to Marley. "I have matchmaking abilities as well and this looks like it's working to me."

Marley put her arm through Kendall's and smiled.

"Life is full of obstacles," Nicole said. "The fun is getting through them together. You'll see." She winked and walked away.

"I like your boss," Marley said.

"Yeah, she cares about us as people, not just her employees." Kendall turned to Marley. "One more dance."

"Oh yeah," Marley replied. "I like this song." She grabbed Kendall's hand and pulled them onto the dance floor as the DJ cranked up the volume to Dua Lipa's "Illusion."

She watched as Kendall jumped and moved to the music. The joy on her face was mesmerizing and Marley knew she was part of the reason it was there. In the same way, Kendall was responsible for the excitement in her heart. Oh, who was she trying to fool? It wasn't just excitement, it was love! She was in love with Kendall Malloy and that made her heart happy.

The song ended and Marley was about to suggest it was time to go when the soft sounds of Muni Long's "Made For Me" slowed down the vibe. She wrapped her arms around Kendall's neck and pulled her close. "One more dance," she whispered.

They slowly moved to the music and Marley swore she could feel Kendall's heart beating as she softly sang, "Body to body, skin to skin... You were made for me."

"How can this night feel even more magical," Kendall whispered.

Marley pulled back so she could see Kendall's eyes. "I think it's time to go, don't you?"

Kendall nodded as the last notes of the song played. She led them off the dance floor and into the elevator.

Once the doors closed Marley put her arms around Kendall's neck once again. "I love dancing with you."

"To elevator music?"

She chuckled. "To any music." Marley kissed just below Kendall's ear and could feel her moan vibrate through her lips.

The elevator doors opened and they jumped into a cab for the ride back to Kendall's apartment.

Marley reached for Kendall's hand and scooted closer. "Are you nervous?" she asked softly.

"No," Kendall replied. "I told you that when I'm with you I feel like I belong. Are you nervous?"

Marley sighed as thoughts raced through her head. She turned to Kendall. "I was going to say this is a big deal and so very important, but you know what?"

"What?"

She chuckled. "It doesn't matter how it goes. This is our first time, but it won't be our last. I'm going to keep doing this with you. Over and over and over..."

"Easy," Kendall said softly, putting her finger over Marley's lips. "You're making me very hot at this moment." She smiled then tilted her head. "Are you saying you'll get through these obstacles with me?"

Marley gave Kendall the sexiest look she had. "I'm giving you my best I-want-to-rip-your-clothes-off look. Tonight there are no obstacles. It's you and me, babe."

They pulled up to Kendall's apartment building and once they were in the elevator, Marley pushed Kendall against the wall and kissed her passionately. "Mmm, I like riding in elevators with you."

"Sexy and beautiful. You should feel my heart now."

"Don't forget bossy." Marley raised an eyebrow.

"Oh, I love my bossy girlfriend," Kendall cooed.

Marley widened her eyes. *Did Kendall just say she loved her?*

"Uh–um," Kendall stammered just as the elevator dinged and the door opened. "Do you remember saying that we're going to be doing this over and over?"

"Yeah."

Kendall led them down the hall to her door. "Well, that

wasn't how I wanted to say that the first time, but I plan on telling you over and over."

Kendall opened the door and Marley quickly shut it and pushed Kendall against it. "I seem to like pushing you up against walls or doors, but I don't care how you say it because I love you, too."

The time for talking was over. Marley claimed Kendall's lips in a heated kiss. Their breaths came quickly, followed by moans and roaming hands.

Marley unfastened the single button on Kendall's blazer and slid her hands over the softest, warmest skin around and up Kendall's back. Marley groaned with such pleasure just being able to touch this amazing woman. She felt Kendall's fingers fiddling with the zipper to her dress and suddenly a rush of air hit her bare back.

Their lips were still in a sizzling battle to nip, suck, and caress, bringing moan after moan. Marley brought her hands around to Kendall's stomach and ran them upward until she cupped both of Kendall's breasts.

"You didn't wear a bra," Marley panted. "If only I'd had this information sooner."

Kendall gave her a sexy smile. "And what would you have done...bossy?"

Marley could feel her brows shoot up her forehead. *Oh, this woman is incredible!* She ran her thumbs over Kendall's already stiff nipples and assaulted her neck with light kisses then sucked at the pulse point below her ear.

Kendall gasped.

"Oh, so you like that," Marley whispered while nibbling on Kendall's earlobe.

A groan echoed in Marley's ear then she swirled her tongue around and inside Kendall's ear.

"Oh, God," Kendall moaned.

Marley ran her hands up and over Kendall's shoulders,

removing her blazer. "I haven't lost my mind completely yet," she said, holding the jacket. "This is too nice to throw on the floor."

Kendall, now bare-chested, took the jacket and laid it on the couch. "Bossy and thoughtful." She surprised Marley by turning around and taking her face into her hands. "I love you."

Before Marley could respond, Kendall kissed her long and slow. Marley thought she knew what the word swoon meant because Kendall's kisses often made her feel weak. But this kiss made her forget where they were and what they were doing.

When they pulled apart, Marley realized Kendall had pulled her dress down and was waiting for her arms to come out of the sleeves. Marley quickly rid her arms of the clingy fabric and was about to step out of her dress when Kendall stopped her.

"Let me," she said softly.

Twenty-Five

KENDALL SLOWLY KNEELED and pulled the dress down Marley's body. She felt Marley's hands on her shoulders as she stepped out of it. Kendall pressed her lips right above Marley's belly button then sighed. She looked up into Marley's eyes and felt her fingers smooth the hair from her forehead.

Kendall stood up and Marley reached for the button to her pants then unzipped them. They slipped down Kendall's legs and she stepped out of her shoes, then her pants. Without her heels, Kendall was now the same height as Marley. She reached for Marley's hand, stepped back and took in the sight of Marley's matching red bra and lacy panties.

"You are beautiful," she said softly.

"As are you," Marley replied just as softly, kicking off her shoes.

Kendall led them to the bedroom and stopped at the foot of the bed. She curled her fingers under the straps of Marley's bra and slid them down as she softly kissed her exposed shoulder. Next, she reached around and unfastened Marley's bra, setting her ample breasts free.

Their eyes met and they both slid their panties off,

standing naked in front of each other, letting their eyes and hearts feast on the sight.

Kendall set one knee then the other on the bed and Marley mirrored her movement. She gazed into Marley's now almost black eyes and saw intense desire but also love. Kendall leaned in, their lips meeting in a smoldering kiss as her hands rested on the curve of Marley's hips.

Kendall had dreamed of feeling Marley's skin on hers. As she pulled her closer, Marley's arms snaked around her shoulders then they were chest to chest. Kendall felt Marley's hardened nipples against her skin and moaned.

They fell to their sides, arms and legs tangling, as the kiss burned even hotter.

Marley rolled on top of Kendall and pressed her leg between hers. Kendall could feel her wetness coat Marley's thigh and the desire to have this woman inside her was all-consuming.

"Marley," she groaned.

This may have been their first time together, but Kendall was sure Marley knew what she needed.

Marley cupped one side of Kendall's face and smiled. "We don't have to say it. I'll show you that I love you."

Kendall felt Marley's hand trail down her neck until she held one of her breasts, gently pinching her nipple between her finger and thumb. Kendall groaned.

Marley gently sucked Kendall's bottom lip into her mouth as her hand slid lower. Kendall never let her eyes leave Marley's. She felt Marley's fingers comb through her hair and when her finger slid through her slit Kendall's hips raised to keep the contact.

"Oh, yes!" Kendall groaned, pleading with her eyes for Marley to push inside.

"Almost," Marley whispered.

Kendall could feel Marley's finger roaming through her

wetness, up and down then circling. Her eyes fluttered shut with sheer pleasure, but she quickly opened them again. She wanted to fall into the inviting warmth and love in Marley's eyes.

Finally, Marley slipped one then two fingers inside and Kendall was in heaven. She began to move her hips to match Marley's rhythm and grabbed her shoulders to hold on. This was going to be the ultimate ride.

Kendall saw the slightest smile on Marley's face as her lips parted with the effort.

"I love you, Kendall," she whispered.

With those words Marley's fingers stopped and Kendall tensed as a deep orgasm shot through her complete with stars sparkling in her eyes. Then Marley's lips were on hers and Kendall held on as wave after wave swept through her body. She finally relaxed her muscles as Marley pulled her lips away.

Kendall saw the softest smile on Marley's face as she released a pleased breath. "I planned to get to know other parts of your glorious body, but I don't think you wanted me to wait."

Kendall simply returned her smile.

"So, I'll just be down here..."

Kendall felt the softest kisses trail down between her breasts then Marley had one of her nipples in her mouth.

"Oh." Kendall exhaled and ran her fingers into Marley's hair.

"Mmm," Marley moaned. "I knew you would taste good."

Warm, wet lips kissed down and across Kendall's stomach and she felt Marley settle between her legs. "Marley."

"It's okay, babe. We've got all night."

Before Kendall could even think, Marley had slid her tongue through her wetness and Kendall felt another orgasm building. When Marley sucked her into her mouth Kendall slapped her hand down on the bed and groaned. Another wave of intense ecstasy flowed through her body. She was sure this had to be Marley's love. Nothing had ever felt this good. This was the love Marley told her about earlier and now Kendall felt it, too.

While Kendall caught her breath, Marley rested her cheek on Kendall's stomach. "I gave you my heart. Don't throw it away."

Kendall raised up and looked down at Marley. "Are you singing "Last Christmas" lyrics to me right now?"

Marley raised up and rested her head on her hand. "I just gave you my heart, but I know you won't throw it away."

Kendall smiled and pulled Marley up so they were face to face. "I won't. This year you'll give it to someone special."

Marley smiled as Kendall said the next line in the song. "I just did."

"We're changing the lyrics to that song."

"Not really," Marley said. "Don't you remember me telling you about the Christmas break-ups I've had?" Marley sighed. "I couldn't help giving you my heart even if I didn't want to, but I do. I know it's safe with you."

Kendall raised up and rolled Marley onto her back. "Feel the love in my heart for you." She softly kissed Marley, taking her time to caress and explore with her tongue.

Marley moaned. "I want you, Kendall."

"You've got me." Kendall kissed down Marley's neck, across her collarbone, then trailed her tongue down between her breasts.

"Good God," Marley whispered.

Kendall swirled her tongue around Marley's nipple. She gently nibbled and sucked as Marley's moans echoed around the bedroom. She felt Marley's fingers in her hair once again as she arched her back.

Kendall kissed her way over to Marley's other breast, giving it the same attention. As Marley's breaths came quicker

Kendall continued her path down Marley's body. She ran her tongue over the sensitive skin just above Marley's bikini line and heard her gasp.

"I found something you like," Kendall murmured.

"Mmm," Marley moaned.

Kendall caught a whiff of Marley's scent and couldn't wait to taste her love. She ran her tongue through Marley's folds, licking and swirling up and down and around her swollen clit. Kendall thought she was in heaven when Marley was inside her, but this was even better.

She could feel and hear Marley's moans as she brought her closer and closer to the edge.

"Oh, yes!" Marley's fingers tightened their hold in Kendall's hair.

Kendall moaned. She sucked Marley into her mouth and let her tongue feather over her sensitive spot. She felt Marley's legs stiffen as her hips rose higher. Kendall held her in place and could feel the orgasm break through. It rushed through Marley's body and back into Kendall. Neither of them moved as they let the waves wash over them.

Marley fell back onto the bed gasping for breath. "Oh, Ken," she muttered between breaths.

"That was incredible," Kendall said as she stopped and kissed Marley's stomach and between her breasts on her way back up her body.

She gazed down at Marley's face where her eyes were closed, her lips parted in a soft smile. Kendall ran her hand up the inside of Marley's thigh and felt the goosebumps in its wake. Her finger lazily found Marley's wetness and she gently circled her opening.

"Mmm," Marley moaned.

"Just breathe, baby." Kendall softly kissed her lips as she slowly pushed a finger inside.

Marley groaned and Kendall added another finger.

"Kiss me," Marley gasped.

Kendall firmly pressed her lips to Marley's as her fingers began to slowly move in and out. Marley matched Kendall's rhythm as their tongues swirled in a feverish kiss. Kendall could feel Marley clamp down on her fingers and she angled them up to find her most sensitive spot. Marley tore her lips from Kendall's and groaned loudly.

Kendall felt the orgasm race through their bodies once again. As the intensity began to wane she gently kissed Marley's neck. "Now you have my heart."

Marley's eyes fluttered open and she ran her hand along Kendall's cheek. "I've never felt anything like that."

Kendall smiled. "I'd love to say it's Christmas magic, but it's not. Our hearts have found where they're supposed to be."

"And it's magical," Marley added.

Kendall nodded.

❄

Marley exhaled a deep breath.

"We get to do this over and over," Kendall said.

Marley giggled. "And I thought pushing you against a wall was fun."

Kendall chuckled. "This is so much better than dancing."

"Oh, we're still dancing." Marley linked her hand with Kendall's where it rested on her stomach. She stared down at Kendall's fingers as they intertwined around hers. They fit perfectly together. She'd felt the same way when they'd kissed for the first time then wrapped their arms around each other.

"What are you thinking?" Kendall asked. "Please don't tell me you're having second thoughts."

Marley quickly shifted her gaze to Kendall's. "I'm not. Are you?"

"Nope," Kendall said immediately. "But you looked rather serious."

Marley smiled. "We're moving really fast, but it doesn't feel that way."

"Are we moving fast?" Kendall raised her brows. "Or are we moving at our own pace?"

"Have you ever told someone you loved them before you had sex?"

"I have not." Kendall rolled on her side to look into Marley's eyes. "That's only because I haven't been in love with anyone before I had sex."

Marley nodded and narrowed her gaze.

Before she could respond Kendall added, "I've been falling for you almost from the beginning. I fought it because of the obvious obstacles and I wasn't sure you were serious."

"You weren't sure? I'm the one who suggested we go to all the Christmas parties together."

"Yeah, but that was helping you, too. You kept mentioning my expiration date."

"That doesn't matter anymore," Marley said. "Our friends are the only obstacle."

"Uh-uh," Kendall said, putting her finger over Marley's lips. "We'll talk about them on the plane tomorrow. Tonight is just you and me."

Marley grinned. "Then why aren't you kissing me?"

Kendall furrowed her brow. "Bossy," she said softly.

"Am I really?" Marley asked as she smoothed the wrinkle between Kendall's brow. "I remember the first time I saw this cute little wrinkle."

"I remember when you ran your finger over it. Your eyes were sparkling and I looked down at your lips." Kendall exhaled. "I wanted to kiss you right then."

"You were afraid you were spending too much time at my house." Marley chuckled and shifted onto her side. "You had no idea how glad I was that you were making daily visits. Frankie and I both were very happy about it."

Kendall smiled.

"Do you know what would make me happy right now?"

Kendall raised her brows.

"One of those deep, slow kisses that make my insides melt then ignite with a fire only you can tame."

"Tame?" Kendall reached over, put her arm over Marley's side, and pulled her closer. "Why would I want to tame that fire? I love my bossy girlfriend."

Marley giggled. "Your bossy girlfriend is through talking."

Kendall's eyes widened and she chuckled. "Yes ma'am."

"It's your fault," Marley said, gently kissing the corner of Kendall's mouth. "You made me feel things I've never felt and I want it again."

"Over and over."

Twenty-Six

KENDALL PRESSED her lips to Marley's and once again Marley felt herself melt. *This woman knows how to kiss.* She thought back to their make-out sessions at home and how she never wanted Kendall to stop kissing her. Tonight they didn't have to stop. Marley was sure she'd have a fire burning in her heart from now on for Kendall Malloy.

"Let's do this together," Kendall said softly, pulling her lips away.

Marley stared into her eyes, reached over, and let her fingers ghost over Kendall's stomach. She moved them lower and lower until Kendall raised her leg so Marley could cup her sex.

Kendall held Marley's chin with her finger and thumb and kissed her softly. Then she mirrored Marley's movements. Marley felt a trail of heat everywhere Kendall's fingers touched.

"Round and round," Kendall whispered.

Marley understood and slid her finger through Kendall's wet folds, circling her clit. She could see the passion and elation in Kendall's eyes as her finger moved. Marley was enjoying watching Kendall's response when she suddenly felt a finger begin to move over her.

Marley gasped and drew in a breath. "Oh my God."

"Mmhmm," Kendall murmured. "That feels so good."

"So good," Marley echoed.

The softness in Kendall's touch along with the way Kendall was gazing into her eyes made the fire inside Marley burn white-hot. She parted her lips and reached for Kendall's. She could feel Kendall everywhere. When their lips touched, an urgency flowed through Marley. She slipped a finger inside Kendall and pushed upward to find the spot she knew would drive Kendall over the edge. At the same time she felt Kendall's finger inside her and for a moment time stood still. They were joined together in the most intimate of ways after building an orgasm that was about to flow through them in waves.

Kendall groaned as they both tensed and let the pleasure burst forth.

Marley pulled her lips away to see the most beautiful look on Kendall's face. This was love in its purest form. Love for her, love from her, love that they'd created together.

Their bodies began to relax as the sweet warmth of their passion eased into the afterglow.

Marley smiled. "That…"

The corners of Kendall's mouth raised slightly. "Yeah, that," she said softly.

After several moments of simply staring into each other's eyes, Marley sighed. She'd been in love before but it had never felt like this. Sure, it could be all-consuming with a desire to touch and be touched yet this was so much more. Her heart felt settled and complete. It was as if no obstacle was too big, no problem couldn't be solved, as long as they were in this together. Maybe that was the difference. She had no doubt that Kendall wanted this, too.

"So, have I made you a believer in Christmas magic?" Kendall said with an amused lift of her brows.

Marley smiled. "Is that what this is?"

"Did you imagine you would fall in love this Christmas?"

Marley scoffed. "Did *you*?"

"Is that the way it happens? Love finds you when you least expect it?"

Marley lifted one shoulder. She exhaled and ran her thumb along Kendall's jaw. "Do you remember the first party we went to when we were talking about my name and Dickens' *Christmas Story*?"

Kendall nodded. "Yeah, didn't Jasmine say something like it was the party from Christmas past? Because so many of the same people were there from our previous Christmas parties."

"Yes, then when we were at the bowling party it was like the party of Christmas present because we'd never done anything like that before."

"Right. Except that's when I became your girlfriend to mess with your ex," Kendall replied. "That's been quite fun."

Marley chuckled. "If they only knew."

Kendall laughed. "Yeah."

"Today it felt like I had several peeks into the future."

"And what did you see?"

"I saw Christmas—I think they called it Christmas yet to come in the story—but nonetheless, I saw Christmas in the future with you and me as happy as could be."

"Together," Kendall said. "That would make my future Christmases very happy."

"Mine, too."

"It sounds like Christmas magic to me."

Marley groaned. "Okay, okay. Would it make you happy if I said I believe?"

"You said when you came here with me you wanted

Christmas magic to show you how things could be. I think from what you just said, it has."

Marley playfully rolled her eyes. "You can believe it's magic. I believe it's in our hearts."

"You know, my heart is so full of love and you put it there. You! With your kindness, and your obvious great choice in Christmas dates." Kendall smirked. "But mostly with the way you care about me. You want to know me. Some things you do know, but you want to know all of me. Not necessarily in a curious way. It's hard to explain."

"I think I know what you mean," Marley said. "It's because I have to know you. It's like you're becoming a part of me. The best part."

"This is so cliché, but is this the 'complete thing' people talk about?" Kendall said.

"I don't know. Maybe." Marley smiled. "What I do know is that I want to keep learning about you and learning about me to make us."

"I really like us," Kendall said. "I want that."

Marley curled into Kendall's arms. "Me, too." She closed her eyes and thought about Kendall's mention of the "complete thing." Marley didn't know about that, but in her heart it felt like she was exactly where she was supposed to be and Kendall was who she was supposed to be with.

Any other time she would be excited to share this with Hector. He would pepper her with all kinds of questions, but also be happy for her. There were times when he didn't really like who she was dating; however, he always supported her and gave the person a chance.

She pushed the thought away until they could figure out how to share this with their best friends. Marley heard Kendall sigh. She pulled her a little closer as sleep captured them both.

. . .

Marley straightened her leg and felt the softest lips placing gentle kisses on her shoulder. She rolled over and gazed into Kendall's sleepy face.

"Good morning," she said with a small smile.

Marley groaned. "Is it time to get up?"

"Do you want to sleep a little longer?"

"No, I want to do this." She pressed her lips to Kendall's, put an arm around her, and kissed her slow and sweet.

"Mmm, good morning to me," Kendall said when their lips parted.

"It's about to get a lot better." Marley raised her eyebrows and crawled on top of Kendall. She began to kiss down her neck and between her breasts.

"I was about to suggest we take a shower," Kendall said between gasps.

Marley moaned. "I can't wait." She kissed her way over to Kendall's breast and took the soft nipple into her mouth. It hardened at her touch which made her smile. After several strokes with her tongue and a little nip, Marley continued to kiss down Kendall's body.

She swirled her tongue around Kendall's belly button then licked all the way down. Marley looked up, seeing anticipation in Kendall's eyes as she put her arms under her legs. "I love you."

Kendall ran her fingers through Marley's hair. "I love you, too."

"Just making sure." Marley winked.

Before Kendall could reply, Marley dropped her head and let her tongue show Kendall just how much she did love her. She kissed her soft folds, her tongue spreading Kendall's wetness over her clit. She swirled her tongue and Kendall raised her hips wanting more. Marley took Kendall into her mouth and sucked gently at first, then with more force.

Kendall groaned and Marley could feel her fingers tighten in her hair.

She flicked her tongue and felt Kendall go over the edge as the orgasm raced through her. Marley loved how Kendall's body responded to her touch and at the same time it somewhat amazed her.

She'd had sex plenty of times in her life, but when she touched Kendall she could feel Kendall's love for her. It was something real Marley could see when she looked at Kendall, taste when she kissed her, hear with her words and moans, smell with her intoxicating scent, and feel all over and through her body.

Kendall moaned as her hips fell back on the bed.

"Race you to the shower?" Marley said, raising up.

Kendall scoffed. "Not fair! I can't move."

Marley chuckled and kissed Kendall on the lips as she swung her legs over to sit on the side of the bed. "You have such a gorgeous glow this morning."

"You put it there." Kendall put her arms around Marley, holding her in place. She kissed her on the thigh and raised up to sit next to her. "I think yesterday may have been the best day of my life."

Marley widened her eyes.

"Don't get scared," Kendall said quickly. "It meant so much to me that you wanted to see my ordinary everyday life and you still want to be here."

Marley laughed. "Oh, babe. There is nothing ordinary about you. The only places I'm going are with you and right now that's to the shower."

A little while later Marley walked out of the bathroom towel drying her curly locks. "That was fun."

Kendall left the bathroom wrapped in a towel. She circled

her arms around Marley from behind, kissing her neck. "That was more than fun."

Marley giggled and leaned into Kendall's touch. "We're in so much trouble," she said. "We can't keep our hands off each other."

"In the infamous words of us both: We'll figure it out." Kendall gasped.

"What's wrong?" Marley asked, turning in her arms.

"I didn't realize how late it was," Kendall replied, staring at the clock on her bedside table. "We've got to hurry or we'll miss our flight."

"Imagine trying to explain that to Jasmine and Hector."

"We'll make it," Kendall said. "I'm going to dry my hair and restrain myself from touching you."

"Are you saying you want me to keep my hands off of you?"

"No. I can't imagine ever saying that, but..."

Marley chuckled. "Go! I'll get dressed and pack."

"One more kiss," Kendall said.

Marley raised an eyebrow. "Are you sure about that?"

Kendall's reply was to press her lips to Marley's in a sweet kiss. "I'm sure." She winked and hurried back into the bathroom.

"Once we get back to my place," Marley said, raising her voice loud enough that Kendall could hear her, "we won't have much time to get ready for the party."

"I know," Kendall yelled over the noise of her blow dryer. "I hoped we'd have time to grab something for breakfast on the way to the airport, but we don't now."

"That's okay, we'll manage."

It didn't take long for them both to get dressed and pack their bags.

"I can make us coffee to drink on the way to the airport,"

Kendall said, setting her bag by the front door and walking into the kitchen.

Marley rolled her bag over next to Kendall's then walked around the living room.

"What are you looking for?"

"I've put the ornament we bought for my tree and my little figurine in my purse," Marley replied. "I'm looking for the perfect spot to put yours. I want you to see it as soon as you walk through the door."

"Put it on that table next to the couch," Kendall said. "I can see it from anywhere in the room."

Marley smiled and placed the figurine on the table. "Until you are holding my hand once again, my sweet," she said quietly.

"Here you go." Kendall handed Marley a travel mug of coffee. "Is that everything?"

"I think so," Marley said, slipping her purse over her shoulder. She smiled at Kendall and kissed her. "I had the best time here and hope to be back soon."

"It won't be the same when I come back without you," Kendall said softly.

"But it's okay," Marley said, raising her brows.

"I know." Kendall chuckled. "We'll figure it out."

Marley opened the door and rolled her bag out. She thought Kendall was behind her, but at the last moment she'd run back into the living room.

"She doesn't have to stay here now," Kendall said, holding up the figurine. "We're together, so they should be too."

Marley tilted her head and sighed as Kendall handed her the figurine. "I love you so much."

Kendall grinned and pecked Marley on the lips. "I love you, too."

Twenty-Seven

KENDALL HELD Marley's hand loosely in her lap. She ran her thumb along Marley's finger and gazed down at their hands. She loved holding Marley's hand and had been doing so for the entire flight.

"I like it when you do that," Marley whispered.

Kendall looked over and gazed into her eyes. "You have the softest skin. I may have been imagining touching you in other places."

Marley smiled. "It won't be long until we land and we haven't talked about the huge obstacle awaiting us."

Kendall sighed. "I've been thinking about it."

"I can tell." Marley reached over with her other hand and smoothed the wrinkle between Kendall's brow. "I'm not worried."

"You're not?"

"No. They may be surprised but after the shock wears off, why wouldn't they be happy for us? I mean, Hector is always saying I'll find the person who will make me happy like Jasmine does for him."

"You're right." Kendall nodded. "Why wouldn't they be

happy for us? We'll be a happy little family. I swear, Jasmine has always wanted that for me."

"I'm the perfect person for that since Hector happens to be my very best friend."

"Exactly." Kendall looked at Marley as the smile faded from her face. "Why does it feel like we're trying to talk ourselves into believing they'll be okay with this."

"We are, but I truly believe they will be happy for us."

Kendall sighed. "I think we should wait until after Christmas to tell them. If they're upset then I don't want to ruin things for them."

"I think we should tell them before Christmas," Marley replied.

"Why?"

"I want you to spend Christmas with us."

"Oh, no," Kendall protested. "They're going to Hector's family home on Christmas Day and returning that night."

"I know that," Marley said, "because my family will be there, too." At Kendall's questioning look, she explained. "I'll be with my family at my parents' house in the morning, opening presents. In the afternoon, we'll all be together at Hector's parents' house. We alternate houses each year. We have a big meal, sometimes play games, but mostly tell stories from the past and laugh a lot."

"I planned to stay at their place with Frankie," Kendall said.

"Right." Marley nodded. "In other words, you'll be working."

"Nope," Kendall replied. "I am not working that day. I'll be hanging out on the couch, watching TV, and I'll call my parents."

"Frankie will be fine alone at their house for the day," Marley said. "I want you to spend Christmas with me." She softened her voice. "With all the magic surrounding us, this will be our first Christmas of many, I hope."

Kendall smiled. "Aren't you coming back that night, too?"

Marley nodded.

"Then you can come to Jasmine and Hector's when you get back and we'll be together on Christmas."

"Not good enough, babe," Marley said.

The idea of meeting Marley's family at a large Christmas gathering was both frightening and exciting. If Kendall wasn't sure before, now she knew that Marley did want to be with her. This wasn't just some fluke or holiday romance that would fizzle out by New Years.

"You know, now that I think about it, I've been to Christmas at Hector's before and I met one of your brothers," Kendall said, sitting up straighter. "I can't remember where they said you were."

"It was five years ago," Marley said. "I was on a Christmas ski trip with my cousins and my other brother. We returned that night."

Kendall nodded. "Makes sense because we came back to their place that night."

"See?" Marley said. "You don't have to be afraid to meet my family."

"Who said I was afraid?"

Marley chuckled. "I could see it in your eyes, babe. Don't forget that I already know you."

"Oh yeah?" Kendall raised her brows. "You saw a hint of fear, but the idea was actually exciting to me. You know I don't love Christmas Day so much."

"And I don't either."

"Aren't we a pair."

"We are." Marley kissed the back of Kendall's hand. "We're going to have happy Christmases from now on."

Soon the plane landed and Kendall glanced out the window as they approached the gate.

"I guess we're telling them before Christmas," Marley said, staring at her phone.

Kendall furrowed her brow. "We didn't decide on that."

"I just got a text from Jane Ann." Marley looked into Kendall's eyes. "She's found Frankie's family and they want to meet us tomorrow."

Kendall gasped. Her heart dropped into her stomach at the idea of losing Frankie, but the goal all along was to reunite him with his family. She gave Marley a half-smile. "I'm happy for him, but a little sad for us."

"I know, honey," Marley said. "I think Frankie is giving us one more Christmas gift."

"What do you mean?"

"In a way he brought us together," Marley said. "Since he'll be with his family, you can spend Christmas with me."

Kendall gave her a genuine smile then her face fell. "Uh oh. That means we have to tell Jasmine and Hector."

Marley nodded.

"What would you say if we skipped the party tonight?" Kendall asked.

Marley's brows shot up her forehead. "Go on..."

"We can't tell them tonight; they'll be at a party," Kendall explained. "That means I won't get to stay the night with you." She took a deep breath. "I think the best part of the weekend was getting to wake up with you this morning."

"Better than last night?" Marley said in a low voice.

Kendall giggled. "There were so many good things from this weekend, but waking up with you after the things we did last night..."

"Oh, I know," Marley said with a loud exhale.

"If we skip the party, we can spend a little time together

before I have to go back to Jasmine and Hector's," Kendall said.

"And what do you propose we tell Jasmine and Hector?"

"We can text them and tell them our plane arrived late, so we'll see them later."

"Hmm." Marley stared into Kendall's eyes. "I think that's a brilliant idea."

Kendall grinned and leaned over to give Marley a quick kiss. "Would you mind if we stopped by Jasmine and Hector's to pick up Frankie?"

"I was thinking the same thing, but do you think they'll wonder why he's not there when they get home?" Marley asked.

"Nah," Kendall replied. "They'll know we picked him up on our way from the airport."

Marley winced. "I'll be glad when we tell Jasmine and Hector the truth. I don't like lying to them."

"I don't either." Kendall sighed. "But Frankie is going to be happy to see us."

A few hours later Kendall was sprawled on Marley's bed in euphoric bliss. "That was amazing," she said, gulping a breath. "I am still humming inside. How do you do that?"

Marley giggled from beside her. "Do you want me to show you again?"

Kendall looked over at her and grinned. "You know I do, but..."

"No buts." Marley raised up to kiss Kendall sweetly. "Aww, look at this good boy coming into the bedroom."

Frankie jumped up on the bed. He walked all over Kendall before plopping down on her chest.

"Were we making too much noise?" Kendall asked the dog, petting his head.

Marley chuckled. "He really is a good dog."

"I can't imagine how much your family has missed you," Kendall said, stroking the dog's head.

His ears perked up and he began to growl.

"Uh oh," Marley said. "He only does that when someone pulls in the driveway."

Frankie began to bark and jumped off the bed.

"I didn't realize it was so late," Marley said. "It could be Jasmine and Hector. Get dressed! Hector has a key!'

"Oh shit!" Kendall jumped up, looking for her clothes.

"Here's your sweater." Marley tossed the garment to her.

"Where's my bra?"

"Put it on without it! We don't have time."

"Yeah, they don't need to find out like this. Damnit, I can't find my leggings!"

"Shit! They're in the living room!"

Marley threw on a sweatshirt and joggers as Kendall ran out of the room. She found her leggings on the floor and quickly stepped into them. Frankie continued to bark as she looked around for her bra. Kendall picked up Marley's shirt. "There it is!" She reached down to pick up her bra as Marley came around the corner from the hall. "Here!" She threw the clothes at Marley. "Hide these!"

Marley hurried down the hall and Kendall put on her socks just as someone started knocking on the door.

"It's us, Frankie!" Hector's muffled voice could be heard through the door.

Marley walked back into the living room and quickly looked around. She began to chuckle as she walked to the door.

Kendall reached out and grabbed her arm. "Don't do that! You'll make me laugh."

Marley took a breath and straightened her face.

Kendall was glad she turned around because she was about to start laughing, too. "Frankie, come here," she called to the dog.

She bent down to pick him up just as Marley opened the door.

"Hey!" Hector greeted them, walking into the room with Jasmine trailing behind.

"Hey!" Kendall exclaimed.

"What's he doing here?"

"You'll never believe what happened," Marley said, shutting the door. "Jane Ann found his family. We're meeting them tomorrow."

"Aww," Hector said, petting the dog's head. "I mean, that's a good thing, isn't it?"

Kendall noticed Jasmine's gaze flitting around the room. "Yeah," she said, still watching Jasmine. "I'm going to miss this little guy." She pulled her gaze away and looked down at the dog.

"How was the party?" Marley asked.

"It was okay," Hector replied.

"It would've been more fun if you'd been there," Jasmine said.

"Too formal?" Kendall asked.

"It wasn't that." Jasmine sighed. "Everyone looked lovely but, I don't know…"

"You couldn't get anyone to do shots with you?" Marley grinned.

"Nope." Jasmine chuckled. "The party was rather subdued. I don't think anyone has to work tomorrow and Christmas is just two days away. You'd think everyone would be ready to let go and have a little fun."

"How was New York?" Hector asked excitedly. "Did you get to meet Stuart?" he asked Marley.

Kendall saw Marley's face light up. "I did!"

"I had a meeting in New York last year and got to spend an evening with Kendall," Hector said. "We went to Stuart's bar and had the best time. That guy is hysterical."

"Did you meet Kendall's boss?" Jasmine asked.

"Yes, and I didn't even embarrass her," Marley said, giving Kendall a grin.

"Why would you think you'd embarrass me?" Kendall asked, surprised by Marley's statement.

"We're small town hicks from Texas," Hector said.

"You're not a hick," Kendall protested.

"I'm sure Marley fit right in with your coworkers," Jasmine said, giving Marley an affectionate smile. "She can put anyone at ease."

"What about when I'm the one who's nervous?" Marley said.

"Trust me, no one ever knows," Jasmine replied. "I envy that about you. When I get anxious, I get these red splotches on my neck."

Hector shook his head. "No one notices it."

"Kendall's seen them before, haven't you?"

"It's been a very long time," Kendall said. "You are so sure about yourself now. Confidence oozes from you."

Jasmine stood a little taller. "Thanks... I think."

"What?"

"I don't know. I appreciate the compliment, but something's going on here," Jasmine said, narrowing her eyes.

Kendall's heart began to thump louder in her chest.

"Oh wait, I know what it is," Jasmine said. "Let me guess, you want to stay over here tonight so you can spend time with Frankie before he goes back home. That's why y'all picked him up from our house."

Thank you to the powers that be! "Uh, well," Kendall mumbled as she winced. "Would you mind?"

"You should be asking Marley," Jasmine said. "You're a big girl and can stay where you want."

"Ha ha," Kendall said sarcastically. "Marley already said I could stay."

"What the?" Hector said. "You sound like you're asking to spend the night with a friend and you"—he turned to Jasmine —"sound like her mother. Fucking weird," he muttered.

Jasmine shrugged. "Take me home, honey," she said. "We have the place all to ourselves."

"Like anything happened while you were gone," Hector said quietly to Kendall.

"Maybe you'll get lucky tonight," Kendall whispered, wiggling her eyebrows.

"What are you two whispering about?" Jasmine asked.

"Nothing, babe," Hector replied, patting Frankie. "It's been very nice getting to know you, boy."

Kendall smiled. "He really is great, isn't he?"

"Yeah, he almost made me want a dog."

"Oh! Hector!" Marley exclaimed. "That reminds me, your mom will be asking about babies when we're at your house on Christmas Day."

"Ugh," Jasmine groaned. "Don't remind me."

Hector chuckled and walked to the door. "Come on, babe. Let's go make babies and we can tell my mom we're working on it!"

Jasmine walked to the door shaking her head. "That's my man. He's so romantic."

Marley laughed. "Oh, Jaz, you have no idea how much better you've made him."

"Yes, I do! I remember the way he was when we met."

Hector gave her the sweetest look and batted his eyelashes at her.

"Those puppy dog eyes get me every time," Jasmine huffed, walking out the door.

"Bye, y'all." Hector winked and followed her out.

Marley shut the door and widened her eyes. "That was so close."

Kendall looked at her and they both broke into fits of laughter.

Twenty-Eight

❦

"THAT'S FINE, JANE ANN," Marley said into the phone. "You can give them my address."

Kendall looked on from where she sat on the couch, stroking Frankie's side. He was asleep, but would occasionally open his eyes to look at Marley.

Marley ended the call and sat down next to Kendall. "His family wants to come here to pick him up."

"You're okay with that?"

"Sure." Marley nodded. "I think it will be better for Frankie. He seemed a little anxious when we took him to the shelter that day to scan his chip."

"Thanks for everything you've done for him," Kendall said softly, looking down at him.

Marley could see sadness along with anxiousness in Kendall's eyes. She put her arm over the back of the couch and gently squeezed Kendall's shoulder.

"I've been explaining to him that his family is coming to get him," Kendall said. "I thanked him for all the love he gave to me this Christmas."

"He's lucky you're the one who found him." Marley continued to run her hand along Kendall's shoulder.

Kendall shrugged. "You know, I really think he found me."

Marley could see tears in her eyes. She leaned over and gently kissed Kendall's hair. "He brought you to me," she whispered.

Kendall looked over at her and smiled. "I'll always be grateful to him for that."

"If I were to believe in Christmas magic," Marley said, smiling, "this would be it."

Kendall nodded. "Do you think he knows?"

"You told him."

Kendall smirked.

"He knows something is going on because he's still and cuddling you the best way he can."

They sat like that until a little while later when Frankie raised his head and his ears perked up.

"I think they're here." Marley got up and opened the front door. She smiled as a man and a woman stepped onto the porch. They both looked to be in their early twenties and resembled one another.

"Hi, I'm Hayden Carillo," the man said. "This is my sister, Ali."

"Hi." Marley gave them a friendly smile. "I'm Marley. Come on in."

They walked into the living room and Frankie stood up on the couch.

"Gary!" Ali exclaimed. "We've been so worried about you!"

The little dog jumped down and went to her. Ali crouched down and hugged Frankie to her.

"This is Kendall," Marley said. "She's the one who found Frank—uh, Gary?"

"Thank you so much," Ali said.

"Have a seat," Marley offered.

Ali sat on the other end of the couch while Hayden sat on the chair.

"He's actually our grandmother's dog," Hayden explained. "Can I ask where you found him? Was it near Caden Court?"

Kendall looked at Marley for help because she was not familiar with the streets around Jasmine and Hector's neighborhood.

"Yes," Marley replied. "It's right behind my friends' house. That's where Kendall was when he came walking up the sidewalk."

"Our grandmother lived there," Ali said. "She died about three months ago."

"Oh," Kendall said. "I'm sorry for your loss."

"Thank you," Hayden said. "He's been living with me in Plano since she passed."

"That's ten miles from here!" Marley exclaimed. "There are expressways and overpasses between here and there."

"I know," he said. "That's why we were so surprised when the woman called us. I can't imagine how he managed to walk all the way over here and knew where to go."

"Yeah," Ali said. "We put flyers out all over Hayden's neighborhood."

Marley smiled with relief that they had tried to find the dog. "Dogs can surprise you. I'm sure he missed your grandmother and wanted to go home. I assure you he's been well loved and taken care of since Kendall found him."

"He was my Gran's faithful companion, but after she died he hasn't been the same little dog."

"But he looks happy now," Ali said.

"I know this is a strange request, but would you mind

giving me your number so I could check on him occasionally?" Kendall asked.

"Of course," Hayden said. "I know he doesn't love us like he did my Gran, but we're trying."

"I'm sure you are," Kendall said. "There's a bag of food and treats you can take with you. He's wearing a collar we got for him and here's a leash."

"He didn't have a collar on when you found him?"

Kendall shook her head.

"Gary," Ali said. "You have to wear your collar so people will know how to find us."

"How about you don't run away again?" Hayden said, getting up and petting the dog.

"Thank you for taking such good care of him," Ali said.

"He's a really good boy," Kendall said, her voice full of emotion. She reached over and stroked his head. The dog whined softly.

"Thanks, Frankie," Marley whispered as she leaned down and kissed his head. He looked up at her with the saddest eyes.

"It'll be okay, boy," Hayden said. "I'll do better." He looked up at Kendall and Marley. "I've been gone a lot in the evenings, but not anymore."

"What's your number?" Marley asked with her phone in her hand.

Hayden and Ali both recited their numbers so Marley could put them in her phone. She sent a quick text and heard Hayden's phone beep in his pocket.

"Got it," he said.

Marley and Kendall walked them to the car. The last they saw of Frankie/Gary was him sitting in Ali's lap as they drove away.

Marley took Kendall in her arms as tears slipped down her cheeks.

"I don't know how you do that," Kendall said as they walked back into the house.

"Do what?"

"Say goodbye to the dogs at the shelter."

"I tell myself they are going to good homes with people who will love them and take good care of them," Marley said.

Kendall plopped down on the couch.

Marley was about to sit next to her when a text dinged on her phone. "How about that," she murmured. "Hector wants us to come over and watch a movie. He knows we're sad having to say goodbye to Frankie—uh, Gary—and he and Jaz want to cheer us up."

"Ah, that's nice," Kendall said. "I wonder if they'll feel that way after we tell them we're together."

Marley chuckled. "We can tell them after the movie."

❄

"I can't believe you're not working today," Jasmine said to Kendall as she sat down on one end of the couch.

"I couldn't concentrate anyway," Kendall replied. It was sad saying goodbye to Frankie, but she was also anxious about sharing the news about her relationship with Marley.

"His name was Gary," Hector said, plopping his feet on the ottoman in front of his chair. "I don't see it. He was definitely a Frankie."

Kendall chuckled. "I thought so too."

"I can see how you'd fall in love with him," Jasmine said. "We only had him for a couple of days and I didn't want him to leave."

"You were with him when we'd spend the evenings at my house," Marley said from her end of the couch.

"Yeah, but he was in Kendall's lap most of the time. He loves you." Jasmine smiled at Kendall.

"He's not the only one," Marley murmured.

"What was that?" Hector asked.

"I agree. Come sit between us," Marley said to Kendall, patting the couch.

"Yeah, we'll make you feel better." Jasmine smiled.

Kendall sat down between them and put one hand on Jasmine's knee and the other on Marley's. "I have the best friends," she said. "Including you, Hector. I just can't reach you."

Hector chuckled. "I got you, Ken."

"Do we need to talk about Christmas Day plans?" Hector asked.

"After the movie," Jasmine replied.

Kendall stole a glance at Marley and widened her eyes. Marley nodded. Kendall knew she was just as nervous as she was, but she was trying to reassure Kendall everything would be all right. Reason number one hundred and thirty-seven why she loved her, Kendall thought. She smiled, thinking she could list reason after reason why she had fallen in love with Marley Jacobs.

She didn't really pay attention to the movie because Marley kept pressing her thigh against Kendall's. It would be the most natural thing in the world to reach over and inter-twine their fingers. That's how they'd sat on the plane for the entire flight back to Dallas. Instead, Kendall sat with her hands clasped in her lap, afraid she'd forget where they were and reach for Marley's hand.

"Relax, Ken," Jasmine said softly. "It's okay to have an afternoon off, especially at Christmas."

Kendall looked over at her and scowled. Jasmine chuckled and continued to stare at the TV. Kendall felt Marley bump her shoulder to hers then pull it away. She sighed and decided it would be better to have Jasmine and Hector upset with them for now than try to sit next to Marley without touching her. *This is brutal.*

When the movie finally came to an end Hector said, "That was cute."

"Yeah, babe," Jasmine said. "Not bad."

"Did it make you feel better, Kendall?" Hector asked with a hopeful look.

"I'm not the only one who will miss Frankie," she replied. "Marley kept him at her house most of the time."

"Yeah, but she's said goodbye to lots of dogs and cats at the shelter."

"I have, but Frankie was special," Marley said, gazing at Kendall.

Jasmine got up and walked to the kitchen. "Does anyone want something to drink?"

"No thanks."

"I'm good."

She walked back into the room and sat on the arm of Hector's chair. "Now that Frankie—"

"Gary," Hector corrected her.

"Whatever." Jasmine rolled her eyes. "Now that the dog is back with his family, that means Kendall can come to Hector's with us on Christmas day."

Kendall looked over at Marley. This was it. Why was her heart beating so fast?

"Before you try to get out of it," Hector said, "I promise it'll be fun. You'll know more people this time. And Marley will be there!"

"Uh, yeah," Marley said, looking at Kendall then facing Jasmine and Hector. "I want Kendall to go with me."

Hector furrowed his brow. "Can't we all ride together?"

"Well, yeah," Marley replied.

Kendall could see her swallow then she reached over and

took Kendall's hand. She gave Kendall a soft smile then looked back at Jasmine and Hector.

"I want Kendall to go with me, as my girlfriend," Marley stated.

"What?" Hector chuckled. "She's your girlfriend for the Christmas parties, not for our family Christmas."

"What we're trying to tell you is that we're together now," Kendall said, holding Marley's hand with both of hers. "We know you're against the idea—"

"I knew it!" Jasmine said angrily. She stood up and stared at both of them. "I could tell something was different last night!"

She paced back and forth in front of them.

"Jaz," Kendall said.

Jasmine held up her hand and stopped in front of Marley. "Come on, Marley. How many dates have you had and complained about no spark? So you couldn't stop yourself and had to go after *my* best friend. You couldn't keep your hands off of her."

"Uh," Marley muttered.

"And you, Kendall!" Jasmine spat, now standing in front of her.

"You won't go out, all you do is work! So the first person who pays you a little attention, you have to sleep with!" Jasmine huffed and pointed at them both. "I know you've had sex, it's written all over your faces."

"Come on, Jaz," Kendall said, standing up. She knew Jasmine and Hector might not be happy about them dating, but she never expected Jasmine to yell at them with such venom.

"No," Jasmine stated with a quiet, deep anger. "I can't fucking believe this." She turned around and disappeared down the hall followed by a slamming door.

Twenty-Nine

"WHAT THE HELL," Hector said, standing up. "Have you been hiding this from us the whole time?"

"No!" Marley exclaimed. "We tried—"

"Save it." He started towards the hallway then stopped to look back at them. He shook his head then walked away.

Kendall sat back down on the couch and exhaled loudly. "I was not expecting that."

"I've never seen her that mad," Marley said.

"She was mad, but there's something else going on," Kendall said. Jasmine's reaction did not change her feelings for Marley, though, and she suddenly turned to her and grabbed her hands. "It'll be okay."

Marley sighed. "I know. I'm not having second thoughts." She scoffed. "It wouldn't matter even if I did. We're adults who are falling in love. This should be a happy time for us."

"Yeah," Kendall said. "And it's Christmas!"

Marley smiled. "This is going to push those bad Christmas memories so far out of our heads. There's only room for happy Christmas times, starting now."

Kendall smirked. "And what will we do with this particular memory?"

"We'll laugh about it one day."

"I hope so," Kendall said softly. "I love you."

"I love you, too," Marley replied. "But I think it's time for me to leave. Are you coming with me?"

"I should stay here. If Jasmine won't talk to me tonight, I'll be here so she has to in the morning."

Marley nodded.

They both got up and walked to the front door. Kendall leaned down and kissed Marley tenderly. "This doesn't change a thing."

"I hope not," Marley said. "I didn't want to break up with my best friend so I could be with Jasmine's best friend."

"We're a family," Kendall said. "They've just forgotten that part."

Marley cupped the side of Kendall's face. "See you tomorrow."

"You will."

Kendall walked Marley to her car and waved as she drove away. She sighed and walked back into the living room.

"Surely you didn't think Jasmine would be happy about this," Hector said, walking into the room.

Kendall sat down on the couch and waited while he sat down in the chair. "No. I didn't think she would react quite like that, though. There's something else going on, Hector."

He nodded.

"We didn't mean for this to happen," Kendall said. "We even tried to hold our feelings back, but Hector, I'm in love with Marley. This isn't just a fling. She loves me, too."

"You know you're family to me," he said. "But I've been friends with Marley longer than I've known you or Jasmine."

"I know. She told me you don't want her to date your friends."

"I don't want to see either of you get hurt."

"We don't want that either." Kendall shook her head. "We didn't want to hurt you."

He nodded.

"You know, if we can fall in love with a dog in an instant then why can't it be the same with people?" Kendall said quietly.

Hector looked up and gazed into her eyes. "Really?"

"That's how it felt when I stood right over there." Kendall pointed to the kitchen. "Marley walked into the room and when our eyes met, something happened to my heart."

"Jaz won't talk to you tonight."

"I know, but I'll be here in the morning because she's my best friend," Kendall said.

The next morning Kendall got up and went into the kitchen. She found Hector already dressed, sipping a cup of coffee.

"Is Jasmine up?"

"She left about thirty minutes ago," he replied.

"Left?"

He nodded. "She said something about last minute Christmas shopping."

Kendall scoffed. "She had her shopping done when I got here."

Hector raised his brows. "That should tell you something."

"We have to talk about this, Hector."

"She knows that, but she's not ready, Ken." He set his coffee cup down and grabbed his keys from the table beside the door that opened to the garage. "I'm going to Marley's. I'll have her come get you when we're finished talking."

Kendall stood there not knowing what to say or do.

"Okay?" Hector asked.

Kendall nodded.

Hector squeezed her arm on the way out of the house.

Kendall let out a deep breath. At least Hector was talking to her. Jasmine would come around. "She has to."

❄

"Hey," Marley said as Hector walked into her living room.

"Good morning," he said.

"Coffee?"

"Nope, I've already had several cups." He sat down on the couch and looked up at Marley.

Marley nodded and sat down next to him.

"Did you even think about telling me?"

"Okay, let's jump right into it. Yes, I've run over several scenarios in my head," Marley said. "Here goes." She set up a little straighter. "I've met someone," Marley said. "I think she's the one."

Hector raised his brows. "Really?"

"Yeah. Then you'd think for a minute and say something like… How could you have met someone when you've only been hanging out with Kendall?" Marley said, imitating Hector's voice. "Then I'd give you that look, like duh!"

Hector smiled. "And then what?"

"Then you'd say, Marley, my dear friend, I'm so happy you found the person who will make you feel the way Jasmine makes me feel." Marley smiled and gave him a hopeful look.

Hector widened his eyes. "You know that's what I want for you."

"Kendall makes me feel like that. I'm in love with her and she loves me," she said. "I know it's fast, but right now, Hector, I don't need you to act like another big brother. I need you to be my best friend." Tears sprang to Marley's eyes and she blinked them away. She didn't expect to be this emotional, but she loved Kendall and she wanted to share this with Hector.

"Oh, shit!" Hector exclaimed. "Don't cry! You know I can't take it when you cry. You never cry!"

Marley sniffed and quickly wiped a tear away.

"You could've told me."

"No, I couldn't," Marley protested. "Not after what you said that night when we were at your house. You talked about your sister and friends dating friends and it ends badly and all of that."

"I thought..." Hector rubbed his hands over his face. "Were you together then?"

"No," Marley said. "The feelings were there, but we were trying to ignore them. But neither one of us could stop them. Can you imagine trying *not* to fall in love with Jasmine?"

"I don't think it works that way."

"It doesn't," Marley said. "I tried to convince myself that Kendall didn't feel the same way and that it was a bad idea. I imagined all the things that could go wrong, but the thought of how right it felt when we were together always won."

Hector sighed.

"I couldn't stop it. Then I decided why? Why would I give up this chance at everything you tell me about how wonderful being in love with Jasmine is?"

"You've been in love before."

Marley nodded. "It didn't feel like this. I'm telling you, Hector, she's the one. I can feel it in my heart!"

"But what does it mean? Are you doing long distance?"

"Kendall's company is thinking of opening an office here," Marley said. "But I'm willing to move to her."

"What? You'd leave here? What about your career?"

"Kendall doesn't know any of this," Marley said. "I haven't told her yet. We wanted to tell you both what was going on between us. After that, I planned to talk to her."

"What exactly are you thinking?"

"You know my life, Hector," she said. "When have I had to make a monumental decision about anything? I have been so fortunate. My family has always supported me, especially when I came out."

"Kendall doesn't have that."

"I know, she told me."

"She doesn't share that with anyone."

Marley raised her brows and looked at him. "The luck just kept happening for me. When I graduated from college I got the job I wanted and have made the most of it."

"And you're willing to give that up?"

"It's a job, Hector. This is a chance at a happy life."

"I've never heard you talk like this," Hector said.

"I've never felt like this," Marley replied. "Did you feel like this when you were first with Jasmine?"

"I remember changing my career path so I could stay near her," Hector said. "She didn't know that until…"

"Until?"

"Until I knew she could see the future I saw for us together."

"I saw our future when I was in New York with Kendall," Marley said. "I want it!"

"Even if it means losing your best friend?"

Marley tilted her head. "You love Kendall," she said. "Are you telling me you'd give up our friendship because of someone I love? Someone who you love, too!"

"Of course I wouldn't," Hector said. "I thought it over last night and the only reason I never pushed you towards Kendall is because I thought you were at different places in your lives."

"We were waiting."

"Waiting for what?"

"Each other," Marley said. "I think our hearts were

waiting to find each other and once they did, they were not letting go."

"No matter how you tried."

Marley shrugged.

"I can't help you with Jasmine."

"This isn't about Jasmine," Marley said. "This is about you and me."

Hector smiled then narrowed his gaze. "If she hurts you…"

Marley chuckled. "Really? What if I hurt her?"

Hector stared. "If you hurt her…"

"That's what I thought." Marley sat back on the couch and chuckled. "You know neither one of us would intentionally hurt each other."

"I know that, but things happen."

Marley nodded.

"Don't let things happen."

"Got it."

Hector took a deep breath. "Why don't you come get Kendall? I think she should stay here tonight. We'll all meet up at my parents' tomorrow for Christmas."

"Don't Kendall and Jasmine need to talk?"

"Yeah, they do, but Jaz ain't ready," he said, lifting his shoulders.

Marley raised her brows.

"Don't ask. It's between them."

"Okay." Marley nodded. "Thanks."

"There's nothing to thank me for, but let's not do this again," he said. "Just fucking tell me next time."

"Next time?"

"I'm sure there will be something y'all are afraid we'll blow up about," Hector said. "So awkward."

"You know, that works both ways."

Hector laughed. "Yeah, I guess it could. Come on," he said, getting up. "Go get your girl."

Marley followed him out the front door and drove to their house.

When they got back to Marley's house, she held the door open for Kendall.

"It's strange walking into your house without Frankie jumping on my leg and wagging his tail," Kendall said.

"I know, babe," Marley said, putting her arm around Kendall. "I'm sure he's at Hayden's being a very good boy."

Kendall nodded. "Yeah, I'm glad he's with his people."

Marley tilted her head. "I don't know," she said. "I think we were his people too."

Kendall smiled and rested her hands on Marley's hips. "I'm glad your talk with Hector went well."

"Yeah, me too. No luck with Jasmine?"

"Hector told me she was prepared to stay away from the house all day." Kendall shrugged.

"Wow, she's really upset."

"Yeah, we have to talk at some point," Kendall said. "I thought I'd wait until we get back from our Christmas celebration tomorrow night."

"Well, it is Christmas Eve and we are together," Marley said with a happy smile.

"I love Jasmine, but I won't let her dampen our Christmas. I can tell this is just the beginning of many more merry ones for us together." Kendall grinned. "Say that three times fast."

Marley chuckled. "Did you have Christmas Eve traditions in your family?"

"Mmm, let's see." Kendall took Marley's hand and they sat down on the couch. "Sometimes we went to church that night and we always got to open one present."

"Let me guess." Marley narrowed her gaze. "New pajamas?"

"How did you guess!" Kendall's face was full of delight.

"Same." Marley chuckled. "It was usually new pjs."

"How about we start our own traditions?"

Marley grinned. "Okay. What are you thinking?"

"We haven't put our jelly-belly Santa on your tree," Kendall replied.

Marley gasped. "I thought about that last night. Since we've been back so much has been going on." She jumped up and grabbed her purse. "I've been carrying it around this whole time. Oh, and there's something else in here."

"I know what it is because mine is in my purse, too."

Marley took Kendall's purse off the table by the door and handed it to her. "This can be our tradition. We'll hang the ornament and then find the perfect place for our girls."

Kendall smiled and held up her figurine. "She's wearing a brown coat and red scarf just like you were that day."

"You remember that?"

"Of course I do."

"You were wearing your big black coat and that pretty white scarf."

Kendall chuckled. "It seems we are both remembering special moments."

Marley leaned down and kissed Kendall softly. "Let's start this tradition."

Thirty

MARLEY GOT up and walked over to the Christmas tree with Kendall. She could feel Kendall's eyes on her as she hung the Santa ornament on the tree.

"He looks so jolly." Kendall chuckled. "I'll see him first every time I look at the tree."

"Now, where shall we put our girls," Marley murmured, gazing around the room.

"How about on this bookshelf across from the front door?"

"I like it."

Kendall walked over and placed her figurine on the shelf then turned to Marley. "She wants to hold your hand."

Marley chuckled and put her figurine next to Kendall's, making sure their hands touched. "Perfect."

Kendall put her arms around Marley and smiled. "Wanna start another tradition with me, but without our clothes on?" She wiggled her eyebrows.

Marley wrapped her arms around Kendall's neck. "Oh, I think I'm going to like this tradition."

Kendall pressed her lips to Marley's in a soulful kiss,

leaving little doubt about what was going to happen. They both wanted to put Jasmine's reaction to their news out of their mind. It was Christmas Eve and they'd fallen in love. For now, that's all that mattered.

"I think I feel more of that Christmas magic you and Hector like to talk about," Marley said, pulling Kendall down the hall as she undressed her.

Kendall chuckled. "She's a believer!"

"Let me show you what I believe in," Marley said in a sexy voice. She pushed Kendall down on the bed.

Moments later Marley found herself on her back, her fingers sliding through Kendall's hair as lips kissed and nibbled a blazing trail across her skin. This woman could turn her body into a puddle of lust then her skilled hands and deft tongue would put her back together again. The entire time an undercurrent of love flowed through their bodies with their hearts whispering, *you're mine, I'm yours, who cares.*

Marley tightened her fingers in Kendall's hair as her tongue swirled around then flattened against her clit. Kendall was everything! How could it even be considered a risk to want this, to embrace this, to hold onto this?

As the orgasm crested then spilled through her, Marley let their love consume her. This was life! The life their hearts had led them to and all they had to do was hold on. "I'll never let you go," Marley whispered as she returned to her body.

"I've got you," Kendall whispered back.

Marley pulled Kendall up and wrapped her arms around her. She smiled and closed her eyes, letting their love rest like a blanket around them. This was definitely a tradition they'd be practicing year-round.

❄

Kendall squeezed Marley's hand and smiled. It had been such a fun day. When they arrived at Marley's parents' home, Kendall met both her brothers Tim and Caden. She was surprised when Caden said he remembered meeting her several years ago at Hector's parents' house.

Marley had stayed right by her side, smiling and holding her hand, making sure Kendall was included in the conversations. Kendall was sure Marley's cheeks would be tired by the end of the night. Marley had assured her the smiles were because she was so happy Kendall was there with her.

They'd gone the short distance down the street to Hector's family home. Marley told Kendall several stories of how she and Hector would sneak out at night and meet halfway between their houses just to talk. She described the times when her brothers couldn't be bothered with their little sister, but Hector shamed them into letting Marley go along with them.

Kendall came out of the bathroom and walked back into the living room. She saw Marley across the room telling a story with Hector. Tim and Caden looked on along with Hector's sister and parents. Everyone had smiles on their faces and were laughing as Marley and Hector took turns speaking.

Kendall hadn't really felt awkward and that surprised her when she thought about it. Hector had smiled and talked to her briefly, but Jasmine looked away anytime Kendall made eye contact. Kendall realized the only uncomfortable parts of the day were because of Jasmine. She was the one who usually made Kendall feel at home and not out of place.

Out of the corner of her eye Kendall saw Jasmine standing alone next to the dining table which was still full of food. This was her chance to at least get Jasmine to look at her. Kendall walked over and was pretty sure Jasmine glanced her way, but she didn't leave.

"Is this the way it's going to be?" Kendall asked, her gaze

on Marley and Hector. "Are you going to stay mad at me instead of being happy for me? It's Marley. Why wouldn't you want us to have what you and Hector have?"

"It's not that easy, Kendall," Jasmine replied.

The tone of Jasmine's voice as she said her name gave Kendall pause. There was definitely more going on here than just this surprise relationship with Marley. This wasn't the time or place, but Kendall intended to sit down with her best friend and figure this out. There was no reason they couldn't all be one big happy family.

Kendall didn't say anything when Jasmine slowly walked away.

"Hey." Marley walked up and grabbed her hand. "Is everything okay?"

Kendall nodded. "I tried to talk to Jasmine."

"Oh." Marley's eyes widened. "I didn't hear any yelling."

"She was very calm, which I think might be worse."

"Oh babe, I'm sorry."

"Hey," Tim said, walking up to them. "We're going back to mom and dad's. Are you coming?"

"No, we're leaving from here," Marley said.

"You might want to get on the road then," he said. "Caden got an alert on his phone that the weather was bad in the metroplex."

"Really?" Marley looked at Kendall. "It was cold when we left this morning, but I didn't know there was a storm coming."

"There was a chance for snow," Caden said, walking up to them. "But it's turned into sleet and freezing rain. The roads are bad."

"Kendall," Tim said, holding out his arms. "It was so nice to meet you. I hope my sister doesn't screw this up and we see you again soon." He hugged her and grinned.

"Oh, she won't." Kendall smiled at Marley.

"It was nice to see you again." Caden hugged her. "Y'all get on the road now or you'll end up spending the night here."

After Marley hugged both her brothers, Kendall felt Marley's hand slip into hers. They walked over to where Hector was staring at his phone.

"Caden told us the roads are bad at home," Marley said.

"Yeah, that's what I'm looking at." Hector continued to stare at his phone. "I lost track of time because we were having such a good time."

"I know," Marley replied. "I thought we'd be halfway home by now."

"Could you tell the innocent bystander what's happening?" Kendall said, trying to lighten the moment.

Hector laughed. "Innocent my ass."

Marley chuckled. "Don't be harassing my girl."

Wide-eyed, Hector looked up at her. "Stop that! If Jasmine sees me laughing with y'all she'll be pissed at me, too."

Marley turned to Kendall. "I thought we'd stay until around five, but time got away from me. It's after seven and getting colder so if the roads are bad then they're just going to get worse."

Hector's mom walked up and put her arm around Marley's shoulder. "I hope you don't think you're going anywhere," she said. "The roads *are* bad, and y'all are staying here tonight."

"Umm," Marley said.

"I talked to your mom and she has a houseful," Hector's mom said. "We have room."

Kendall met Marley's gaze then glanced over at Jasmine who was staring at them. "We really need some Christmas magic, Hector."

"Yeah," Marley agreed. "Now!"

Hector sighed. "Don't I know it."

They passed the time playing with Hector's nieces and

nephews as well as playing games with his sisters and parents. Kendall smiled as she watched Jasmine having a tea party with Hector's nieces. She knew Jasmine and Hector planned to have children someday and she couldn't wait to spoil them.

When it was the kids' bedtime, Jasmine helped corral them to their bedrooms.

Kendall had met a lot of people today, but everyone had been welcoming, including Hector's sisters and brother-in-law. She'd been around all of them before, but she'd always felt a little awkward. However, with Marley by her side she was almost comfortable. The Jacobses and Hernandez were one big happy family and Marley made sure Kendall was part of it now.

"Okay." Hector's mom came walking into the living room with Jasmine. "Here's what we're going to do. Hector and Marley can sleep out here on the couches. It will be like the sleepovers you used to have as kids."

"Uh, Mom—" Hector started.

"Don't worry," Hector's mom said. "Jasmine and Kendall can stay in your old room. I'm sure they'd like a little time without you."

"I've been traveling all month," Hector protested.

"It's fine," Jasmine said. "You know what your mom says goes."

"I'll get you blankets and pillows," Hector's mom said.

"Let me help." Marley followed her into the hall.

"Night, babe," Jasmine said, walking past them. "Are you coming, Kendall?"

Kendall stopped in the hallway as Hector's mom walked past her. "Uh, I'll see you in the morning?"

Marley smiled and kissed her on the cheek. "If not before."

Kendall walked into the bedroom and Jasmine threw her a T-shirt.

"You can sleep in this," Jasmine said.

As Kendall put the shirt on and took her pants off, Jasmine turned down the bed. She turned off the light and Kendall stood in the dark. Kendall waited a moment for her eyes to adjust then got in the bed next to Jasmine. She took a deep breath.

"You know how hard it is for me with my family, and that you feel more like family to me than they do. Of all people, I thought you'd be happy Marley and I have found one another. We're who we've both been searching for all this time."

"Have you been searching? Really?" Jasmine replied sarcastically. "You have to go out with people and share parts of yourself. When have you done that in the last few years in New York?" Her voice was stern. "If you have, then you haven't told me about any of these dates. And I'm supposed to be your best friend!"

There it was. Jasmine felt threatened in some way that she wasn't still Kendall's best friend.

"You *are* my best friend," Kendall said.

"How can you be sure about this thing with Marley?" Jasmine continued. "You haven't had sex in forever. I know you're having great sex now and this is all new and fun, but you know it won't always be that way. The newness will wear off."

"Of course I know the newness will wear off," Kendall replied. "I am sure because Marley has my heart and that's exactly where I want it to be."

"I get all of that, but what about Marley?"

Kendall raised up and rested her head on her hand. She could see Jasmine's face in the dim light coming through the window. "Marley is your friend, too. I'm not sure I understand why this is such a big deal now. I'm telling you, Jaz, we are in this all the way. It's not a fling. It's not a holiday thing."

"Then why do you need me?"

"What? I need you because you're my family. You're my best friend!"

"Don't you have Marley for that now?"

"No one could ever take your place as my best friend," Kendall said, reaching over and putting her hand over Jasmine's. "Who am I going to talk to when I need advice on my relationship? I can't talk to Marley about that."

"Whoa, you probably should. She's the one you're in the relationship with," Jasmine said.

"Like that's what you do with Hector."

Jasmine scoffed. "Why didn't you tell me?"

"I was afraid you'd have all these reasons it was a bad idea and when I didn't listen, you'd leave me. I didn't want to lose you," Kendall said.

"Uh, why would you think that?"

"Because of what you said that day we watched the movie,"

"Oh God!" Jasmine exclaimed. "We were talking what-ifs! I didn't know you really meant it."

"We were trying to hold back our feelings, but love doesn't work that way. Aren't you going to tell me it's too fast? You've already pointed out my loser sex life."

Jasmine chuckled. "You had a loser sex life because you chose it." She sighed. "Kendall, you've always known your heart. This might be fast for some people, but when you know, you know. That's who you are."

"She has my heart, Jaz, and won't let go," Kendall said.

"Do you want her to?"

"No!" Kendall exclaimed. "I just told you. I want her to hold it tight and never let go."

Jasmine smiled. "I want that for both of you."

"You do?" Maybe it was going to be all right.

"Now you've really gone and done it," Jasmine said.

"What do you mean?"

JAMEY MOODY

"If y'all have a fight, Hector and I will be in the middle of it all until you make up." Jasmine groaned. "We're committed with y'all. We won't let you give up."

"Then how could we not make it?" Kendall smiled.

"Come with me," Jasmine said, getting up. "I love you, but you're not the one I should be sleeping with."

Jasmine quietly opened the door and Kendall followed her out of the bedroom. The living room was dark but Kendall could hear Marley and Hector talking quietly.

"Come on, babe," Jasmine whispered.

"Jaz? What are you doing?" Hector said, sitting up.

"You're sleeping with your wife." She turned to Kendall. "The couch Marley is on is big enough for two people, trust me." Jasmine chuckled. "Just make sure you're back on your couch before Hector's mom comes into the kitchen to make coffee in the morning."

Kendall nodded and was sure her smile lit up the room.

Jasmine started to walk away then turned around and hugged Kendall tightly. "You're home," she whispered.

Kendall felt a knot in her throat as Jasmine let her go.

"Babe?" Marley said quietly. "Are you okay?"

Kendall turned around and smiled at Marley with tears in her eyes. "I'm home."

Marley grinned and held the blanket up so Kendall could crawl in next to her.

Thirty-One

"Look at all this food." Kendall glanced into Marley's back seat. "Your mom sent enough for days."

Marley chuckled. "She loves to send us back home with food. It's her way to show us her love."

"Did you see that pecan pie?"

"I did." Marley checked her rearview mirror to be sure Hector was behind her. "She may have known how much you liked the pecan pie I made at Friendsgiving."

"Oh?" Kendall glanced over at Marley and reached for her hand. "Have you been talking about me?"

"Maybe."

Kendall giggled. "My sister has heard your name a few times lately."

Marley gasped and glanced over at Kendall. "Did you call them yesterday?"

"Yes." Kendall smiled. "I called them when we got to Hector's house. His mom took me into her bedroom so I'd have privacy."

"She's the best."

"I had so much fun and it wasn't awkward," Kendall said.

"That's because you fit in with everyone."

"You made sure of that."

"It wasn't me, babe," Marley said. "It was you. They like you. Don't be so surprised. I like you, too."

Kendall chuckled. "I like it when you call me babe."

"Oh yeah?" Marley smiled.

Kendall nodded. "And when you get bossy."

"Ugh, I am not bossy!"

Kendall laughed and kissed the back of her hand. "Okay," she replied nonchalantly.

A couple of hours later they were putting the food in the refrigerator when Marley's phone beeped with an incoming text.

"We've been invited to a sleepover at Jasmine and Hector's."

"A sleepover?" Kendall gave her a confused look.

"Jasmine says we're having family time, a sleepover, and breakfast in the morning. She wants to know all about our trip to New York." Marley looked up from her phone. "I wonder why she didn't text you."

"Y'all haven't really talked since our big announcement."

"We were fine this morning," Marley said.

"I think this is her way of saying she's not mad at you."

"Oh." Marley frowned. "Do you think she was mad at me?"

Kendall shrugged. "You mean more to her than you know."

"I know we're friends, but I was always Hector's friend." Marley made air quotes with her fingers. "But these last few weeks with the three of us hanging out most nights, I do feel like *her* friend now."

Kendall smiled. "We're a family."

"We are." Marley was about to kiss Kendall when there was a knock at the door. She furrowed her brow and went to answer it.

When she opened the door, Frankie jumped up on her legs then disappeared into the room to find Kendall.

"What the?" Marley exclaimed.

Hayden and Ali were standing on Marley's porch. "Hi," Hayden said, hesitantly.

Marley turned around to see Frankie in Kendall's arms, licking her face. She laughed. "Come in."

"We should've called first," Ali said.

"But we didn't." Hayden shrugged.

Marley walked over and stroked Frankie's head. "Hey, buddy." He licked her hand and she chuckled. "I swear, he's smiling."

Kendall laughed. "He is!"

"He hasn't been this happy since we picked him up the other day," Ali said.

Kendall sat down on the couch with Frankie on her lap. Marley sat on the arm of the couch and continued to pet him. "Y'all have a seat."

"He's been so sad since we brought him back to my house," Hayden said.

"We thought he might be sick," Ali added. "I let him stay with me one day while Hayden had to work, but he was just as mopey at my house."

"He seems happy now," Kendall said.

"What can we do to help?" Marley asked.

Hayden and Ali shared a look. "He could live with you," Hayden said, shyly.

Kendall looked at Marley with surprise on her face, but also hope. Marley knew Kendall missed Frankie and she did too.

"He's obviously happy with the two of you," Ali said. "We aren't his people."

"Yeah, we promised our grandmother we'd take good care of him," Hayden said. "But he's so unhappy."

"You want him to come live with us?" Marley asked.

"I know it's a lot to ask, but if he's happy here and..." Ali trailed off.

"Yes!" Kendall exclaimed.

Marley looked over at Kendall and the excitement, delight, and hope on her face made Marley's heart jump in her chest. As if to seal the deal Frankie crawled into her lap. She chuckled and smoothed the hair on top of his head.

"Would it be okay if we called him Frankie?" Marley asked.

"He seems to like that name." Hayden grinned.

"What do you think, boy?" Marley asked the dog, cradling his face between her hands. She was sure the smile on his face was his way of saying yes.

"That looks like a yes to me," Kendall said.

"Thank you so much!" Ali said.

"I'll get his food out of the car." Hayden jumped up and was out the door in a flash.

"I think my grandmother would be pleased with us," Ali said. "All of us."

"Are you sure?" Kendall asked Marley softly.

Marley nodded. "I'm sure."

Kendall grabbed Frankie and looked him in the face. "Welcome to the family, boy."

The little dog wiggled in her arms.

A few minutes later Hayden and Ali said their goodbyes and Marley walked them outside. When she came back into the living room Frankie was sitting beside Kendall.

"Aren't you two a happy sight." Marley laughed.

"He belongs with us," Kendall said. She patted the couch next to her.

Marley sat down beside her and smiled.

"*This* is Christmas magic," Kendall said.

Marley chuckled. She'd planned to tell Kendall about her idea of moving to New York before they went to Jasmine and Hector's and this was as good a time as any.

"There's something I wanted to talk to you about," Marley said, taking Kendall's hands in hers. "I know we haven't discussed what happens next, but long-distance isn't going to work for me."

Kendall's eyes widened. "Uh, okay," she mumbled. "Let me—"

"It's okay, babe," Marley said. "Just listen to me for a minute. I've been doing a lot of thinking and I've taken a look at my life." She smiled and continued. "I've been so lucky to have a supportive family and friends. I've never had to take a big risk with anything. Coming out was not necessarily difficult and my career path has worked out just as I planned."

"But that's a good thing."

"I know, but instead of hoping your company will someday expand to Dallas, why can't I—well, now Frankie and I—move to New York?"

"Oh, babe," Kendall said. "I would never ask you to do that. You'd have to leave your family, your friends, your job."

"You're not asking me. I want to do this." Marley raised her brows and nodded.

"I don't know, Marley. You are so good at your job. You take that giant puzzle each day and put it together to make everything run smoothly."

Marley chuckled. "I do and there are other opportunities with my company, but maybe I want to work on a new puzzle.

"A new puzzle?"

"Yeah, the puzzle of us. I want to work on putting our life together. What could be better than that?"

"This is such a big leap."

"That's the thing, it doesn't feel like a big risk to me. This is it. We're it. This is my path to happiness. Kendall, I want to be with you through all the happiness and sometimes the not-so-happiness."

"We've just made it through one of those not-so-happy times with Jaz and Hector."

Marley nodded. "We'll make it through the others together."

Kendall stared into Marley's eyes. Marley knew she was looking for the slightest hint of doubt or apprehension, but she'd find none.

"Let's do this," Marley said.

Kendall took a deep breath and slowly let it out. She looked down at the dog. "What do you think, Frankie? Do you want to move to New York with Marley and me?"

Marley couldn't believe the happiness in her heart. She grabbed Kendall's face and was about to kiss her when Kendall stopped her.

"Are you sure?"

Marley nodded. "I've never been so sure of anything in my life. We're supposed to be together. Let's make it happen."

Kendall crushed her lips to Marley's, pushing her back against the couch. Marley laughed at her exuberance when Kendall wrapped her arms around her in the biggest hug.

"I can't believe this!" Kendall exclaimed, looking into Marley's excited face.

"How's that for Christmas magic!"

"Oh, I love you so much," Kendall murmured. She placed kiss after kiss on Marley's cheeks, her lips, her forehead, and then hugged her tight once again.

"I love you, too, babe," Marley said, finally able to speak through the laughter and kisses.

"Have you talked to your family about this?"

Marley shook her head. "I mentioned it to Hector when he was here the other day."

Kendall sighed. "What did he think?"

"He understood because he had a chance at a big job when he first graduated from college and turned it down to be near Jasmine."

Kendall tilted her head. "I remember that. Jasmine tried to convince him to take it, but he gave her several reasons why it wasn't the right fit for him."

Marley chuckled. "Yeah, because he fit with Jasmine and she was here."

Kendall stared at Marley for several moments.

"What is it?"

"I—I can't believe you would do this for me," Kendall said softly. "No one has ever done anything like this for me."

"I'm doing it for us," Marley said. "Look what I get out of this deal. A cute apartment in New York City."

Kendall smirked.

"And Stuart!"

"Oh my God," Kendall said. "He will lose it!"

"Mrs. K and her deli!"

Kendall widened her eyes. "She'll think she somehow made this happen."

Marley laughed. "Most of all." She paused. "I get to wake up with you every morning."

Kendall gasped and Marley saw tears pool in her eyes.

"Oh, baby," Marley said. "Don't cry."

"These are happy tears," Kendall said. She leaned in and kissed Marley tenderly.

"I'd better text Jasmine and let her know we're bringing another guest with us," Marley said.

"I don't think they'll mind."

. . .

"Do you think they're going to be mad at us all over again when we tell them I'm going to New York with you?" Marley asked as they walked onto Jasmine and Hector's porch.

"Nah, I think they'll be happy we're not doing long distance," Kendall replied.

"Look who's here!" Hector exclaimed. "Frankie, have you come back to us?"

Marley and Kendall quickly told the story of how Frankie was now part of the family.

"We have so much to celebrate," Jasmine said. "I want to hear everything about your time in New York. First, we need drinks. Marley, will you help me?"

"Sure." Marley looked at Kendall and raised her eyebrows.

Once they were in the kitchen, Jasmine turned to Marley and gave her a big hug. "I'm really happy for you and Kendall."

"Thank you."

"I know I didn't handle it well at first, but honestly I was shocked," Jasmine said, uncorking a bottle of wine. "And then I got to thinking about all the missed connections between the two of you."

"It feels like it's meant to be," Kendall said from the entrance to the living room.

"Or Christmas magic," Marley said, looking at Hector.

"Oh, my God!" Hector exclaimed "Did you just say—"

"Stop!" Marley raised her voice. "I'm beginning to believe in this Christmas magic thing, but really us getting together is all y'all's fault."

"Our fault?" Jasmine frowned.

"Yeah, you kept us apart so long. If you'd let us meet years ago I wouldn't have had to have my loser sex life," Kendall said.

Jasmine chuckled. "Sorry about that."

"And I wouldn't have had to go on all those first dates! Ugh!"

"Okay, I shouldn't have said that." Jasmine laughed.

"No, you're right," Marley said. "I never have to go on a first date again."

"Let's drink to that." Jasmine raised her brows and smiled at Hector. "So," she said, leading them into the living room. "I want to hear all about this first date and how you snuck around behind our backs."

"It wasn't like that," Kendall protested.

"Uh huh." Jasmine smirked.

They all chuckled as Marley and Kendall sat down on the couch and told them everything, including their romantic day in New York City.

Thirty-Two

MARLEY GLANCED down at her watch and sighed. She looked at the door to the bar when it opened but in walked two guys wearing suits who had probably stopped in for a drink after work. Marley wasn't the only one working the day before New Year's Eve. She'd offered to work a couple of days between Christmas and New Years so the people traveling during the holidays could be with their families.

Kendall had gone downtown to meet with two prospective analysts as well as a client. She'd explained that this was the only time the analysts could see her, so she didn't mind working over the holiday. Although she only had a few clients of her own, one lived in Dallas and they usually met on a video call. When the client was available for an in-person meeting, Kendall jumped at the chance to see her.

Marley had received a text from Kendall earlier that afternoon suggesting they meet at a nearby bar for a drink. They'd spent most of the holiday with Jasmine and Hector. When they weren't with them, they were at Marley's house. She certainly didn't mind that because most of the time they were naked and making love all over the house.

Marley smiled at the thought of how they'd woken up that morning.

"With that kind of look on your face, I hope you were thinking of me," Kendall said, sliding into the booth opposite her.

Marley felt her cheeks heat up and thought about a clever retort, but she knew it was obvious that she'd been thinking of Kendall. "I had to think of something to pass the time."

"Sorry." Kendall winced. "I think everyone must be out on the roads exchanging their Christmas gifts."

"It's okay." Marley smiled. "I haven't been here long. I ordered you an old fashioned."

Right on cue the server brought their drinks.

"Ahh, this is perfect," Kendall said, sitting her drink down after a generous sip. "Is that a martini?"

Marley nodded. "It's a chocolate martini. Kyra, my assistant, loves them and keeps asking if I've tried one yet." She picked up the drink and took a small sip. "Whoa," she said, blinking her eyes.

"Good?"

"Yeah, it's different," Marley said. "It's like a milkshake with alcohol. Try a sip." She slid the glass towards Kendall and watched her eyes brighten as she sipped the drink.

"That's strong."

"I'll only need one of these." Marley chuckled. "How did your meetings go?"

Kendall smiled and Marley could see anticipation in her eyes. She was excited, but there was something else.

Marley raised her brows. "Did something happen?"

"My meeting with the analysts went well," Kendall said. "I think they will both join our team."

"Oh good," Marley said. "I know you thought they would be a good fit."

"It was wonderful to see my client in person. I hope you

can meet her sometime," Kendall said, reaching for her drink. "I think you would get along well. She's very interested in investments in supply chain corporations."

"Ah." Marley smiled. "Does she like puzzles?"

Kendall chuckled. "Probably."

Marley watched Kendall sip her drink. There was something else. She could see it in Kendall's eyes.

"Nicole wanted to have a video call after I finished with my client," Kendall said. "That's one reason I'm a little late."

"Oh, did she have a nice Christmas?"

Kendall nodded. "We had a long conversation about Dallas and the market here. The projections for the wealth that is going to be in the hands of women in the coming decade is astounding. The baby boomers are turning over vast inheritances and the like."

"And a lot of these women will need skilled advisors on how to manage this wealth," Marley commented.

Kendall nodded. "The numbers are amazing and Nicole thinks this area would be perfect for a satellite office."

Marley gasped. "Does that mean what I think it means?"

Kendall leaned over the table and reached for Marley's hand. "I know you would leave your job and move to New York with me, but what if we stayed here?"

Marley raised her brows. "Does Nicole need a very skilled analyst to run this new satellite office?"

"She does."

"Well." Marley exhaled a deep breath. "I'm looking at a woman who happens to be very skilled in many areas," she said with a grin.

"You are."

"Are you the new boss?" Marley raised an eyebrow.

"Oh, babe, you'll always be the boss."

Marley chuckled. "You know what I mean!" she exclaimed. "Tell me! Are we staying in Dallas?"

"Only if you want to," Kendall said, suddenly serious.

"Honey," Marley said softly. "Isn't this what you hoped for?"

"It's not just my hopes any longer, Marley. What are your hopes?"

Marley got up and slid into the seat next to Kendall. "I'm good at my job and I'm moving up. If you're here, beside me, how can I hope for anything more? If this job is what you want then I'm just fine staying right here."

"Are you sure? That was a big decision to uproot your life and move to New York with me."

Marley cradled Kendall's face between her hands. "We're starting our life together. What better place than right here with our friends and family nearby." She smiled. "Honestly, I don't care where we are as long as we're together. It's funny how career ambitions aren't as important when you're no longer doing this alone. My happiness is with you."

"Oh, babe," Kendall said. "That's what I think, too. As long as I'm with you, that's all that matters."

Marley leaned in and kissed Kendall softly. "It would be nice to stay here. We have a house, good jobs, friends, and a sweet little dog."

Kendall chuckled. "I'll never forget that you were going to move for me. I can't tell you how much that means to me."

"You don't have to tell me." Marley grinned. "You've been showing me since I told you."

"There is a perk if we decide to do this," Kendall said.

"I'm listening."

"I'll have to go back to New York once every month or so for a couple of days," Kendall explained. "Of course, you will have to come with me."

"Of course." Marley nodded.

"Those trips would be like mini honeymoons."

Marley's eyes widened. "Honeymoons usually happen for married people."

Kendall nodded. "We're going to be together forever so why not?"

Marley chuckled. "If that was a proposal, it rivals the first time you told me you loved me."

Kendall smiled and waited.

"Yes, we are going to be together forever, so I accept your proposal of mini honeymoons every month."

The smile on Kendall's face was like the brightest star on a moonlit night. Marley pressed their lips together in a kiss of love, promise, and imminent happiness.

❄

"Who knew that six months ago this brown and withered backyard would be so vibrant and green now? All these pops of color; red and orange and yellow. I didn't know there could be this many shades of red and pink," Kendall said as she watered the pots of flowers around the back porch.

"The colors are so bright because you're in love," Marley said, sitting on one of the chairs.

"What?" Kendall gave her a confused look.

"I'm telling you, these flowers were not this bright and beautiful before you came to live here," Marley said.

"So our love is making them more beautiful?"

"Well, it isn't Christmas magic. It's the end of June."

Kendall walked over and sat in Marley's lap. "I think our love is the magic."

"Oh yeah?"

Kendall nodded. "When I first came here back in December I thought I was lonely, but now I don't think that was it at all."

Marley ran her fingers through Kendall's hair, brushing

the strands off her forehead. The touch was so familiar and Kendall knew it was a way that Marley showed her love.

"What was it then?"

"I think you were reaching out and pulling me to you."

"Then why did it take you so long to get here?" Marley said.

"It had to be the right time," Kendall said quietly. "All along I was looking for love—not just love, but my forever love. The real love that makes you want to grow old with someone, the kind of love that doesn't scare you to be with another person that long, but makes you excited about it." Kendall smiled and continued. "I was missing what I didn't have, but I knew my heart would know when it was time."

"That's what I was doing with all those dates," Marley said.

"Sometimes I would think about it and consider going on a date, but with whom? Other times I would tell myself that my love was out there and she would find me."

"I found you," Marley whispered.

"And we're not letting go."

"No way."

"Hearts don't know about shouldn'ts and expiration dates," Kendall said.

"Our hearts knew they'd finally found each other."

Kendall nodded. "And the magic of our love pushed us together when we were ready."

"And got us through when things got a little iffy with our best friends."

"Magic," Kendall said softly as she leaned towards Marley's lips. "And to think it all started with a Christmas date."

"My heart still happily sighs every time I see you." Marley smiled. "Are you going to kiss me?"

"You know I love it when you're bossy," Kendall replied

and pressed their lips together. The passion and love exploded when their lips touched. Kendall's hand was behind Marley's neck, keeping them close. She felt Marley's mouth open slightly, inviting her to deepen the kiss. Kendall could kiss those lips from then on and that's what she intended to do.

They heard Frankie huff as he laid down beside the chair.

Kendall pulled away and looked down at him. "Yep, we're kissing again."

She felt Marley's hand pull her chin back until their lips met again.

They were both breathing hard and letting the kiss take them away when Marley's phone beeped on the table. Neither of them moved, languishing in the kiss that had now become soft, gentler.

Kendall pulled away and smiled while Marley reached for her phone.

"It's Hector," she said, reading the text. "He wants us to go to the lake with them."

Kendall raised her brows. "Want to?"

Marley tapped her screen, replying to the text, then looked up at Kendall. "I told him we'd be there in a little while."

Kendall felt Marley gently push her up to standing. "Come on."

A knowing smile crossed Kendall's face as Marley led them into the house. She loved her bossy girlfriend.

Five Years Later

"I can't believe it's taken you two five years to get married," Jasmine said, smoothing her hands down Kendall's shoulders. "Why did you decide to wear a suit instead of a dress?"

"Because Marley loves to see me in a suit." Kendall smiled.

"Mmm, I do." Marley grinned.

"It's taken us this long to have the actual wedding because we were busy," Kendall said.

"Yeah, Kendall was opening the new office for her company."

"And Marley was promoted and that took a little time to get used to," Kendall added.

"We've taken some little honeymoon trips to New York." Marley winked at Kendall. "Plus, we had to wait and have a Christmas wedding."

"Besides, someone had a baby, so then we had to wait until their perfect little girl could walk up the aisle with Frankie," Kendall said.

"She is perfect," Hector said, gazing down at his four-year-old where she played with Frankie.

"I always thought it was dumb for people to have their

dogs in their wedding," Kendall said. "But then came Frankie and now I understand."

"Yeah," Marley said. "He's so much more."

Frankie looked up at both of them and smiled.

"Okay," Jasmine said, "Stuart is about to take his place. We'll walk down the aisle and wait for you two."

Stuart had jumped at the chance to officiate their wedding. He and Marley had become good friends and his bar was their first stop every time they went to New York.

"Thanks for standing up with me, Jaz," Kendall said.

"Of course, you're my best friend."

"I'll be waiting for you," Hector said to Marley.

"I know," Marley said. "I've always been able to count on you."

"We'll give you two a minute before we walk down," Jasmine said.

Marley turned to Kendall and pulled her away from the others. "Do you remember all the Christmas miracles that got us here?"

"We've had so many, but I remember those in the beginning. They came in threes."

Marley smiled and tilted her head. "Go on."

"First, it was a bit of a miracle that got me to come here for the entire month of December. Then came Frankie, and finally, my company started a new office here."

"Okay." Marley nodded. "For me, it was pausing the dating apps over Christmas, feeling the connection I was searching for when I looked into your eyes, and then seeing our future on that first trip to New York."

"You know, that trip was when we got married. My heart vowed to always be with yours that first night."

"The first time we had sex?" Marley asked.

"That first time was so much more than sex."

"It was hard to stay present in the moment because I felt

276

like I was looking into the future." Marley raised a brow and grinned at Kendall. "But then you did that thing with your tongue and whoa baby, was I ever in the moment."

Kendall laughed.

"Did you really tell Hector that if we can fall in love with a dog with one look, like we did with Frankie, then why couldn't we do the same with people?"

"I did." Kendall smiled. "My heart fell in love with you the moment our eyes met in their living room."

Marley chuckled. "It just took us a minute to listen to them."

"We've been listening ever since and it's given me a life even better than I'd dreamed."

They stared into each other's eyes for a moment and smiled.

"You're still not afraid of growing old with me?" Kendall asked, rubbing her lips together.

"Oh, babe. I can't wait!"

They could hear the music begin to play and Jasmine and Hector walked down the aisle with their beautiful little girl leading Frankie right beside her.

"Oh, wait. I have something." Kendall pulled a sprig of mistletoe out of her pocket and held it over their heads.

"Christmas magic is all the things that transport you to a world where anything is possible," Marley said, kissing Kendall softly.

"Our world is beautiful, sometimes messy, and full of love," Kendall said, gazing into Marley's eyes.

"Love is our magic."

Their lips met in a kiss full of love, magic, and their forever.

About the Author

Jamey Moody is a bestselling author of sapphic contemporary romance. Her characters are strong women, living everyday lives with a few bumps in the road, but they get their happily ever afters.

Jamey lives in Texas with her adorable terrier Leo.

You can find Jamey's books on Amazon and on her website: jameymoody.com

Join her newsletter for latest book news and other fun. Join here.

Jamey loves to hear from readers. Email her at: jamey moodyauthor@gmail.com

On the next page is a list of Jamey's books with links that will take you to their page.

Jamey has included the first two chapters of Until We Weren't: A Story of Destiny and Faith. This is an enemies to lovers, second chance love story full of romance. In the lush world of landscaping, Destiny and Faith once thrived in love until Faith vanished without explanation. Now, Destiny seeks reconciliation to win a career-defining project. But past wounds fester, leaving Destiny to wonder: how deep does their love truly grow? A tale of redemption, forgiveness, and flourishing romance.

f X ◎ ⑥ **a**

Also by Jamey Moody

Stand Alones

Live This Love

One Little Yes

Who I Believe

* What Now

See You Next Month

Until We Weren't: A Story of Destiny and Faith

The Your Way Series:

* Finding Home

*Finding Family

*Finding Forever

The Lovers Landing Series

*Where Secrets Are Safe

*No More Secrets

*And The Truth Is ...

*Instead Of Happy

The Second Chance Series

*The Woman at the Top of the Stairs

*The Woman Who Climbed A Mountain

*The Woman I Found In Me

Sloan Sisters' Romance Series

*CeCe Sloan is Swooning

*Cory Sloan is Swearing

*Cat Sloan is Swirling

Christmas Books

*It Takes A Miracle

The Great Christmas Tree Mystery

With One Look

Meant to Be Christmas

*Also available as an audiobook

Until We Weren't: A Story of Destiny and Faith

CHAPTER 1

"Those are doing well despite this heat."

Faith looked up and smiled. "Hi, Mrs. Baker. How are you?"

"Oh honey, I'm just out enjoying this sunshine," Mrs. Baker replied. "I'm glad to see you. I've told the boy who cuts the grass he'd better take care of these plants or you'll be after him."

Faith Fields was the owner of Lush Fields Landscaping. She had planted the grass and created the flower beds for this retirement home several years ago when she was working for another company, but she still stopped by occasionally to check on the plants and shrubs.

Faith chuckled. "Sometimes plants die, Mrs. Baker."

"It's been years since you've planted these and not one has died. The way you lovingly tend to the delicate plants to make sure they thrive makes me wonder if you give that kind of attention to other parts of your life," Mrs. Baker said.

Faith was on her knees and stopped to look up at the older woman and smirk. "You know this was one of the first projects I was able to create and put in. It's special to me and that's why I come by to make sure I chose the right plants for this area. I want you to have something beautiful to look at on your daily walks. Besides, I get to see you."

Mrs. Baker smiled. "Your friend from The Green Thumb came by earlier this week and checked on that very flower bed."

Faith bristled and paused for a moment then she stabbed her small shovel into the earth around the vinca plant she was tending to.

"I still don't understand why you two don't come by together anymore," Mrs. Baker said. "It seems to me you'd be finished a lot quicker with two of you."

Faith pushed the dirt around the tender plants then looked up at Mrs. Baker. "You know why. We both have our own companies now and don't work together any longer."

"Yet you both still come by and check on these plants," Mrs. Baker said, raising one eyebrow.

Faith sighed and tried to push down the knot that had formed in her stomach.

"Why is it again that you two opened separate companies? You did everything together to make this place beautiful," Mrs. Baker said.

"Now, Mrs. Baker, it's been years," Faith said, standing up and dusting off her pants. "You know we had our own ideas about things and decided to go off on our own. Some things don't flourish no matter how much attention you give them."

"Mmhmm," Mrs. Baker muttered, staring at Faith. "It seems to me that sometimes these plants get a little brown or wilt and you think they're gone, but lo and behold there are still little shoots of green at the base. There's still life."

Faith put her hands on her hips and tilted her head. "When did you become a horticulturist?"

"I've watched these plants grow since you put them in, dear," Mrs. Baker said.

Faith reached down to pick up her other tools.

"Some of them have withered, but you haven't had to replace them because they keep coming back," Mrs. Baker continued.

Faith looked into Mrs. Baker's eyes and knew she wasn't just referring to the plants.

"Sometimes plants aren't the only things that wither," Mrs. Baker said. "I live in a place where I see that happen every day. Hell, I experience it because of my age."

"But you're not," Faith said with a smile. "You're thriving."

Mrs. Baker scoffed. "And your business is thriving, but are you?"

Faith smirked. "I'll see you again soon, Mrs. Baker."

"Think about it, Faith," Mrs. Baker said. "It hurts my heart to see my friends wither away before their time."

Faith smiled and walked back to her truck. The last thing she wanted to do was think about *her friend* as Mrs. Baker had called her. Destiny Green was the furthest thing from a friend. It made Faith's stomach queasy that she ever let that woman touch her, much less trust her with her heart.

Mrs. Baker was right that they did work well together. As time passed they became more than co-workers and led their own teams within the company. Faith trusted Destiny with her ideas of how they could turn a piece of ground into something beautiful.

In turn Destiny befriended Faith and they began to spend time together outside of work. They had fun and Faith felt like she'd found a true friend. As their friendship evolved into more, Faith was hesitant at first. Her past was full of people who were supposed to care for her, yet always let her down.

But Destiny could see past Faith's walls and had been patient as well as caring. When Faith moved in with Destiny, she finally relaxed and let herself be loved.

"You were such a fucking idiot," she muttered. She shook her head, put the truck in gear and sped out of the parking lot.

❄

"They aren't supposed to award the contract until tomorrow. I don't know why you keep checking for an email."

Destiny Green looked up from her computer and smirked at her assistant, Monica. They were friends long before Destiny started The Green Thumb, so when Destiny needed someone to run the office, Monica asked for the job. She was tired of the long hours and stress as a paralegal. Destiny welcomed her to The Green Thumb; they worked well together and had remained friends.

"I know." Destiny sighed. "I was hoping maybe if we won the bid they'd let us know today."

"Mmhmm," Monica murmured. "I know what you're doing."

Destiny met her eyes and raised her eyebrows.

"You're making sure Lush Fields Landscaping doesn't get it."

"I didn't say that," Destiny said defensively.

"You didn't have to," Monica said. "I'm not sure what you hope for more. That we get the job or Faith doesn't."

Destiny scoffed. "Of course I want us to get the job."

"Come on, how long have we been working together?" Monica said. "Who knew the landscaping business was so cutthroat? I think I need to pitch a reality show. We could call it Landscape Wars."

"What!" Destiny exclaimed.

"You and Faith are the perfect enemies."

"That's not funny."

"It's not supposed to be funny," Monica said. "As much as y'all hate each other it'd make for great TV and probably put both our companies on the map. You'd be turning jobs down."

"I don't hate Faith," Destiny stated.

"Okay, whatever you say." Monica grinned. "I've only known you for ten years and we've worked together for three. It's not like you and Faith weren't both my friends at one time."

Destiny stared at Monica. She could feel her cheeks getting warm.

"You know, they say there's a fine line between love and hate," Monica said.

Destiny looked back at her computer. "I'm actually doing a little research. Do you know that new construction off Interstate 35? It's going to be a huge business complex."

"No comment and a subject change," Monica said. "Okay, that conversation is closed. Yes, I know the area you're talking about."

"They plan to take bids to do the landscaping for the entire complex, but they're also looking at breaking it into different sections and tying them all together in some way. If I can come up with something creative and different, this job could boost The Green Thumb's exposure and make it one of the top landscaping businesses in the state."

"But that place is huge. Can we pull off something like that?"

"We'd have to put everyone on it, but I think we can," Destiny said.

"Is that where you were this afternoon? I wondered why you had dirt on your pants when you came in. You rarely have time to work in the field anymore."

"Uh, no," Destiny replied. "I had to check on something else."

"Don't tell me you were at the retirement home again." Monica shook her head. "What is it with that place? The

Green Thumb does not get a penny from that estab-
lishment."

When Destiny didn't say anything, Monica continued.
"Before starting your own company, you were working for the
Galloways at Landscape Artists, right?"

Destiny nodded. "Yes, and they taught me to not only
take pride in my work, but also to be attentive. The land can
change over time and sometimes your design needs to
change with it. Going back and checking on projects I did
when I worked for them is valuable in how I bid on jobs
now."

"I wonder if Faith does the same thing. She worked there,
too, right?" Monica said.

Destiny sat back in her chair and stared at Monica. "If you
must know, I go back there not only to check the grounds, but
also to visit with one of the residents." She smiled just
thinking about Mrs. Baker. "When Faith and I were putting in
the flower beds we made a friend. Every time I go back, Mrs.
Baker appears while I'm tending to the plants and we have a
nice visit."

"Maybe I should ask her what happened between you and
Faith because no matter how many times I ask, you won't
enlighten me," Monica said.

"Maybe because it's none of your business," Destiny said.

"Oh, but it is. I'm concerned with your well-being and I
know Faith has a lot to do with that."

Destiny laughed sarcastically. "How so? It's been three
years since Faith and I were together."

"Three long years since you've been on a date or smiled
when talking about another woman," Monica said. "I've tried
to set you up several times."

"If you haven't noticed, I'm trying to run a company,"
Destiny said defensively. "That leaves no time for dating or
much else."

"Oh, you could make time. That's what I'm for. As your assistant, I'm supposed to take some of the burden off of you."

"And you do," Destiny said.

"Why did you and Faith break up again? I forget," Monica said. "Was it because you worked all the time? Because that's all you've done since you two broke up. Come to think of it, you and Faith didn't do much with us or our friend group when you were together."

Destiny looked back to her computer. "You'd have to ask her," she muttered.

"What was that? I should ask her? Come on, Destiny. This is the closest you've come to telling me what happened," Monica pleaded.

Exasperated, Destiny sighed. "I said, you'd have to ask her. She never told me why she left."

Monica stood in front of Destiny's desk with her mouth hanging open. "Really?"

"Yes, really."

"All this time, she has never told you why she left?" Monica said, unbelieving. "I thought you'd eventually open up about it, but you really don't know?"

Destiny shook her head. "Please don't ask me about this again, Monica." She could feel the familiar stab of loss in her stomach. It was accompanied by sadness now that the anger had washed away.

"Okay, Des," Monica said softly.

"It's time to close up for the day. You go ahead," Destiny said, still staring at her computer screen. "I'm going to stay for a little longer."

"Don't stay too long. We'll be busy in the morning starting that new job we're going to win."

Destiny smiled. "That's right."

"See you tomorrow," Monica said, walking out of the office.

Destiny sat back in her chair and sighed. It had been three long years since her life imploded. She knew that was a little dramatic, but that's how it felt. She had to work late one night and when she'd gotten home, Faith was gone along with most of her things. When she tried to call her, she discovered Faith had blocked her number.

She tried to find her at work the next day, but Faith had cleaned out her locker and quit. Destiny began to call their friends including Monica and her wife, Kim, but they didn't know what was going on either. She finally cornered a worker on Faith's crew who was also a friend. Destiny could still remember the sad look on Mark's face and the hurt in her heart was just as sharp today as it was back then.

"She said to tell you that you know what you did," Mark said.

Destiny looked at him with such confusion, but he shrugged.

"That's all she told me," he said.

"But what did I do?" Destiny pleaded.

"I don't know," Mark said. "She just said, 'she'll know what she did.'"

Three years later and Destiny still didn't know what Faith was talking about. She had tried over and over to get Faith to talk to her and even asked their friends to help, but Faith only told them the same thing she told Mark.

Destiny had run into Faith a few times since their break-up because they both had their own landscaping businesses now and bid on some of the same projects. The first time she saw Faith after she'd left, Destiny remembered the pain then the anger flashing in Faith's beautiful blue eyes, the same eyes that used to light up whenever they met Destiny's. But now Faith avoided her and wouldn't meet her gaze.

Destiny could feel tears burn the back of her eyes. "Oh no you don't, Faith Fields," Destiny whispered. "I'm done crying unanswered tears for you."

Chapter 2

FAITH YAWNED THEN TOOK a sip of her coffee as she waited for the light to change. It had been a long evening followed by a fitful night of sleep littered with snippets of dreams.

Sometimes after she'd had a visit with Mrs. Baker, thoughts of Destiny Green would not leave her head. No matter how many times Faith pushed them away another memory would surface. How long does it take to get past the hurt of betrayal? She may never get over it, but surely it would eventually go away so she could live her life in peace.

Faith took another sip of her coffee and scoffed. "What life?" she muttered. All she did was work, but that's what it took to run a small, yet successful, landscaping business. Lush Fields Landscaping didn't just maintain outdoor spaces, Faith also created concepts with beauty in mind for this sprawling urban area she served.

Her company provided more than just mowing and trimming the grass. She designed areas with color that were uplifting and others with subdued plants inviting calm and relaxation. The landscape around a building could set the tone for the business inside. It was more than just grass and shrubs.

Faith pulled into the parking lot and drove around to the loading area of her favorite wholesale nursery. She was meeting Mark, her longtime friend who ran the installation crew for Lush Fields. Faith dreamed up the designs, went over them with Mark, and he and his team made them come to life at the project site.

When she'd quit her previous job and decided to start her own business, Mark was the first person she asked to come with her. He believed in her vision and took the leap. They had built a thriving company with a steady client base, but Faith was ready to go after bigger jobs.

"Hey, where were you last night?" Mark asked, walking up to the truck. "I thought you were going to come by and have a beer with us."

"I was, but I heard about a big job off I-35 at that new office park," Faith said. "I started looking at the area on the internet and—"

"The next thing you knew it was midnight. Is that why you look so tired? I know you couldn't possibly be out with anyone." Mark said, giving her a pointed look.

Faith smirked. "It wasn't quite that late, but it was too late for a beer."

"Faith, it's never too late for a beer," Mark said seriously. "One of these days I'm going to convince you that it's okay to smile and have a good time."

Faith shook her head and rolled her eyes.

Mark leaned in and lowered his voice. "There are beautiful women out there who would love to show you a good time."

"I can show myself a good time and these flowers, plants, and shrubs are all the beauty I need."

Mark sighed. "You have a big birthday coming up. I refuse

to let you turn forty without some kind of fun. Prepare yourself because I'm not taking no for an answer."

"It's not a big deal."

"Oh yes it is. We'll talk more as it gets closer," Mark said. "Check out these butterfly shrubs."

"Oh, those are nice," Faith said. "I texted Abel and asked him to pull the Black Knights. These dark purple blooms will be beautiful."

"Yeah, he had them waiting when I got here. I'll start loading them," he said. "I've already loaded the rest of our order into my truck."

"I want to look at his gardenias," Faith said. "I really want to try a few of them sprinkled throughout that bed against the building. They smell so good, but can be finicky."

"Not with your green thumb." Mark grinned as he began to put the shrubs in Faith's truck.

Faith chuckled and walked into the nursery. She wandered through the rows of shrubs until she found the gardenias.

"Those would look nice with the butterflies Mark's loading," Abel said, walking up beside Faith.

"They would, but..." Faith said, turning one of the plants around to examine it.

"You can get them to thrive," Abel said. "Everything grows for you."

Faith shrugged. "Most of the time."

"How many do you want?"

"Let me have these," Faith said, pulling four pots into the aisle.

"Come sign for your order and I'll get a cart to load these," Abel said.

Faith followed him over to the counter and looked over her order as Abel loaded the gardenias. She signed the receipt, turned around, and looked straight into the dark brown eyes that once made her melt with the slightest glance. For a moment everything stopped and she was whisked back to a happier time.

"I'll be with you in a minute, Destiny," Abel called from behind them.

Faith's heart started to pound in her chest and she was instantly irate at her body's betrayal.

Where was it, she wondered. She couldn't see the slightest hint of guilt which should be shimmering in Destiny's eyes. Instead, for just a flash, she saw softness, but then Destiny took a shaky breath and stood a little taller. The corner of Faith's mouth slightly turned up from seeing Destiny falter somewhat before regaining her composure.

"I don't guess you're buying supplies for that Sims job," Faith said with a smirk.

Destiny scoffed. "You didn't get it either."

Faith smiled. Lush Fields Landscaping may not have won the job, but knowing The Green Thumb didn't get it either had eased the sting a little.

"At least they gave me a reason why they went with the other company," Destiny said, looking into Faith's eyes.

Faith could feel the heat of Destiny's stare. Was that sadness in her eyes? Surely not.

"We've got plenty to do," Destiny continued, looking away and shuffling her feet. "Besides, I've got my eye on something bigger."

"Surely you don't mean the business complex up the Interstate," Faith said. "That's more my size."

Destiny huffed. "Oh yeah? Because you're such a big player in the landscaping business in the Austin area?"

Faith furrowed her brow, set her feet and folded her arms across her chest. Destiny was a couple inches taller than Faith and heavier. Where Faith's frame was slight and willowy, Destiny was muscular and athletic. Years of moving dirt and planting shrubs and flowers had made both women strong.

Faith remembered how Destiny once marveled at her body.

"You are such an enigma," Destiny said. "Your beautiful, lithe body is so strong and powerful. People don't see that by simply looking at you, but I know. I've felt your strength. I've experienced your power." She ran her fingers through Faith's light golden strands of brown hair.

They were naked in bed when Destiny had told her that. Faith had proceeded to give Destiny another taste of her strength and they'd made love late into the night.

But here they were about to face off—in what, Faith wasn't sure.

"Oh, stop!" Destiny exclaimed. "You don't have to get all big and bold with me, Faith."

"You'll find out how big and bold I can be if you fuck with my company, Green," Faith said, venom in her voice.

"I'm not fucking with you or your company. Why would I do that?" Destiny shrugged and furrowed her brow.

"Why wouldn't you?" Faith said. "It's not like you haven't done it before."

"What?" Destiny exclaimed with a confused look on her face.

"Hey," Mark said, walking up looking from one woman to the other. "Everything is loaded, Faith." He looked at Destiny and smiled. "Abel is taking your order to your truck, Destiny."

"Fine," Faith said, walking past Destiny giving her shoulder the slightest nudge with her own.

❄

Destiny closed her eyes and fisted her hands where they hung at her side. She tried to calm her pounding heart before she talked to Mark. It wasn't his fault that his boss was such a bitch.

"You okay?" Mark asked quietly.

Destiny opened her eyes and smiled. "Hi, Mark. How's it going?"

Mark grinned. "Oh, you know. Just watching two people that could've had the most amazing life together totally fuck it all up."

Destiny looked at him with shock on her face.

"The air crackles with electricity when you two are near one another. I used to wonder if you were going to tear each other's clothes off and now I'm wondering if you're about to get into a fist fight."

"I would never hit her," Destiny exclaimed with shock in her voice.

Mark smiled and nodded. "She wouldn't hit you either."

"I don't know." Destiny blew out a deep breath. "What the fuck," she said, frustrated.

"Have you ever considered apologizing?" Mark asked.

Destiny's brows flew up her forehead. "For what? Breathing the same air?"

"Uh, no," Mark said slowly. "That's not what I meant."

Destiny tilted her head then realization covered her face. "Oh, you mean..." She sighed. "Don't you think I've thought of that? I don't know what I have to fucking apologize for, Mark!"

Mark winced and led them over to a bench at the side of the counter. "You really don't know?"

"That was probably the longest conversation I've had with her in three years. She never told me what she thinks I did. If I knew what it was and could apologize, I don't know how I'd even do it." Destiny threw up her hands in defeat. "If she saw me come into your shop, I'm quite sure she'd either leave or throw me out."

"Man, what could you have done that's unforgivable?" Mark said.

"I know you don't believe me and you, like everyone else, think I'm hiding something, but I swear, I don't know what I could've done. I was head over heels in love with Faith. I wanted to spend my life with her."

"Was?"

Destiny glanced over at him. "It doesn't matter if I love her or not," she said with a sad smile.

Mark sighed. "All she does is work. I can't even get her to have a beer with the crew. She rarely smiles. Micromanages everything. She trusts no one and if it wasn't for her assistant, Amy, I'm not sure anyone would work for us."

"It's hard starting then running a business," Destiny said, in Faith's defense. "It takes all your time and energy. When you're not at the office or a job site you're thinking about the next job."

Mark gave her a sarcastic smile and chuckled. "You're defending her?"

Destiny shrugged. "Like it matters."

"This morning she was talking about the big office complex over on Interstate 35," Mark said.

"Yeah, I'm going to have a look and work up a bid on it," Destiny said. She whipped her head towards Mark, wondering if she should've told him that.

He chuckled. "It's okay. I'm your friend, too, Destiny, and I would never give up your plans. I'm sure Faith is doing the same thing. It won't be the first time the both of you have bid on the same job."

Destiny nodded. "I've missed you, but I'm afraid if Faith knew we were talking to each other she might fire you."

Mark chuckled. "No she wouldn't. You don't worry about me. And I have a feeling you've been doing the same thing she has. All work and no play."

Destiny grimaced. "I have no desire to give my heart to anyone. When Faith up and left like that I was devastated and it still hurts. That's just the way it is. Believe me, I wish I could get past it all. One of these days, I'll wake up and decide I don't have to stay busy for the next sixteen hours in order to take a deep breath."

"Aww, Des," Mark said, putting his arm around her. "I'm so sorry."

As good as it felt to have Mark's sympathy, Destiny knew she'd burst into tears if she didn't get up.

"Thanks," she said, jumping up and swiping under her eyes. "My mom keeps telling me it will all work out."

"Your mom is a pretty smart lady," Mark said. "You should listen to her."

Destiny shrugged. "What choice do I have?"

Get Until We Weren't: A Story of Destiny and Faith

Printed in Great Britain
by Amazon